SYMPHONY IN A MINOR KEY

SYMPHONY IN A MINOR KEY

SCIENCE FICTION TALES OF TIME AND SPACE

H. G. STRATMANN

Starship Press, LLC
Springfield, MO
www.starshippress.com

Symphony in a Minor Key
Science Fiction Tales of Time and Space

Copyright 2010 by Henry G. Stratmann

Manufactured in the United States of America

"Symphony in a Minor Key" appeared in *Analog Science Fiction and Fact*, October 1996.

"Jurisimprudence" appeared in *Analog Science Fiction and Fact*, October 1998.

"To Him Who Waits" appeared in *Analog Science Fiction and Fact*, December 1999.

"When All Else Fails" was co-written with Henry Stratmann III and appeared in *Analog Science Fiction and Fact*, March 2009.

"Tempora Mutantur" appeared in *Analog Science Fiction and Fact*, July/August 1999.

"Going Home" appeared in *Analog Science Fiction and Fact*, April 1999.

"The Invasion" appeared in *Analog Science Fiction and Fact*, April 2009.

"Naked Came the Earthling" appeared in *Analog Science Fiction and Fact*, July/August 2001.

"Achromomorph's Burden" appeared in *Analog Science Fiction and Fact*, February 2000.

ISBN: 978-0-9790480-3-6

LCCN: 2007904382

Published by
Starship Press, LLC
4319 S. National, #135
Springfield, MO 65810-2607

DEDICATION

To my wife, Maryellen, for her love and inspiration

To our sons, Henry III and Joseph,
for teaching me what it means to be a father

ABOUT THE AUTHOR

Henry G. Stratmann, M.D., F.A.C.C., F.A.C.P., F.C.C.P. is Clinical Professor of Medicine at St. Louis University in St. Louis, Missouri. He is board-certified in Internal Medicine and in the specialties of Cardiovascular Disease and Nuclear Cardiology.

Henry has been a cardiologist for more than twenty-seven years. He has either authored or co-authored over seventy peer-reviewed scientific publications. He and Maryellen, his wife and a fellow physician, have also co-authored a book for the general public, *Sex and Your Heart Health: A Cardiologist Tells All.*

A lifelong reader of science fiction, Henry is a frequent contributor of both stories and science fact articles to *Analog Science Fiction and Fact.* He is a longstanding member of the Science Fiction and Fantasy Writers of America.

Henry lives with Maryellen and their two teenage sons in the Missouri Ozarks.

PREFACE

I didn't start out to be a science fiction writer.

True, I've been *reading* science fiction as far back as I can remember. During my first years in grade school, way back in the early 1960s, I discovered the colorful comic book adventures of superheroes like Green Lantern and Superman. Starting with those examples of simple but imaginative SF, I later graduated to the literary classics of Asimov, Heinlein, Bradbury, and other authors that I found in local libraries. From high school onward I've kept up with modern SF mainly through magazines like *Analog Science Fiction and Fact*.

Occasionally, as I went through college, medical school, and beyond I dreamed about writing SF myself. However, as the years passed and I became a physician, husband, and father, I never had time to create my own stories. Instead, my writing was confined to the considerably drier genre of research papers published in medical journals.

My career as a science fiction writer started unexpectedly when, on impulse, I sent a letter to *Analog* commenting on a story I'd enjoyed. My first surprise was seeing my letter printed in that magazine. My second and even more delightful surprise was receiving a letter from the story's author. He thanked me for my comments—and asked me if I'd like to co-author a story with him dealing with futuristic medicine.

Our collaboration, "Tin Angel," was later published in *Analog*. The experience of helping to write a successful SF story whetted my appetite to try writing more. Rereading some of my first "solo" efforts still makes me wince at how steep my learning curve was. Nevertheless, with the generous help and inspiration provided in particular by three individuals, I've managed to create and publish stories that I hope you will enjoy.

First and foremost, I want to thank G. (Gerald) David Nordley. He wrote the story that prompted my first letter to *Analog* and started me on my career as an SF writer. Besides his many other accomplishments, Gerald excels at writing both "hard" SF stories and nonfiction dealing with the science of space travel.

Although Gerald and I have actually met in person only a handful of times over the years, we've corresponded frequently, first by traditional mail and then later by e-mail. We've also had a second collaboration on a science fact article for *Analog* describing the biological hazards of space travel. Gerald has always shown himself to be not only a brilliant thinker and scientist but also a fine person in every way. He is truly, in the classic phrase, a gentleman and a scholar.

The second person I'm indebted to is Dr. Stanley Schmidt. Both as a writer and especially as the editor of *Analog*, Stan is one of the most influential people in modern SF. He is also extremely personable and a true professional in the best sense of the word.

One of Stan's many talents is his ability to inspire other writers, including me, to stretch their skills and produce the best stories they possibly can. He combines a requirement for stories of the highest quality with a style of kind, constructive criticism that encourages his writers to aim high. Even when he's declined one of my stories or suggested revisions to ones he eventually did buy, he's done it in such a gentle and encouraging manner that I've wanted to run back to my computer immediately, determined to make him happy with my next effort.

Finally, I'd like to thank Kevin J. Anderson. Kevin is well known as an extremely prolific writer of high-quality SF. He not only personally answered a letter I sent to *Analog* commenting on one of his stories, but he also generously sent me a large package containing autographed copies of several of his novels. Since then I've had the privilege of returning his thoughtfulness by giving him advice regarding medical issues for several of his novels, including *Climbing Olympus* and *Fatal Exposure*.

Table of Contents

I love classical music. I've spent countless hours listening to the great masters, studying the scores of their masterpieces, and reading books analyzing their works. I particularly enjoy the music of the Baroque and Classical periods, with Joseph Haydn, J. S. Bach, and Ludwig van Beethoven being my favorite composers.

"Symphony in a Minor Key" reflects the sadness I feel that so much music of the great composers is lost to us. We'll never hear as much as a third of what J. S. Bach wrote. Such intriguing works as Haydn's piano sonatas in B major and D minor and all but a small fragment of Beethoven's early Oboe Concerto in F major are probably lost forever. My story is a "wish fulfillment" dream of recovering this unheard music, and more.

I modeled "Symphony in a Minor Key" on the type of sonata form that's used in the first movement of many symphonies. The story opens with a recurring "Introduction," similar to how the music of the slow introduction returns in various guises throughout the first movements of both Haydn's *Drumroll* Symphony and Schubert's *Unfinished* Symphony. The subsequent parts of the story have headings indicating the standard three sections of sonata form. The story then concludes with a "coda" whose beginning is indicated by alluding to a piece by Haydn that contains a long and tragic coda itself.

I hope you enjoy my potpourri of "musical" science fiction.

Symphony in a Minor Key

Introduction

*A*s he emerged from the alley the front of the building on his right exploded. Knocked down by the blast, Robbins staggered back to his feet, unable to comprehend what he saw.

The city was deserted and in ruins. Most of the nearby buildings were at least partly destroyed. A few were on fire, spewing acrid black smoke into the cold air. The wide street he stood on was pockmarked with craters and littered with broken wood, glass, and the torn bodies of dead animals. In the distance he heard unintelligible cries and screams, sharp firecracker-like snaps, and faint whistling sounds like descending skyrockets followed by thunderous explosions.

Suddenly a horse-drawn wagon whipped around the nearby street corner and bore directly down on him. Both the driver and the gray-faced woman at his side looked terrified at he lashed the horses to greater speed. The wagon grazed Robbins' arm as he jumped aside just in time.

Before he could catch his breath, a portly red-faced man puffed around the same corner and sprinted toward him. As the stranger ran past, Robbins grabbed the man's arm and shouted at him in German, "What is happening?"

The fat man's eyes bulged. "Let go of me, you fool!" he screamed. "They're right behind me, they'll kill us all!"

Before he could ask who "they" were, the other man broke free and resumed his headlong flight. As Robbins started after him an arcing shriek tore through the air. Suddenly the part of the street just in front of the fleeing man exploded, flinging him backwards high into the air, arms flailing wildly, until he landed on his head with a sickening thud. Robbins ran to him. The man lay on his back, bloodied mouth gaping wide, unmoving eyes staring up at the sky. Dead.

Then Robbins heard more hoofbeats coming from the other end of the cobblestone street. Recalling the dead man's last words, he looked around for a place to hide. The closest shelter was the crater just blasted in front of him in the middle of the street. It made a shallow foxhole, deep enough to let him duck his head below street level by lying on his stomach. Ignoring the mud staining his clothes, he peeked over the edge of the crater.

Four horsemen turned the same street corner from which the wagon and the dead man had just come. They wore identical tall black woolen hats, brown shirts open at the neck, wide red sashes around their waists, and dark pants stuffed into high military boots. A long saber hung from each one's side. Their bearded faces too seemed identical, with coarse menacing features.

Seemingly oblivious to his hiding place or the distant thunder of cannons, they trotted their horses down the street at a leisurely pace, directly toward him. Every few meters they would stop momentarily and peer at the surrounding buildings, as if looking for someone.

Quickly Robbins ducked his head back down, heart pounding. The alley from which he'd emerged—the one containing the portal back home—was too far away. If he tried running to it, they would see him and could cut him down with their sabers long before he reached safety.

And if he did nothing, in a few minutes they would, literally, be right on top of him.

The melody of the Russian dance from Tchaikovsky's Nutcracker *ballet flashed through his brain. He was about to be killed by—* Cossacks?

Confused, desperate, Robbins closed his eyes. Like the bass part of some diabolical passacaglia, a single thought repeated itself in his mind.

What in God's name is going on?

Exposition

"—and we have no right to play God!"

H. L. Robbins, head of the Musicology Section, looked anxiously at the other members of the Humanities Committee seated around the conference table. Then he sighed with relief. Except for Billingsley, who was grinning at her, the other Section Chiefs seemed unmoved by Brentano's tirade.

At the head of the table, the chancellor of the Institute for Transcosmic Studies frowned at Brentano. "Thank you for your comments, Dr. Brentano. However, before we discuss whether Dr. Robbins' proposal should be carried out, we need to establish whether it is even feasible. That's why I've asked our distinguished guests from the Science Committee, Drs. Everett and Harrison, to come to this meeting."

She nodded toward the elderly woman seated at her right.

Catherine Everett, Ph.D. glared back. "I gave my opinion in the report I sent to your Committee." Her eyes flashed around the table. "I assume you all read it?"

From the embarrassed looks on the faces of his colleagues, Robbins doubted any of them had been able to figure out what Everett's report said either. He for one had no idea what terms like "closed temporal loop" and "quantized timelines" meant. And as for the equations—

The chancellor said diplomatically, "Perhaps you could summarize your conclusions about the possible dangers of traveling back in time and changing the past."

"No, no, no!" Everett shouted back. "There's no danger anything we do on Transcosmic Earth can affect us! Translocating there may seem like simple time travel into the past, with all the possible paradoxes and violations of causality that implies, but it's actually much more complicated! Anything we change there would simply replace TCE's current history with one of a nearly infinite number of different 'shadow histories' and make it the 'real' one instead. But *our* history would stay the same!"

She launched into an arcane monologue about "temporo-quantum discontinuities" and "branching universes" that Robbins couldn't even begin to follow.

But even if he didn't understand it, Everett must know what she was talking about. She had originated the theory of "transcosmology" that let them travel to Transcosmic Earth. Apparently, Everett and the other physicists at the Institute disagreed about what TCE was—their own Earth's past, a "parallel" world, or something else. Whatever it was, you could "translocate" to anywhere on it within a roughly four hundred year "temporal window," stay as long as you liked, then return to "their" Earth an equal amount of time later.

Nobody he talked to seemed to know why you couldn't travel back farther than the mid-17th century, or sooner than 1998. Rumor was that the last six decades were "off-limits" because the members of the Executive Committee who oversaw the Institute didn't want anyone alive today to be embarrassed by anything discovered by observing their younger analogs on TCE—especially themselves. Unlike his colleagues, Robbins didn't feel those limits hurt his work. In fact, it was because of his expertise in pre-21st century Western music, whose "golden age" fell within those years, that he'd been invited to join the Institute for Transcosmic Studies.

The Institute was the result of an international effort to use and reg-ulate translocation. Its purpose was to "go back in time" on TCE and collect information and "cultural artifacts," like music, that had been lost on their own Earth. Along with a monopoly on its use, the Institute was responsible for ensuring translocation wasn't misused. There was one particular rule, the "First Law of Contact," that every member of the Institute was required to obey at all cost. Anyone going to TCE was to have as little contact with the people there as possible and not do anything that might change its "past."

It was this rule that Robbins was proposing to break in a very big way.

"—and that should answer your question!" Everett folded her arms.

The chancellor looked as confused as the rest of them. "Then I take it you believe we can alter TCE's past without changing our own?"

Everett's face turned crimson. "Of course! That's what I just said! Weren't you listening?"

Cowering like everyone else, Robbins thought it amazing that this short, grandmotherly woman with silver hair pulled back severely into a tight bun could make the lot of them—all experts in their fields, and several nearly her age—feel like grade-schoolers being scolded by a strict teacher.

Everett sighed. "Let me put it even more simply. Transcosmic Earth was the timeline that initially produced us. But ever since a temporo-quantum event made our current universe branch off from TCE, there's no longer any 'causal' relationship between our timeline and TCE's. Now, TCE is no longer 'the' past, but only 'a' past—one we can change without affecting the unique past, or the present, of our own branch universe. To use a crude analogy, just as a newborn baby, once its umbilical cord is cut, exists completely separately from its mother and continues to exist despite what may happen to her, our Earth and its timeline now exist independently of TCE.

"What Dr. Robbins proposes will prove what I've been telling my denser colleagues and the Executive Committee for years. We won't change our own 'remembered' history, we won't 'blink' ourselves out of existence by changing TCE's history!"

The chancellor nodded politely. "Thank you, Dr. Everett." She turned to the white-haired man seated on her left. "Dr. Harrison?"

Cecil L. Harrison, M.D. began, "Dr. Ertmann, the physician on my staff with the most experience in field work on TCE, made a series of nocturnal visits to the subject's apartment starting two years before he died and collected blood samples while he was sleeping. Postmortem tissue samples and ascitic fluid were also obtained a few hours after his death. Our analysis of the specimens confirmed the opinion of his own physicians that he had died of liver failure. However, they erroneously believed that it was due to alcohol abuse or syphilis. Using tests not available in the 19th century, Dr. Ertmann and I found it was actually caused by chronic active hepatitis, from an infection with the hepatitis B virus that he contracted no more than fifteen months before he died.

"Thus, to prevent his death, we only need to give him an injection of an appropriate medicine at least a month before he was infected. Nanoscrubbers block entry of viral DNA into cells and have a success rate of nearly 100%. However, 'scrubbers stay in the blood and other bodily fluids, and anyone else exposed to them after he was injected could also become immunized. Since it was emphasized to me that only the subject himself should be affected by what we do, I suggest immunoboosted hepatitis B vaccine should be used instead. Its average success rate is still 95%, and it wouldn't affect anyone besides him."

Harrison coughed. "Bear in mind, however, that at the time he died he had other significant medical problems that, even if we prevent him from dying of hepatitis, will still eventually kill him. I estimate he'll live about five, and certainly no more than ten extra years."

"Thank you, Dr. Harrison." The chancellor continued, "Our guests tell us there's no technical reason why Dr. Robbins' proposal can't be done. Now we must consider whether we *should* do it. Drs. Robbins and Brentano have already expressed their positions. Are there any other comments?"

Now, Robbins thought, was the moment of truth. Brentano was adamantly against it. However, right now it was dangerous, politically speaking, for anyone to side with her. She and the Philosophy and Theology Section that she headed had been in disgrace with the Executive Committee since their report on what really happened at Lourdes in 1858 had leaked to the public. The Vatican had shrugged it off, saying no official articles of faith were involved, just a popular tradition. But the crowds protesting outside the Institute compound, and whoever had sent the bomb threats, clearly disagreed. That formal complaint sent by the French government, presumably on behalf of their tourism industry, hadn't helped either.

Lytton and Shimura should be on his side. If his proposal were approved and set a successful precedent, they had similar proposals of their own to submit.

Billingsley, as always, was an enigma

Shimura said, "Dr. Lytton and I both strongly support Dr. Robbins' proposal."

The chancellor nodded at Billingsley. The latter, easily the youngest person at the table, adjusted his bow tie and horn-rimmed glasses and ran a hand through greasy crew cut hair. He shrugged. "I'm ambivalent. If Howie's plan works, I can think of projects I'd like to do too. Like go to Earth-Two and tell the Big Bopper and his pals to not get on that plane."

The big what? Robbins thought.

"But Toni"—he nodded at Brentano—"is afraid we're not smart enough to know what will happen if we change Earth-Two's past, and that we might screw things up. Based on the kind of literature I know best, I have to agree with her that violating the Prime Directive wouldn't be a good idea. We shouldn't risk turning the people there, or maybe even us, into lizards."

Into what? Robbins found Billingsley's sophomoric obsession with "popular culture" of the previous century to be very irritating. While the other Humanities sections were recovering things of real cultural value on TCE, the Sociology Section Billingsley headed wasted its time scanning old "films" and recording episodes of twentieth-century radio and television programs that were all probably better left lost. Billingsley defended the "scholarly" nature of these projects, saying, "The best way to understand a society is to see what its people enjoy, what they consider entertainment."

But, Robbins suspected, the real reason the powers-that-be tolerated it was that those samples of pre-Digital Revolution "entertainment" were wildly popular on the Internet—and the Institute collected a royalty each time one was downloaded. Besides, how much scholarship could you really expect from someone whose doctoral thesis was entitled, "The Role of the Tropicana Club as a Microcosm of Early 1950s American Society in 'I Love Lucy'"?

And Robbins hated it when Billingsley used obscure terms he didn't understand. He made a mental note to run a net search on what "Prime Directive" referred to.

The chancellor said, "Dr. Velikovsky?"

Robbins tensed. Velikovsky, of the History Section, was the pivotal vote.

The latter began, "This is not an easy decision. Even a tiny, critical change in TCE's past could have great, perhaps very negative repercussions for its later history. I can't be certain whether saving this particular individual would be such a change. Those 'extra' ten years Dr. Harrison referred to were relatively quiet, politically speaking, in his own country—though not elsewhere in Europe. While the subject himself was something of a political revolutionary, it's difficult to see how he could affect the course of the various revolutions that occurred in Europe in 1830 and 1831. Conversely, if he were to live to 1848 or 1849, when even more critical events occurred—well, that would be even harder to predict. In that case, I would have to vote 'no' to Dr. Robbins' proposal.

"However, since Dr. Harrison is convinced he'll die no later than the 1830s, at this time I'm inclined to favor Dr. Robbins' proposal."

The chancellor said, "Any other comments?"

Brentano again. "I'd like to remind everyone that the decision we make today might, as Dr. Robbins said, 'enrich' both our world and TCE—or it could destroy them. Even if we do have much to gain, is it worth such a terrible risk?"

Robbins said, "Although I appreciate Dr. Brentano's concerns, as I said before, and as Drs. Everett and Velikovsky have just confirmed, the risks do indeed seem minimal. And oh, how much we and TCE stand to gain! Genius, whether it is in music or some other field, is a rare and precious thing. Those individuals blessed with such great powers of creativity and original thought are given to the rest of humanity only briefly, but what they do far outlasts their own lifetimes. It is tragic when one of them is taken away from us prematurely by an accident of Nature, leaving his work undone—the masterpieces he might have created unfinished or stillborn. We have the means to correct one of those tragedies. I believe we should do it."

"Any more comments? No?" The chancellor continued, "Is there a second for Dr. Robbins' proposal?"

"Seconded!" Lytton and Shimura spoke simultaneously.

"Those in favor of Dr. Robbins' proposal, raise your hands."

Robbins' own right arm went up immediately, followed by those of Lytton and Shimura. After some hesitation, Velikovsky's joined them.

"Opposed?"

Brentano and Billingsley raised their arms.

"Let the record show that the Humanities Committee has voted 4 to 2 in favor of Dr. Robbins' proposal."

For the first time since the meeting started, Robbins relaxed. He'd won! The hardest part—getting the Executive, then the Science, and now the Humanities Committee to approve his proposal—was over. The rest should be simple—just go to TCE and do it. Robbins could barely contain his excitement.

Soon he would travel to Vienna in 1825 and save the life of Ludwig van Beethoven.

"Congratulations."

Robbins sighed. He'd known this was coming.

Antonia had asked to come to his apartment in the Staff Quarters that evening. "Just to talk," she'd said. But he knew what she wanted to talk about.

"Thank you," he replied.

"When are you going?"

"Tomorrow morning."

"I don't suppose there's any way I can talk you out of it."

"No, there isn't."

The muted lights in the apartment cast a lustrous sheen to Antonia's long brown hair. Though they were both toward the middle of middle-age, unlike his own her hair was just starting to show a little gray. And as for the rest of her—he knew all too well how heartachingly beautiful she was.

He and Antonia Brentano had been among the first of the Humanities staff to come to the Institute. Though different in many ways, they found they both shared a great passion for classical music. Acquaintance had turned to friendship, and then they'd discovered something else they shared—loneliness. Neither of them had ever been married or had any close family. Immersed in his work for so many years, until he met her he hadn't noticed what was missing from his life.

In retrospect, it was natural that they'd drifted into a brief but intense love affair—and just as natural that it should end. They'd soon realized they were both too dedicated to their work to have enough time and energy left for each other. Afterwards, they'd still maintained a cordial, platonic friendship. But now they might lose even that.

They sat on the couch together silently for a while, just listening to the music playing in the background. A large bust of Beethoven frowned at them from atop the Steinway grand piano that filled a good part of the living room. Pictures of some of Robbins' other favorite composers hung on the walls. The one of J. S. Bach seemed to be smiling in approval at the piece Robbins had selected—the master's Concerto for Three Violins and String Orchestra in F-sharp minor. Absorbed in the first movement's intricate counterpoint, it took him a few seconds to realize Antonia was speaking.

"Why, Howard? Why do you have to do this?"

"It's just like I said at the meeting. I want to allow a genius whose life was cut tragically short to create new works for the benefit of all humanity."

"Oh, cut the melodrama! If you're really serious, you have the worst case of *hubris* I've ever seen. Is it an ego thing with you—a way to bask in Beethoven's reflected glory by being the instrument for his 'resurrection'? If that isn't 'playing God,' I don't know what is!"

"But I really mean it! There's nothing selfish in this!"

The expression on Antonia's face told him what she thought of that.

"Listen," he began, "over the last four years my staff and I have traveled to TCE and recovered thousands of scores by the great composers that were lost for one reason or another centuries ago. We knew about some of them from surviving fragments or the *incipits*— the first few measures of the main theme—in catalogs of their works that the composer or a near-contemporary compiled."

"Like the Köchel catalog for Mozart's works?"

"Exactly. Since we knew about when those 'lost' works were composed, we've been able to go back and retrieve them. When we did that, however, we also found many 'new' works that nobody knew anything about!"

The concerto had entered its heartrendingly lyrical slow movement, a Largo in A major. "The piece by Bach we're listening to now is one of them—unknown, forgotten for over three centuries until I went to Cöthen in 1722 and scanned a copy of the score. By going to TCE we've managed to nearly double the amount of his music we had before the Institute was formed!"

"I don't understand. How did all that music get lost?"

"Several reasons. After Beethoven's time, we already had nearly all of the music the 'major' composers wrote. Unless they destroyed what they considered to be 'inferior' works, like Chopin. Or if they were very careless with the manuscripts."

Robbins smiled to himself. After methodically rummaging through Schubert's closet at various times during the mid-1820s, he had finally found the completed third and fourth movements of the composer's B minor symphony—the one that *used* to be known as the "Unfinished."

"But before Beethoven's time, however, very little of a composer's music was published. For the most part, the scores of their works existed in only a small number of handwritten copies, all of which could easily be lost by accident or neglect. Plus, the major composers before Beethoven were very prolific. Bach himself wrote nearly two thousand works. They wrote so much music that it was hard even for them to preserve or keep track of everything they wrote!

"But now my staff and I have become the victims of our own success. We've managed to recover just about everything those composers wrote. At the rate we're going, soon we may not need to go to TCE anymore."

"So that's it!" The anger was back in Antonia's eyes. "This proposal is just your way to justify staying at the Institute!"

The concerto began its fiery third movement, back in the tonic minor.

"No, that's not it at all! Until now, all we've been doing is acting like scavengers. We've been retrieving those lost works for ourselves, *we* now have them—but the 'First Law of Contact' forbids us to give them back to the people of TCE! What I'm going to do will benefit both us and them!

"Lytton understands. Think of all the poets and writers who died 'before their time'! Like Percy Shelley—drowned at age 29 in a stupid boating accident. Or John Keats, who died at age 25 from tuberculosis, something that Harrison could prevent easily. Edward says the first thing he'd do is give Charles Dickens a few more years of life, so he can finish *The Mystery of Edwin Drood*. The point is that, if any of them lived longer on TCE, anything new they created would become part of both our cultural heritage—and theirs!

"And Shimura—his list has van Gogh, and—"

"All right, all right! I don't disagree with you about the possible benefits, just the risks."

She glanced at the brooding plaster figure on the piano. "But why Beethoven? Why not someone who died younger, like Mozart? He'd probably live even longer and write more music than Ludwig."

"But that might backfire! If Beethoven lived too many years longer, his career would overlap those of Chopin, Schumann, and other major composers who were all active in the late 1830s and 1840s. If he were still alive and writing constantly greater masterpieces himself then, they might feel discouraged, unequal to the task of reaching his standard of excellence, and not write much themselves! Although we'd still have them, TCE could be deprived of their greatest works. The same thing could happen if we saved Mozart, only worse—because Beethoven himself would be one of the composers who might be 'discouraged'!

"But remember, Harrison said Beethoven won't live much longer even if I do temporarily 'save' him. So, both we and TCE should get the best of both worlds—a few more works by one of the greatest composers of all time and no bad effects on his contemporaries. Plus, we'll prove we can do something good for the people of TCE, too."

"But that's the real question, isn't it. How do we know we'll do something *good* for them?"

Antonia took a piece of paper from her purse. "Billingsley asked me to give you this. He says you haven't answered his messages, and he's been too busy making trips to TCE to catch you in person."

She smiled grimly. "He said he wants to salvage as much of the 'pop culture' as he can from the 20th century before you 'screw things up and wipe it out.'"

How typical, Robbins thought. He took the note and stuck it in his pocket.

The Bach concerto sounded its final cadence. In the silence that followed Antonia sighed, "It's getting late, and I have to leave."

Robbins walked her to the door. In the open doorway she said, "I don't care at all for what you're going to do. Even if the chance of something bad happening is small, it's still too much."

She hesitated. "But I do care about you. Whatever happens, take care of yourself."

Then she gave him a brief hug, brushed her lips chastely across his cheek, and was gone.

The scent of her perfume lingered in the empty room. Sitting down at the piano, he played "Für Elise," mentally changing the title to "Für Antonia." "You don't mind, do you?" he asked the bust of Beethoven.

The composer scowled back at him.

Then he remembered about Billingsley's note. It read, "Dear Howie, Please read these stories. They just might make you change your mind about changing history on Earth-Two."

There was a list of ten titles and authors. Well, why not?

"Computer?"

"Yes?" a warm contralto voice answered from the walls.

Robbins looked at the first title on the list. "Access story, 'A Sound of Thunder.'"

"Category, science fiction?"

Robbins frowned. "I suppose so."

"Author, Bradbury, Ray?"

He checked the note. "Yes."

"Would you like it read to you, or would you like a printout?"

"Printout."

Robbins watched as sheets of paper spat out of a slot in the nearby wall into the small wire basket attached beneath it. When the printout stopped, he read the first few pages—and then threw the papers down in disgust. Hunting dinosaurs—how ridiculous!

He should've known better. Once he'd asked Billingsley why he always used the term "Earth-Two" instead of the standard "Transcosmic Earth." The latter had replied very seriously that it was a term used in a series of "graphic novels" written in the last half of the 20th century. He'd given Robbins a list of titles and authors then too.

Intrigued in spite of himself (What was so "graphic" about them? And what did those strange titles like *Flash of Two Worlds* refer to?), he'd asked for printouts from the Internet then too. His surprise at receiving pages of small crudely colored and lettered pictures turned to anger when, at his query, the computer said those so-called "graphic novels" were more commonly referred to as "comic books." It was so—typical of Billingsley, quoting from simple-minded stories written for children!

Robbins read more titles on the note. *Timescape. By His Bootstraps. The Men Who Murdered Mohammed. Appointment in Berlin.* Then he crumpled the note and tossed it on the floor. Probably more of the same. Not worth wasting his time over.

Fingers poised over the keyboard, he hesitated. Right now he didn't feel in a heaven-storming, Beethovean mood. No, something lighter—like Chopin. Playing through several of the master's etudes from Opus 25, some of his tension drained away. As the last fluttering strains of the delightfully delicate Etude No. 9 in G-flat major, the one nicknamed "The Butterfly," faded away in the quiet room, he addressed the bust on the piano again. "Do you think I'm doing the right thing?"

Beethoven scowled at him even more disapprovingly.

Development

"Look's good from this side, Dr. Robbins."

Robbins examined himself in the changing room's full-length mirror and then nodded in agreement. The "Night Operations Camouflage" suit that Miles, the Portal Technician on duty, had just helped him put on resembled a deep-black wet suit, covering him from shoulders to ankles with an opening for his head. A wand-like digital scanner hung from a black belt around his waist.

Miles continued, "I calibrated and focused the portal just before I came here. You can translocate as soon as you finish getting dressed."

Robbins sat down on a bench and tugged a pair of black boots on. "We'll have to wait for Harrison. He's bringing the vaccine I'm going to use."

Miles frowned. "Dr. Harrison's bringing it?"

"That's what he told me. Why do you ask?"

"Because just before I left the Portal Room to help you, Dr. Ertmann came in. I assumed she had it."

"Well, as long as one of them brings it."

He stood up, and Miles handed him a black hood. It covered his entire head except for small circles at his eyes and slits for his mouth and nostrils. Robbins pressed the edges of the hood and suit together. Their magnetic strips made a tight seal.

Miles then gave him a pair of black goggles. Securing them with a strap behind his head, Robbins turned them on. A multicolored display appeared at the top of the left lens. "Fully charged, diagnostics check out," Robbins reported. "Lights off."

In the darkened room the goggles switched to "NightVision" mode. Though it was like looking through green-colored lenses, everything in the room could be seen as clearly as in normal light.

"Lights on." Robbins checked himself in the mirror once again and smiled. Billingsley called the NOC suit a "cat burglar outfit"—not a bad description for what it was designed to do.

To avoid contact with the people of TCE as much as possible, most of the work done there consisted of searching through rooms at night for manuscripts or other documents. Should a "native" happen to enter one of those dark rooms unexpectedly, the NOC suit was supposed to keep the wearer undetected long enough to hide or escape.

"Don't forget this."

Robbins took the bracelet from Miles and snapped it around his left wrist. No, he didn't want to forget that. Without the retrieval bracklet, he couldn't activate the portal from TCE and return to their Earth.

They walked back through the short corridor to the Portal Room.

Harrison was there, bending over a young woman wearing a white lab coat who was slumped forward in a chair near the main control console. Robbins didn't recognize her. She seemed to be in her early thirties, with cascading red hair and pale skin. Sobbing violently, she buried her face in her hands.

Harrison looked up at Miles and him, obviously worried. "Do either of you know what's wrong with Dr. Ertmann?"

Miles shrugged. "Beats me. She was fine when I left her about ten minutes ago."

Harrison bent down again, close to the woman's ear. "Dorothy, what's the matter? Are you sick? Do you want me to get some help?"

Slowly Ertmann looked up at Harrison. Her face was drawn, her eyes red and moist. When she wasn't crying, Robbins thought, she was probably quite pretty. "I'm so sorry," she said, "I should have known better than to—"

She stopped suddenly, staring hard at Robbins. "Who is he?" she demanded.

"That's Dr. Robbins." Harrison said. He frowned at Robbins' black, hooded form. "That is you, isn't it?"

Robbins nodded.

"Dr. Harrison, do you mind if I leave now?" Ertmann pleaded. "I'm sure *he*"—she pointed at Robbins—"will tell you what happened!"

"Do you feel up to walking? I can get a wheelchair—"

"No, that's all right."

With an effort Ertmann lifted herself out of the chair and headed toward the exit. "I just need to go to my room and—lie down for a while."

"Well, if you're sure you're up to it—"

"I'm sure. Please, I just need to be alone!"

After she left, Miles said, "Doc, what was that all about?"

Harrison shrugged. "I don't know. I arrived just before both of you came in and found her sitting there crying!"

He paused. "Dorothy has always been very—sensitive. When things don't go right she can get quite flustered. But I've never seen her this upset before."

Shaking his head, Harrison picked up a small white box from the floor, saying, "I'll go check on her after we finish here."

He opened the box, then carefully extracted a small bottle filled with clear fluid and a device that resembled an automatic pistol. Flipping its metal tab off, with a twisting motion he inserted the top of the bottle into a round slot on the bottom of the body of the pistol-like device, then gave it to Robbins. "Any questions?"

"No." Robbins hefted the transcutaneous injector in his hand.

Yesterday Harrison had demonstrated how easy it was to operate by using it on him. *Press the tip of the injector firmly against the upper arm like this, release the safety catch, and pull the trigger.* Robbins had felt only a slight tingle as the sterile water Harrison had loaded it with passed through his skin, leaving only a small red spot that quickly disappeared.

Robbins nodded to Miles. "Ready when you are." The latter moved toward the control console, pausing to pick up several objects off the floor and replace them on a nearby shelf. Glancing over the displays on the console, he said, "The portal is still stable and active. Local time on TCE is now...1:10 a.m., November 17, 1825."

Robbins trod nervously to the entrance of the portal. It was a large cylinder a bit over six meters long and laid on its side. It was flattened a little where it touched the platform and its entrance was some three meters in diameter. When the portal was active, as it was now, at the near end of that cylinder was pure blackness. From past experience Robbins knew better than to stare into that utter emptiness. It made him dizzy, as if he were looking down over the edge of a high cliff into a bottomless chasm.

Here goes. Walking into the portal wasn't painful. It felt like his whole body had been turned into a mildly vibrating tuning fork, re-sonating at middle C. Miles had told him the sensation was due to his passing through "low-level phase-inverted force fields" used to keep air molecules and microorganisms from passing from Earth to TCE. Those fields did, however, let "slow-moving, macroscopic objects" like him through. And the portal was basically a one-way path from Earth to TCE. With a few exceptions, like the oxygen bound in his blood when he breathed there, no matter or energy originating on TCE could come into their world—

Suddenly those thoughts were interrupted—he was there. His first breath brought a multitude of very unpleasant smells. The NV goggles activated automatically in the dark room.

He was standing in the kitchen of Beethoven's quarters. A fireplace filled with musty ashes was set into one wall. The room had several tables and open shelves, with plates, bowls, and utensils on them. In one corner stood a dusty, dilapidated pianoforte. Robbins smiled slightly. It was ironic that the composer, who had started out as a piano prodigy and contributed so much to the literature for the instrument, had become so indifferent to it in his final years. After finishing his last sonata and the Diabelli variations a few years before, he wrote no other major works for it. Maybe it was because he couldn't hear and enjoy his own playing, or he was too preoccupied with major projects like the *Missa solemnis* or the Ninth Symphony. Whatever the reason, it was sad to see his piano so badly neglected. Given extra years of life, maybe he would write for it again.

He didn't notice the knife lying on the floor until he accidentally kicked it. It skidded across the floor and rattled into a corner. Robbins froze instantly, straining to hear anyone talking or moving, alerted by the noise. But everything stayed silent.

Slowly, he entered the main living area, carefully avoiding bumping into the small writing desks and chairs scattered around it. He was tempted to examine the partially notated sheets of staff paper on the desks, but refrained. First things first.

The door to Beethoven's bedroom was open. Moving even more cautiously, he entered it.

The composer was lying on his right side in a small wooden bed, snoring quietly. A thin blanket covered him up to the waist. He wore a plain nightshirt that was torn in several places. A fringe of unruly gray hair peeked out from beneath his nightcap.

Robbins contemplated the sleeping figure. Here, he knew, was one of the greatest musical geniuses of all time, one who set a standard of excellence that no later composer had ever surpassed. Superficially, though, all he saw was a paunchy man, prematurely old at 54, with a homely, pockmarked face.

With a grunt the man on the bed strained and farted loudly. Robbins froze again, expecting him to wake up at any second. Instead, a smile came to the man's face. He resumed his melodious snoring.

Robbins searched carefully for a good place to inject the vaccine. Fortunately there was a large tear in the nightshirt over the upper left arm. He cautiously raised the triangular flap of cloth upward, exposing the skin beneath. He released the safety on the injector and pressed it down—

There was a faint click as the injector fired. Robbins jumped back, watching anxiously to see what the composer would do. But the latter only snorted and kept on sleeping.

Robbins carefully retraced his steps back out to the main room. There he succumbed to temptation and ran his scanner over those sheets of music he'd seen before. Back in the kitchen again, he rechecked the chronometer display in his NV goggles. He'd been on TCE about ten minutes—and was right on schedule. Since an equal amount of time had passed for Harrison and Miles on the other end, they would be expecting him to return about now.

The next step was to reactivate the portal now, return temporarily to Earth, and then translocate back to see if the composer was still alive in Vienna on March 27, 1827—the day after he was "supposed" to die. He excitedly pressed a stud on the retrieval bracelet. The air shimmered in front of him, like heat waves above a hot street, indicating where his end of the portal was located. He stepped into the shimmer...

Robbins took another peek over the rim of the crater. The Cossacks were still coming slowly toward him—about seventy meters away now. Ducking his head back down, his mouth slid wetly across the muddy side of the crater. A few measures from "The Beautiful Blue Danube" lilted through his brain before he could shut it off. He was going to have to make a run for it and take his chances. Not a great choice, but better than just staying in the mud and dying on his belly—

Suddenly he heard the Cossacks yell excitedly. Glancing up again, he saw them pointing toward the barrel of a rifle poking through the second-floor window of a building on his left. There was a sharp crack! *and the tall black hat of one of the Cossacks went flying off.*

Immediately two of them dismounted and ran into the building. The other pair quickly brought themselves and all of their horses close to the front of the building, out of range of the rifle. Robbins braced himself to make a run for the alley containing the portal while the Cossacks were distracted, but thought better of it. The two by the building were directly across the street from the entrance to the alley. They would probably see him before he reached it—and he doubted they were in any mood to take a prisoner.

From the building Robbins heard men shouting—and then a woman scream "No!" A moment later the two Cossacks emerged dragging a young man, and a woman Robbins assumed was his wife. She was in her late teens, with auburn hair, and obviously pregnant. She pleaded with their captors not to hurt her husband Josef, her baby, or her. The young man just shouted curses at them.

The Cossacks laughed harshly. One of the pair still on horseback dismounted and said something to the couple in broken German. Robbins couldn't make out all of it, but what he did understand made him feel sick. Then the Cossack nodded to the one holding the woman. The latter pulled her down on her back to the dirty street, pinning her arms and grinning wolfishly in patient anticipation as she struggled futilely. The other one knelt beside her, and roughly pulled and ripped her long skirt high above her waist.

Paralyzed with horror, Robbins stared open-mouthed at the scene playing out in front of him. The bare thrashing legs and waist of the woman. Glimpses of her protruding, pregnant abdomen. The husband, locked in a viciously tight bear hug by the Cossack standing behind him, no longer cursing but pleading with them in the names of Jesus and the Blessed Virgin. The other Cossack, standing with his back to Robbins just in front of the young woman's feet, slowly, methodically, pulling down his pants.

Robbins clenched his fists, reflexively praying to God himself to tell him what he could do to help her. He wasn't a fighter, he didn't have any kind of weapon. If he tried to stop them they'd just take a minute to kill him and then get on with it.

What could he possibly do to change things—

"Nothing changed."

Robbins slumped down into the cushioned chair in the chancellor's office. He was still dressed in a long coat, coarse woolen trousers, white shirt, and vest—typical dress for a Viennese bourgeois circa 1827.

The chancellor sat behind her desk, a look of concern on her face. Everett sat in a chair next to him.

Robbins said, "I translocated to Vienna again a little after dawn on March 27, 1827. After I came out of the alley containing the portal, I walked several blocks and found a street vendor selling newspapers."

He paused dejectedly. "A headline on the front page said, 'Yesterday afternoon, our beloved Herr Beethoven passed on to his reward.' After returning briefly to our world, I translocated back to Vienna on the afternoon of March 29, 1827." Robbins described how he'd blended in with a large crowd of mourners as the composer's funeral procession wended its way through the streets of Vienna.

He looked at Everett. "Why didn't it work?"

The latter shook her head. "I don't know. From the standpoint of transcosmological physics, there are two possibilities. One is that I've been wrong all these years about the 'pliable' nature of TCE's history.

The other is that, by injecting Beethoven with the vaccine, you may actually have prolonged his life—but in a new 'sub-branch' universe you created by that intervention. The problem is, if that were so, we might be able to translocate only into the 'original' universe where he died on the same day as in our history. Thus, from our point of view, we will seem to have done nothing."

So that's that. Robbins loosened the collar of his starched linen shirt and sighed. So close—

"But there is another possibility."

He looked at Everett again.

"The reason may not actually be transcosmological, but medical. Maybe Harrison's opinion that Beethoven died of hepatitis is wrong. Maybe you didn't give the vaccine properly."

Robbins frowned. Well, he thought he had—

"Also, Harrison said the success rate with the vaccine was 95%. That means it would fail 1 time out of 20. Maybe we've just been very unlucky."

Robbins looked thankfully at Everett, feeling like a condemned prisoner who had received, if not a full pardon, at least a stay of execution.

The chancellor asked, "What do you propose we do?"

Everett shrugged. "Harrison's the expert on the medical possibilities. I suggest we discuss them with him."

She paused. "Speaking of Harrison, wasn't he supposed to be at this meeting too?"

Just then the office door opened and Harrison walked unsteadily into the room. He collapsed into an empty chair and wiped a pale forehead with his palm. Right now, Robbins thought, he looked more like a patient than a physician.

"Sorry I'm late," he mumbled. "I—Dr. Ertmann is dead."

The chancellor frowned. "Who?"

"Dorothy Ertmann. She's been with me for five years."

"I'm sorry to hear this." The chancellor looked truly concerned. "How did it happen?"

"She killed herself." Harrison massaged his eyes. "At least she knew what to inject herself with to make it quick. Relatively painless."

Everett said, "Do you know why she did it?"

"She left a note. But it wasn't very specific. Something about her being so sorry that she'd betrayed the Institute and all of us. Especially me." Harrison sighed. "Her closest relative is a younger sister in Des Moines. I'll have to call her."

The chancellor said, "I know how upset you must be, and we won't keep you here any longer than necessary. Before you arrived, we were discussing why Dr. Robbins' project failed."

Harrison listened patiently as Everett then repeated *sotto voce* what she'd told them earlier. He said, "Based on our tests, I'm certain our diagnosis of the cause of Beethoven's death is correct. And I taught Dr. Robbins to use the injector myself. It's so simple to use, it's virtually idiot-proof."

He glanced at Robbins. "Sorry, that didn't come out right."

Robbins shrugged. "No offense taken."

Harrison continued, "Also, the vaccine won't work if the recipient can't generate a good immune response, or if the infection is simply too severe."

Everett said, "Could the dose itself have been defective in some way?"

Harrison shook his head. "No. I tested it myself shortly before giving it to Dr. Robbins. It never left my possession until I gave it to him."

"Then what do you suggest, Dr. Harrison?" the chancellor asked.

Harrison shrugged. "Dr. Robbins should go back again and inject Beethoven with nanoscrubbers. Barring prior treatment with a specific blocking agent, they're essentially fail-safe."

Everett looked pensively at Harrison. "While I was listening to you

I thought of another possibility."

She frowned. "Deliberate sabotage."

Harrison sat straight up in his chair. "What are you suggesting?"

"It strikes me that both the transcosmological and medical reasons for this failure are so remote that we can't rule out the human factor."

"I told you, Dr. Everett, I tested the vaccine myself and kept it with me until—"

"I'm not accusing you of anything. Or Dr. Robbins either."

Me? Robbins thought. *This is my project. How could she think—*

He wrinkled his forehead. *Unless she suspects I'm so diabolically clever that I proposed it just to sabotage it, so no one else would try to change TCE's past.*

Robbins felt a trickle of sweat form under his armpits. *I know I didn't sabotage it. But how can I prove it to them?*

Everett continued, "Do you know anyone else who had both the technical knowledge and opportunity to sabotage the project?"

Harrison frowned. "Well, I suppose—"

"Dr. Ertmann."

They all looked at Robbins.

"Remember, Dr. Harrison? She was in the Portal Room just before I translocated. Could she have done something?"

Harrison glared at him in a way unbecoming someone dedicated to the saving of lives.

"Madam chancellor," he said, "I find Dr. Robbins' insinuation to be in very poor taste, considering the person in question has just died under tragic circumstances and cannot defend herself."

"We understand, Dr. Harrison," Everett said. "However, try to put your personal feelings aside and give us an honest answer."

Harrison's shoulders sagged. "Dr. Ertmann was very—idealistic. She was truly one of the most caring and dedicated physicians I have ever worked with."

He paused. "However, I must say this too. When Dorothy went back and obtained those specimens from Beethoven, she was under the impression it was a standard pathology project to discover his cause of death—the kind she and I have done on so many other historical figures before. After Dr. Robbins' project was approved, I…told her what its real purpose was. And yes, I know that information was only supposed to be given on a strict 'need to know' basis. But I believed that, considering the dangerous work she'd done, she had the moral, if not technically the legal right to know."

Everett said, "And how did she react when you told her?"

"She became very angry. She cited the potential risks of erasing our own world or of causing some unforeseen catastrophe on TCE—much like Dr. Brentano did at our recent meeting. She even accused me of lying to her and betraying her."

The chancellor asked, "But—what does this all mean?"

"It means," Everett answered, "that we try again. But this time, it's going to be a little more complicated. And,"—she looked at Robbins—"a lot more dangerous."

After putting on his NOC suit, Robbins reentered the Portal Room. Miles was talking to Everett and Harrison. "Now that you mention it, I did pick up a pair of NV goggles and a retrieval bracelet off the floor after Dr. Robbins and I came back into the Portal Room."

Everett looked at Robbins. "The technician says Dr. Ertmann was left unattended at the active portal for about ten minutes. So she had enough time to enter TCE and do something to sabotage your attempt to vaccinate Beethoven. Harrison tells me she probably injected him with a blocking agent that would prevent him from responding to the vaccine you gave or any nanoscrubbers we might inject later."

Harrison nodded.

Robbins said, "Tell me again. What exactly am I supposed to do?"

Everett explained, "The technician has just set the coordinates to translocate you to Beethoven's apartment about five minutes before we believe Dr. Ertmann arrived. What you need to do is—stop her. Confront her when she arrives. Convince her to return without doing what she came to do."

A grim smile formed on Everett's lips. "Be creative."

Robbins replied, "But how is that going to change anything? You're saying that if I stop Dr. Ertmann, the vaccine I injected should work then, and Beethoven will live longer. But, I know he didn't live longer, because when I went to TCE the day after he was 'supposed' to die, he *was* dead. Therefore, I won't succeed, I can't succeed in stopping her! Do you understand what I'm trying to say?"

Robbins frowned. He wasn't sure *he* understood what he was trying to say. "It sounds like I'm supposed to change what's already happened. And I remember you said it's impossible to change our past."

"No," Everett answered patiently, "we can't travel back along the timeline of our own branch universe and change its past. But, as I said at your meeting yesterday, we can change the 'past' of TCE without running into the kind of causality problems you're trying to describe. In other words, from our current 'past' and 'present' perspective, Dr. Ertmann did succeed in preventing the vaccine from working and prolonging Beethoven's life. However, if you go back 'now' and stop her, from our 'future' point of view—which will become the 'present' when you return through the portal after stopping her—at that time, from our perspective, she will have failed, and the vaccine you gave will work. Is that clear?"

Robbins knew she couldn't see his face through the black hood of the NOC suit, but she must have guessed how bewildered it looked.

Everett said sympathetically, "Even if you don't understand, just take my word for it. If you do what I tell you, it will work."

Then a real smile flickered on her lips. "Trust me, I'm a physicist!"

Robbins and the other two men blinked. *Now's the time she decides to show she has a sense of humor,* he thought.

Recovering first, Miles said, "The portal is stable and active, Dr. Everett."

The latter said, "Good luck, Dr. Robbins."

Sounds like I'll need it. Robbins walked to the portal entrance—

"One more thing."

Caught with one leg in the air, Robbins teetered on the threshold of the portal before righting himself.

The grim smile was back on Everett's lips as she continued, "Make sure you stay on TCE no more than fifteen minutes. Otherwise you might—literally—run into your 'past' self coming through to inject the vaccine. I'm not sure what would happen if that occurred, but some of the possibilities are very—unpleasant."

Robbins sighed. *As if I didn't have enough to worry about already.*

At least the translocation went smoothly—no rude surprises so far. The kitchen in the composer's apartment was almost exactly as he remembered it. His NV goggles guided him back to the main studio room. He positioned himself in the corner of the room farthest from the bedroom door—and waited.

After what seemed like an eternity, he heard a faint rustle from the kitchen. A few seconds later, a slim figure came stealthily through the open doorway. Ertmann was dressed just as he'd last seen her in the Portal Room. She was wearing the NV goggles and bracelet Miles had mentioned. In her left hand she held an injector like the one he'd used to inject the vaccine—or was that "going to use"?

Robbins let her get halfway to the bedroom door before he whispered, "Stop."

Ertmann froze like a statue. While the rest of her remained immobile, her head swiveled slowly towards the direction of his voice.

41

"I know what you're planning to do, and I can't let you do it." Robbins hoped he sounded menacing.

"Dr. Harrison sent you, didn't he," she whispered back.

"Yes."

Shoulders slumped in resignation, she placed the injector in a pocket on the side of her lab coat. "I should have known it wouldn't work."

"Now we're going to go back to the kitchen together, activate the portal, and leave. Understood?"

The expression on her face was so forlorn he had to suppress an urge to go over, give her a hug, and say, "There, there, it's all right."

Ertmann shrugged. "Why not?"

Moving quietly to her side, Robbins steered her back toward the kitchen. As they entered it he started to activate the retrieval bracelet on his wrist—and then she broke away from him and screamed, "No!"

Startled, Robbins froze. What if she'd just woken Beethoven up—

"What you and the others are planning to do is wrong!" she shouted. "It could destroy our world, and this one! Billions of living, breathing human beings—on our Earth, this one, all of us—might be snuffed out like we'd never existed, or maybe suffer something worse than we can possibly imagine! I can't let you do it!"

She snatched a wicked-looking, vaguely familiar knife from a near-by table and pointed it at him.

Robbins stared at her. What was he supposed to do now? He was taller than she was, probably stronger. But he was no fighter, she was about fifteen years younger than him—and she had a knife.

"Don't be foolish," he said. "It's over. Just what do you think you're going to do with that knife?" Remembering too late that she was probably an expert at surgery, he hoped she'd take it as a purely rhetorical question. "We're on to your plan, and you can't fight all of us!" *Of course,* he added to himself, *the rest of "us" don't happen to be here right now—*

The knife in Ertmann's hand drifted slowly downward. "You're right," she whispered. "I can't fight all of you."

You've got her on the ropes, now finish her off! "Harrison took you into his confidence. He *trusted* you—and you betrayed him! You betrayed all of us at the Institute—but most of all you betrayed him. He's been like a father to you all these years—and you still betrayed him!" He wasn't sure if the "father" part was true, but it sounded good.

The knife clattered to the floor. Robbins glanced over his shoulder, expecting to hear curses in German and see an irate composer storm out of the bedroom to confront the prowlers in his home.

"You're right," Ertmann repeated. The NV goggles covered her eyes so he couldn't see the tears, but she was sobbing. "What do you want me to do?"

"Activate the portal and leave—now!"

It was hard to act so cruel. He had to suppress another urge to give her a comforting hug. Quietly, she fumbled with the bracelet on her wrist. The portal snapped to shimmering life—and then she was gone.

Robbins exhaled slowly. *Didn't know you had it in you.*

Then he tensed again. Just because Beethoven hadn't made a dramatic entrance into the kitchen didn't mean that he wasn't stumbling around in his bedroom trying to light a candle to see who was making the commotion. Robbins walked cautiously towards the bedroom and peeked in.

The great man was snoring heavily, lying in the same position Robbins had seen (would see?) him in when he came with the vaccine. Robbins mentally kicked himself for forgetting something so basic. Ertmann could have shouted and made noise all night and it wouldn't have woken Beethoven up!

He went back to the kitchen. He wasn't sure how much time he had before "he" would come through from the other side. And he certainly didn't want to find out firsthand what kind of unpleasant things Everett was alluding to if he encountered his "earlier" self.

As Robbins started to activate the portal a sudden thought stopped him. When he reemerged back on Earth Ertmann would still be alive—wouldn't she? He'd assumed that, by going back into the "past" to confront her and change what she'd done, he'd also be preventing her from committing suicide. Now, trying to remember what Everett had said, he wasn't so sure. But you couldn't talk to a "dead" person like that—could you?

Then he remembered what he'd told Ertmann about how she'd betrayed everyone, especially Harrison—and where he'd heard those words before. If she *was* still dead when he returned to Earth—

Feeling sick, he activated the portal and stepped through.

"Was it worth it?"

Robbins smiled at Antonia. "I think so."

He sat down next to her on the couch in his apartment. The last ten days had definitely been the most exhausting—and exhilarating—of his entire life. He'd made thirty-two trips to TCE since translocating a second time to Vienna on March 27, 1827—and this time finding the newspaper headline was about somebody named Metternich, and not Beethoven's death. Then daylight trips to music shops, more nighttime excursions to the composer's home during his additional lifetime—by now Beethoven's apartment seemed as familiar to him as his own.

After the composer finally died in 1834, Robbins and his staff made scouting excursions every one to two years to see what effect his "new" music had produced on other composers. So far the survey had reached 1847—and found no significant changes. Chopin, Schumann, Mendelssohn, Berlioz—the new masterpieces that Beethoven created hadn't significantly affected their music. Maybe it was because those final works were so distinctly in Beethoven's own individual style—an apotheosis of everything he had previously written. A musical valedictory, rather than breaking new ground like the *Eroica.*

Antonia said, "When can we hear this wonderful music?"

"Soon." Late this afternoon his staff had finished downloading all the scores he'd scanned from the composer's manuscripts into the Musicology Section's own computer system. After assigning digitized instruments to each part, and adjusting the dynamics and tempos, they now had versions of the music ready for playback.

Antonia smiled. "I have to admit, I am curious. What did he write during those 'extra' years?"

"Most of it was chamber music. The remaining movements of his unfinished String Quintet in C major. Three string quartets. Two piano sonatas. Three trios for piano, violin, and cello."

Robbins paused. "And one work for orchestra."

Antonia arched her eyebrows.

"You and I will be the first people on our Earth to hear Beethoven's final symphony.

"The A minor.

"The Tenth."

Raising his arm as if holding a baton, Robbins brought it down with a sudden downbeat. "Computer—begin!"

The slow introduction to the first movement began with a series of crashing dissonances by the full orchestra. Finally the clashing chords resolved themselves into a quiet, gentle theme in C major, introduced by a solo clarinet and supported by pizzicato strings. Gradually the melody was taken up by the rest of the orchestra, underwent a brief development—then suddenly disappeared in a dark descent into A minor as the main Allegro section began. A short exposition presented two tragic themes. ("Both," Robbins whispered, "are derived from ones in works by J. S. Bach. The Crucifixus section of the Mass in B minor, and also a cantata entitled *Christ Lay in the Bonds of Death*.") The development section kept almost exclusively to minor keys, the sense of pain, foreboding, and heroic but futile struggle in the music becoming more and more intense. The recapitulation brought no relief, finally ending in a whisper of hopeless resignation in the tonic minor.

The Andante second movement was a set of alternating variations on two themes, one in F major and the other in C minor. (Robbins smiled at the quizzical look on Antonia's face. "Sound very familiar, don't they? Both melodies are similar to ones in the oratorio *Messiah*. The aria 'He Was Despised,' and the chorus 'Surely He Hath Borne Our Griefs.' Beethoven once said Handel was his favorite composer.") The movement's initial quiet, pastoral mood eventually gave way to darkness and despair in its last measures.

The third movement Scherzo was a Presto in C minor that sounded like a *danse macabre*, a hideous joke. ("The main theme is like the one Mozart used in the Dies Irae section of his Requiem.") Each return of the prayer-like melody ("More Mozart—from the *Masonic Funeral Music*.") in the A-flat major Trio sections was, just as a glimmer of hope seemed to appear, abruptly trampled by the reappearance of the dark theme of the main section.

And then—the work's fourth and final movement, initially marked "Moderato." It opened with the reappearance of the original gentle C major theme from the beginning of the symphony, but played this time in A minor. The higher strings and woodwinds played it softly, tentatively. Just as it swelled into a tragic sigh a harsh new theme played fortissimo by the trombones and lower strings tried to overwhelm it. ("That new theme," Robbins whispered, "is a verbatim quote of music Beethoven's old teacher, Haydn, wrote to honor the Emperor of his native Austria.")

Despite this onslaught by the second subject, the primary theme returned again and again, each time more forcefully, until it and *The Emperor's Hymn* seemed locked in a titanic struggle full of clashing dissonances. Then, after a sudden and dazzling modulation to its original key of C major, with trumpets blaring and timpani thundering the primary theme overwhelmed the "imperial" one, shattering it into scattered notes and crushing it out of existence. Its true power and strength finally revealed, the full orchestra took up the melody in a coda of orgiastic celebration and joy that made the ending of Beethoven's own preceding symphony seem tame and restrained by comparison. Finally, amid martial fanfares by the brass and percussion of barbaric intensity, the strings and woodwinds played the victorious C major theme in a massive contrapuntal *tour de force* that brought the symphony to a triumphant close.

They sat together in silence for a long time, with the music echoing in their ears and hearts.

Finally Antonia spoke. "You're right. It was worth it."

"Actually," Robbins said, "Beethoven started a new symphony, in C minor, in 1826. But it never got beyond some sketches. Then, in 1831, he started this work, and finished it early in 1834. He wrote in his diary that he'd been inspired to write it by some recent events, such as the Poles rising up and trying to free their country from Russian rule. And especially by a gift his nephew Karl gave him on his 60th birthday—a German translation of Shelley's *Prometheus Unbound*. He said the music depicts the triumphant struggle of the human spirit and Life against tyranny and Death—the ultimate victory of freedom over oppression. Like the Fifth Symphony, or the *Leonore* Overture No. 3, only more so.

"Interestingly enough, a few years after it was first performed, the primary theme from the fourth movement, the one that closes the symphony so dramatically, was used as the basis for a very popular patriotic song. Just about every music shop I've gone into on TCE from 1837 on had copies of it for sale. The last time I went to Vienna, in 1847, a crowd was even singing it at some kind of street rally."

The lyrics were by an obscure Hanoverian poet. In the original

German, they were hardly great poetry. Lytton had written a version in English for him that was no better. Like the first verse—"Arise, ye German sons, unite! / No foe can stand before thy might! / The future now belongs to thee, / In union lies thy destiny!"

Robbins continued, "It's like the way new words were written about the same time to Haydn's *Kaiserhymne* too, praising Germany instead of the emperor of Austria. *Deutchland über alles*, which became the German national anthem."

"Did Beethoven get to hear the symphony before he died?"

"Well, he could never have 'heard' it. Towards the end of his life he was almost completely deaf. Remember the story, that when he conducted the first performance of the Ninth Symphony, someone had to turn him around to see the audience applauding? But if you mean, did he ever attend a performance—no. He died just before a set of concerts was going to start. It was first played a week after his funeral."

He smiled at the bust of Beethoven on the piano. The composer scowled angrily back at him.

Robbins frowned disappointedly. *I thought you'd like hearing your symphony!*

"What exactly did he die of, Howard?"

He blinked. "From injuries he suffered in a tragic street accident." *Run over by a runaway wagon carrying offal*. Never heard it coming. TCE had lost the Romanticized story of the composer leaping from his deathbed to shake his fist in defiance at the lightning-filled sky. But, he believed, it had gained far more.

Antonia looked dreamily ahead, the music still playing within her. "When are you going back?"

Tentatively, Robbins draped his arm over her shoulder. "Tomorrow morning. We're right on schedule with our survey, up to the year 1847. Velikovsky says there were major political disturbances in Vienna in

1848 and 1849, so he told me to 'jump ahead' to 1852, when things should be safe."

She replied, "So you're free for the night." Antonia's eyes gazed deeply into his, a shy but gently inquisitive smile on her lips. He had last seen that look in her eyes far too long ago, and knew she wasn't planning to go back to her own apartment tonight.

Much later, with Antonia lying asleep in his arms, Robbins gazed contentedly up at the ceiling of his bedroom. Memories of the music, of Antonia's body moving rhythmically against his, wafted through his thoughts like a slowly played fugue. It was moments like this that made Life worth living. Now, even if he were to die tomorrow, he would die happy.

But as he drifted off to sleep, memories he'd suppressed for the past ten days seeped back into his mind. Of Everett saying, "No, there was nothing you could have done to save her." Of Harrison, Ertmann's mentor, reassuring him, "No, it wasn't your fault. She did it to herself."

Maybe they were sincere, maybe they were even right. But as hard as he tried, he couldn't rationalize it or forgive himself. So young, so beautiful... He'd wanted to hug her, comfort her—not kill her! Remembering those things, the exuberance he'd felt from listening to the Tenth Symphony, from making love with Antonia, faded and died.

His semiconscious mind tried to block those memories by replacing them with more music. But the melodies it played were from tragic symphonies. Unlike those of Beethoven, some symphonies in a minor key, like Tchaikovsky's B minor or Haydn's E minor, did not finish in a bright, triumphant major key, but maintained the darker minor tonality and a mood of *Sturm und Drang* tragedy and despair to the very end. Sometimes, in music as in the real world, Death did defeat Life.

As Antonia pressed warmly against him, sleep finally claimed him too. But he slept poorly. All through the night more music haunted his dreams. Motifs from Schumann's overture to *Manfred*, especially the one representing Astarte. And the second movement of Schubert's String Quartet in D minor. The one with the nickname, "Death and the Maiden."

Robbins pounded the sides of the crater with his fists frantically. There had to be something he could do to help her! The Cossack's pants were around his ankles now, his bare buttocks quivering as he laughed, relishing the woman's terror—in no hurry to turn the horror of anticipation into the greater one of reality. Robbins raised himself higher over the rim of the crater, his eyes desperately scanning the ground for a rock, a stick, anything he could use to fight them, even if he died trying!

And then he saw it—a flash of metal against the waist of the fat dead man lying nearby. Tucked into his belt.

A pistol.

Suddenly he heard music once again in his mind. The whole Tenth Symphony, compressed into an almost instantaneous burst of sound and power. The dramatic battle of the human spirit against evil and Death, always fighting back, never giving up no matter how much pain and suffering it had to endure, until finally winning its ultimate victory!

In an instant, like a Titan unchained Robbins raised himself up from the ground, ran toward the dead man, pulled the gun from his belt, and sprinted towards the group ahead. The tiny bit of his mind that remained rational tried to tell him that he'd never fired a gun, that he didn't even know how many bullets it had, but he ignored it. He screamed in Russian, "Stop!"

The Cossacks stopped laughing and looked at him.

Holding the pistol outstretched with both hands, Robbins stood just far enough away so he could cover all four of them. The music within

50

him started to fade as the reality of the situation sank in.

"Let go of them, you bastards!" The gun swiveled from one to the other. For the first time Robbins got a good look at the weapon. It looked like the kind he'd seen in that violent, century-old "Western" Billingsley had shown him once. Remembering what the hero of that "movie," Shane, had done with his six-shooter, Robbins cocked the hammer of the gun with his thumb.

The Cossack directly in front of him slowly bent over, pulled his pants back up, and turned around.

"Peace be with you, my friend," he said through broken yellow teeth. "The Czar has sent us to free you from your oppressors. Certainly not to harm you!"

He gestured toward the woman on the ground. "There is enough here for us to share. Let us all pleasure ourselves, and be brothers."

Even from five meters away Robbins could smell how foul his breath was.

The Cossack bent down again and seemed to brush some mud off his boot, curling his hand. Straightening up, he began to walk slowly towards Robbins. "Let me shake your hand in friendship—"

"Stay back!"

The other man's face looked wounded. "Surely you would not shoot down an unarmed man, one who only wishes to be your friend, like a dog! Surely you, a man of the German people, who are known even in our land for their courtesy and gentleness, would not do such a thing!"

Something glinted in the hand the Cossack had used to clean his boot. As the Russian raised his arm back to throw the knife he'd taken from the scabbard hidden in his boot, Robbins' finger squeezed the trigger of the gun. The recoil staggered him. He recovered in time to see the other man and his knife begin a slow fall to the ground, the top of his head blown away in a scarlet shower of blood, bone, and brain.

The Cossack still on his horse tried to spur it at him. Two shots, and he too lay sprawled and bloody on the ground. The one pinning the woman down leapt up and pulled out his saber. It clattered to the street after a bullet tore through the center of his face.

The last one was still holding the woman's husband, using him as a shield. As the Cossack tried to pull his saber the man twisted away from him. Robbins put a bullet into the Russian's belly.

The sound of the Cossacks' horses whinnying and striking their hooves hysterically against the cobblestones snapped Robbins back to reality. The young man was at his wife's side, brushing off the blood and gore that had splattered on her bare flesh. Gently pulling her skirt back down, he hugged and comforted the sobbing woman in his arms.

In a daze Robbins walked slowly toward each of the bodies in turn, careful not to step in the spreading red puddles on the street. He didn't need Harrison here to tell him they all looked very dead. The gun at his side dangled from his finger, then dropped to the ground.

"Will you be all right now?" he asked the man, who'd raised his wife to an unsteady standing position.

"Yes, if you help me," the man said, glancing toward the nearest horse.

Robbins helped him lift the woman onto its back, sidesaddle. Then the man led the horse down the street, avoiding the crater Robbins had just vacated. He watched the couple turn the corner at the other end of the street and heard the woman shout over the distant rumble of artillery, "God bless you, and thank you!"

Then, trying not to look anymore at what was on the ground, Robbins walked slowly toward the entrance to the alley—and the portal home. So much for the "First Law of Contact," he thought darkly as he reached for the bracelet on his left wrist—

Suddenly there was a sharp bang! *and a tearing pain ripped through his body under his right shoulder. Knocked down by the impact, he looked back toward the front of the alley and saw one of the Cossacks—the one he'd shot in the belly—lying on his side, pointing the smoking barrel of the gun at him. The Cossack grimaced, dropped the gun, and then lay still.*

His upper back now burning like acid, Robbins stared in disbelief at the red stain slowly spreading on the front of his shirt. Somehow he managed to stand up and stagger farther into the alley, fighting the urge to faint. When he tried to raise his right arm more pain lanced through him, and it was getting harder to breathe. Swinging his left wrist over toward his right hand, his numb fingers fumbled with the retrieval bracelet.

Suddenly the air in front of him shimmered and the welcoming darkness of the portal appeared. Gasping for breath, legs feeling like lead, he stumbled into it. Blackness surrounded him, a peaceful oblivion without beginning or end...

Recapitulation

When he woke up the pain was gone, and he could breathe again. The room was bright and decorated in white. He was in a strange bed, in an unfamiliar place—

"Don't try to get up, Howard."

He sank back into the sheets and smiled thankfully.

Antonia sat by the edge of the hospital bed. "Dr. Harrison says the surgery went fine, and soon you'll be as good as new."

Robbins saw the relief in her eyes as she kneaded his hand. Life is so short and uncertain, he thought. It was time to get his priorities right. Cut back on his work, convince Antonia to do the same—and find time to build a life together.

Suddenly he felt very tired. As much as his heart wanted to gaze into Antonia's eyes, the rest of him just wanted to sleep.

"You won't leave me, will you, Antonia?" he croaked.

"Never, Howard. I'll never leave you."

He drifted back to sleep, Schumann's *Träumerei* wafting through his mind.

But when he woke up, Antonia was gone.

The nurse who came in a few minutes later told him that he'd been in the Institute's hospital for over four days. Then Velikovsky walked in. The latter asked him to describe what had happened on that street in Vienna in late 1852. Though eager to listen to every detail of the incident, he brushed aside Robbins' queries about what it all meant with "It's still too early to tell."

After Velikovsky left, Robbins tried to think it through himself, but couldn't. As many times as he'd traveled to TCE, his knowledge of the non-musical history of the places he visited was too sketchy.

Harrison saw him the next morning. "Everything seems to be healing well."

He paused. "Velikovsky asked me to tell you that there's going to be a special meeting of the Humanities Committee at four o'clock this afternoon. Medically speaking, it should be safe for you to attend."

"What's the meeting about? That—incident on TCE?"

Harrison hesitated. "Yes. Velikovsky and his people started investigating it right after you returned, and he's presenting their preliminary findings and suggestions to the Executive Committee this morning. He'll meet with the Science Committee at 2:00 p.m. and then your Committee after that."

He looked at Robbins with an expression that resembled pity. "There are many rumors circulating as to what he will say."

"Such as?"

Harrison shook his head as he left. "I always try to deal with facts, not things that may or may not be true. Life is so much simpler that way."

A little before 4:00 p.m., two nurses helped him get dressed and into a wheelchair. The orderly who scooted him through the underground tunnel to the Institute's main building got him to the meeting room just on time.

The others were already there. He took the last empty seat, between Billingsley and Antonia. She didn't respond to his greeting but instead stared stonily ahead. Before he could speak again the chancellor said, "Thank you all for coming here on such short notice. As you know, Dr. Robbins was seriously injured during his last translocation to TCE. We all wish him a speedy recovery."

Then Velikovsky spoke. "For the last five days my staff have been traveling to TCE investigating the historical anomaly experienced by Dr. Robbins. Many of them were given missions that would normally have been considered far too dangerous. Some have actually been injured—several of them fatally. Through their dedicated efforts, we now know that Transcosmic Earth has suffered a major catastrophe."

Everyone in the room glanced at Robbins. *What happened? What did I do?*

Velikovsky continued, "Except for a surge in nationalistic activity in the various German states in the preceding decade, we did not discover any significant deviations in the history of TCE until 1848. In that year, in our history a number of popular and nationalistic movements threatened to or, in several cases, succeeded in changing the political structures of many countries in Europe."

Robbins listened as Velikovsky described events that he only vaguely recalled from the historian's orientation lectures. Demonstrations and riots in Vienna and Berlin in March, 1848 that forced the royal family of the Austrian Empire, the Hapsburgs, to flee their capital and threatened to topple the other major German state, the Kingdom of Prussia. The calling not long afterwards of the Constituent National Assembly in Frankfurt. Its purpose was to try to unite all of the many independent

55

German states—Prussia, a hodgepodge of much smaller principalities and cities in central and southern Germany, and the Hapsburgs' large empire composed of Austria, Hungary, and much of central Europe— into a single nation.

In the end, Velikovsky said, that attempt failed. By 1849 the reactionary factions, the ones who supported the political *status quo*, had won. The first successful steps towards German unification were delayed until the mid-1860s. Through the *realpolitik* policies of Prussia's "Iron Chancellor," Otto von Bismarck, that kingdom and the smaller German states were united in 1871 into the German Empire with the king of Prussia, William I, as its Emperor. The Hapsburgs continued on their own separate path, their Austro-Hungarian Empire marked by a growing decadence and military weakness until its political incompetence helped touch off the First World War in 1914. Except between 1938 and 1945, the Germans in Austria never were a part of the nation that became "Germany."

"That is what happened in our history and," Velikovsky continued, "until recently, on TCE. But while our history has not changed, that of TCE most certainly has. There, in 1848, Prussia, the smaller German states, and the entire Austrian Empire were all united together into the Pan-German Empire, with the Hapsburg ruler Ferdinand I assuming the title 'Emperor of All the Germans.'

"Such a major change in the political structure of Europe—a new nation of over seventy-five million people in the very middle of the continent, much larger than any except Russia—produced a history far different from ours. The event that almost cost Dr. Robbins his life in 1852, one that never happened on our Earth, was the near-capture of Vienna, the capital of the new empire, by the army of Czar Nicholas I. The German forces under Prince Alfred von Windischgrätz were finally able to repel it, and a week later won a decisive victory over the Russians at the Battle of Olmütz. The French, under the newly self-crowned Napoleon III, also launched an attack as the Russians were threatening Vienna. Their army was more successful, defeating the Germans near Cologne. After an armistice, the French forced the Pan-German Empire to cede all its territory west of the Rhine to their own Second Empire."

He went on, adding more details. The Franco-German war of 1868, ending with the execution of Napoleon III and the installation of a German prince on the throne of France. The successful invasion and subjugation of Russia in 1878 by a general named Moltke, with a member of the German royal family placed on the throne of the Czars.

"And then, with the formation of the Anglo-German Confederation in 1892, all of Europe, North Africa, the Middle East, and Australia were under the direct or indirect control of the Pan-German Empire. Over the next two decades the Confederation extended its influence to include all of Africa and, after a bloody war with the Empire of Japan, Asia. By 1912, except for those countries in the Western Hemisphere that were not possessions of formerly independent European nations like Great Britain and Spain, a 'Pax Germanica' extended across TCE.

"Except for different patterns of immigration to it in the late 19th century and, of course, no war with Spain in 1898, until 1912 major events in the United States were very similar to those on our Earth. That year, Woodrow Wilson was elected President on an 'antimonarchist' platform. It included his 'Ten Points,' calling for the 'liberation of the enslaved peoples of the world, the establishment of democracy, and the right to national self-determination.'

"That began a period of forty years during which the U.S. waged an ideological, indirect war against the Confederation that included fomenting civil unrest, terrorism, and even guerrilla wars using proxy 'national democratic liberation front' groups within its borders. In the early 1950s, however, this 'cold war' reached a final crisis after the successful invasions of Cuba and Canada by the United States, and the overthrow shortly thereafter of the republican government of Mexico by a Confederation-backed local faction and its replacement by a monarchy headed by a Hohenzollern prince."

Velikovsky paused. "To understand what happened next, remember that nearly all of the important scientific figures from 1848 on we are familiar with still existed on TCE. For example, Albert Einstein, Edward Teller, and Wernher von Braun did similar pioneering work, but never emigrated to the United States. Those born in America, like the Wright brothers, J. Robert Oppenheimer, and Robert Goddard had careers even more successful than in our history. Thus, the technology on TCE in the middle of their new 20th century was as advanced or, in some cases, more advanced than at the corresponding date on our world."

Velikovsky looked at Robbins and said quietly, "On December 1, 1953 the United States of America launched a massive preemptive nuclear strike with its full arsenal of aircraft and missiles against all the major cities and military installations of the Confederation. The latter retaliated in kind."

There was a long silence. "It was difficult to assess the full range of destruction produced immediately, and by the later effects of residual radiation, plague, and the great famine caused by the resulting 'nuclear winter.' We estimate that three billion people—85% of the total population of TCE when the war began—had died by the end of 1954. After 1996, we've been unable to find any survivors."

I did it, Robbins thought to himself. *I don't know how, but I killed all those people*. Eyes closed, he didn't dare look at the rest of them. Especially Antonia.

From a distance he heard Velikovsky say, "There are two important questions we must answer. What caused this catastrophe? And can we do anything to change it? I will defer the latter question to Dr. Everett. As to the first, I would like your opinion, Dr. Robbins."

Reflexively he opened his eyes.

Velikovsky said, "Computer, display."

A holographic display appeared in the middle of the table. He continued, "This is a recording made in Frankfurt on July 4,1848 at the official announcement of the formation of the Pan-German Empire."

The recording must have been taken from the top of a tall building. Robbins looked down at a sea of cheering humanity in the great open area, and a dais on which stood bemedaled dignitaries. At ground level, near one end of the raised platform, he noticed a military band that seemed ready to start playing.

"The man who is speaking," said Velikovsky, indicating the walrus-mustached figure talking softly in German in the middle of the image, "is the same Baron Otto von Bismarck I mentioned earlier. In our own history, he was one of the many nobles in the Prussian and Hapsburg courts who opposed German unification in 1848. In the revised history of TCE, however, for reasons we still do not fully understand, they were among its most enthusiastic supporters."

The small figure in the display concluded his speech with a generous sweep of his arm toward "our new Kaiser." As if on cue the military band started to play a powerful, triumphant, martial tune.

Robbins felt his flesh turn cold. *Now* he understood. As they sang together, the faces of the tiny figures in the recording showed a mixture of pride, fervor, and single-minded patriotism. Workers, peasants, aristocrats—men and women, people from every level of society, different in so many ways, but all united in a common cause—in their love for their new country. Right arms raised in a loyal salute to their leader, they shouted the words to the song passionately, in complete fanatical unity—as if they were now inspired to go out and conquer the world.

It all made sense. He thought of the armies of Revolutionary and Napoleonic France, marching out to the strains of *La Marseillaise* to overrun Europe. Or the Germans of the 20th century on their Earth, with *Deutchland über alles*. Even the English, perhaps, during their days of Empire, with *God Save the King*. A memory from his early childhood came back to him—the time his father had taken him to a baseball game. The swelling pride he'd felt at being an American, standing with the rest of the crowd, as he'd heard *The Star-Spangled Banner* sung for the first time.

Those people in the recording seemed to feel that same emotion, but many times more intensely as they sang their own anthem. *Aufstehen!* ("Arise, ye German sons, unite!") A song whose melody was based on the primary theme of the fourth movement of Beethoven's final symphony.

The A minor.

The triumphant Tenth.

"Dr. Robbins?" Velikovsky was speaking to him. "Dr. Brentano says you're familiar with the song these people are singing, and that it might have a bearing on the question we are discussing. Is that correct?"

"Yes," Robbins said. "But first—could you please turn off that recording?"

After the others had a little time to absorb what he'd told them, Robbins turned to Everett, who was sitting by herself in the far corner of the room. "Is there any way we can undo all this? Change things back the way they're supposed to be?"

She nodded. "I think that we can. At the Science Committee meeting earlier this afternoon, Harrison told us that the vaccine-blocking agent the late Dr. Ertmann tried to use would still be effective even if it were given up to twenty-four hours after you injected the vaccine. All you have to do is to translocate to Beethoven's apartment again, say about thirty minutes 'after' you gave the vaccine, and inject this neutralizing agent into him. Theoretically, that would undo what's been done to this point, and TCE would return to 'normal.' I propose you do just that."

That's all? That's all I have to do? He looked down at his hands, clenched them, then opened them. *I destroy worlds, then I create them again—*

But not anymore. He had no desire to play God. After this one last time, he swore he'd never to go back to TCE again.

The chancellor said, "Is there a second for Dr. Everett's proposal? All in favor? Any opposed? Let the record show that the Humanities Committee has voted 6 to 0 in favor of her proposal."

Robbins sighed. The sooner he did it the better he'd feel—

"And that," the chancellor continued, "brings us to the second item on our agenda here. Dr. Velikovsky has submitted a proposal that was approved by the Executive and Science Committees earlier today. It involves setting up a special Task Force to review future projects for changing the history of TCE. The applicability of this proposal is, of course, contingent on Dr. Robbins' anticipated success in returning TCE to its original state. If he does, and this proposal is approved by the Committee today, the Task Force will—"

"What?" The chancellor looked startled at Robbins' interjection. "Are you saying that, if I do make things right on TCE, you're going to let someone else go back and change them again?"

Velikovsky said, "Precisely. You have shown that it is possible, with appropriate manipulations, to change TCE's history without changing our own. Thus, instead of only passively retrieving lost information as we have done in the past, we now know that we can use TCE as a vast laboratory for studying the effects of carefully selected changes on subsequent political, scientific, and artistic developments. After each such experiment is finished, we can go back and, as you will be doing, undo that change and reset TCE's history to its 'default' condition."

He smiled warmly at Robbins. "Although the change you caused had, in that particular history of TCE, disastrous consequences for its people, we here on our Earth have benefited greatly. The dynamics of what is to us an 'alternate' history will provide enormous material for analysis and review for years to come. And this is just the beginning. We all owe you a debt of gratitude for showing us what can be done."

Robbins wished he still had that gun he'd dropped on TCE. "Do you realize what you're saying? You're talking about deliberately manipulating, possibly destroying billions of innocent people for the sake of an 'experiment'!"

Velikovsky looked pained. "Not real people, like we are. 'Shadow people,' in a 'shadow history,' without a real existence of their own. As Dr. Everett has said, they live in a 'pliable' past that is not truly 'real'—"

"Don't you dare misquote me!" Everett interrupted. "You know what I think of your proposal!"

Robbins glared at Velikovsky. "They are real! Flesh and blood! I saw them! I touched them!" *I killed four of them personally!* "They can be hurt, they can feel pain just like us—and we have no right to play God!"

"Order, order!" The chancellor looked angry. "We must discuss this proposal in a civilized manner. You and Dr. Velikovsky have had your say. Does anyone else wish to comment?"

There was another round of shouting, this time with Antonia on one side and Lytton and Shimura on the other. For every "Shelley" that Lytton mentioned or "van Gogh" that Shimura brought up, Antonia countered with "And how many billions of people have to suffer and die to get those few extra poems and paintings?"

Billingsley said nothing. Just fiddled with his bow tie.

After the arguing died down the chancellor said, "Is there a second for Dr. Velikovsky's proposal?"

"Seconded!" Lytton and Shimura spoke simultaneously.

"All in favor?"

Velikovsky, Lytton, and Shimura raised their hands.

"Opposed?"

Robbins' arm shot up first, then Antonia's. Billingsley raised his lazily.

"Let the record show that the Humanities Committee has voted 3 to 3 on Dr. Velikovsky's proposal."

The chancellor paused. "As per our by-laws, I must now cast the tie-breaking vote. Based on the positive recommendations made earlier today by the Executive and Science Committees, I feel that I too must vote in favor of the proposal. Let the record show that—"

"That does it!" Antonia's face was crimson. "You little tin gods can play your games with peoples' lives by yourselves! I have nothing but the utmost contempt for you and refuse to be a part of it!"

She stood up. "I resign from the Institute! Good-bye!"

Antonia glared at Robbins and sneered in a low voice, "You and your damn music!" Then she left the room.

"What a woman," Billingsley said suddenly. He stood up. "I didn't say anything before we voted because everybody already had their minds made up. Now, I'll just say that a person can stand a lot of push-ing if he has to."

He frowned. "But there are some things a person can't take. I resign too."

He moved toward the door. "It's sad. I used to think we were the good guys. That we were Earth-One. Looks like we're really Earth-Three.

"And for those of you who don't get that allusion, here's another 20th century term that seems appropriate right now. AMF!" Billingsley's last words as he left the room were what that acronym meant.

Robbins blinked. He'd never seen the chancellor blush before.

Recovering her composure she said, "Any more business? Then this meeting is adjourned."

The others began to stand, say their own good-byes, and then leave. But Robbins stayed in his chair, alone with his memories and regrets. Faintly, deep within him, his mind played through the final Adagio of Haydn's *Farewell* Symphony. As each instrument played its plaintive "auf Wiedersehen" and left, all the things he had hoped and lived for, everything that brought meaning to his life, seemed to go with them. Finally, as the two remaining muted violins closed the work softly in the distant, lonely key of F-sharp major, he got up and left too.

Back in his own apartment, Robbins felt a little better. Harrison had sent a message for him to get a good night's sleep before going back to deliver the vaccine-blocker in the morning. He sat down at the Steinway and, though wincing occasionally from the pain in his wounded upper back, began to play. But the pieces his fingers selected just made him feel depressed again. The third movement of Chopin's Sonata no. 2 in B-flat minor, then Haydn's Andante and Variations in F minor. As the last questioning notes of the latter work's coda faded away, the doorbell rang. Praying it was Antonia, he opened the door—

It was Everett.

"May I come in?"

She sat down on the couch. He settled down beside her.

"Nice piano."

"Thank you."

Everett looked at him sadly. "You look depressed."

"Of course I am!" Everett's hair shimmered like spun silver in the muted light. Almost like an older version of— "If I go to TCE and manage to undo all the damage I've done, Velikovsky and the others are going to use all those people as guinea pigs for their 'experiments'!" *But isn't that what you did? No, I was trying to do something good for them and us! Tell that to all the people you killed.* "And if it doesn't work, I'll still be responsible for the death of billions of people—the whole human race there! Either way, it's all my fault!"

"No, it isn't. It's more my fault than yours. I could have vetoed your proposal anytime. You wanted your music, I wanted to prove we could change TCE's history without changing ours. We both got want we wanted. Just not what we expected."

Everett moved closer. "How much of that report about TCE I sent out three weeks ago did you understand?"

Robbins rolled his eyes.

Everett grunted. "Oh. That much. Well, I'm really not very good at asimoving, but I'll try. The key thing you have to understand is, at any instant in time, 'choices' are being made. At the smallest scale, a radioactive atom may 'choose' to decay or not decay. When you get up in the morning, you choose to part your hair on the right or the left. The 'present' is the sum of all the specific choices and decisions made in the past. Nearly all those choices are 'trivial,' in the technical sense that they don't lead to any 'significant' difference in the history of the universe. They might affect only an atom or, at the macroscopic level, only a tiny portion of the cosmos. But, occasionally, one of them makes a 'critical' difference."

She paused. "On September 17, 1666, someone or something made a choice that—God, Nature, whatever you want to call it—considered so important that it caused our universe to split into two branches. In one branch, one 'choice' was made, some event occurred—and in the other branch, it didn't. On November 9, 1998, the same thing happened, due to some other choice. What we perceive as the 'real world' is just one of those latter two 'branch' universes. What we call TCE is the discreet timeline, the 'history,' between those two branch points in 1666 and 1998.

"If you're wondering what the actual choices were that made the universe split in those two particular years—well, I wish I knew too. But I do have some guesses. In 1666 Isaac Newton—you've heard

65

of him, haven't you?—was doing some of his most important work."

Everett smiled wryly. "It's supposed to be a myth but maybe, in the other branch universe, the apple 'decided' *not* to fall.

"As for 1998—well, I've never told anyone this before. People think I have delusions of grandeur as it is. I was in my high school library that day looking for a copy of *Little Women*. I went down the wrong aisle and happened to see a set of the *Feynman Lectures on Physics*."

A sad, faraway look came to her eyes. "Perhaps, in that other branch universe, there's no transcosmology. Maybe, at this moment, I'm a retired English teacher playing with my grandchildren."

She sighed. "We can't physically travel to any of those other branch universes or back into the 'past'—that is, from 1998 to 'now'—of our own particular branch. Actually, we might be able to do it someday, if you believe in stable wormholes—which I don't. On the other hand, folding space-time to travel to TCE, which is in a null energy state relative to our branch universe, is fairly easy. It's like temporarily re-connecting an umbilical cord between a baby and its mother. We use a—"

She noticed the blank look on Robbins' face, then muttered a word that sounded like "reason." "Never mind. You don't really need to understand why this should work, just what you have to do."

Her face moved closer to his. "I have a plan. It's more dangerous than anything we've done so far. Depending on how strict Nature is about violating causality, it might not even work at all. But it's the only way we can make everything right on TCE, and here."

Robbins' eyes opened wide. "How?"

"As I said, we can't physically travel back into the past of our own branch universe and change things that have already happened. But, by using TCE, we might be able to change them by a less direct method."

She smiled. "Actually, this idea isn't very original. I first read about it in some old science fiction stories when I was in college."

"Science fiction?"

Everett looked at him quizzically. "Do you read science fiction too?"

"No, but maybe I should." He started to ask her if the idea she was referring to was also in "graphic novels," but thought better of it.

Everett reached up and took a book of piano music from the top of the Steinway. Taking a pen from her purse, she began writing on the book's blank back cover. "This is what you need to do—"

Robbins' eyes opened wider as she explained her plan.

"But didn't you say it was dangerous to—"

"Believe me, I wish there was another way!" She handed him the book. "Will you do it?"

Robbins looked at the instructions she'd written on the book, then turned it over. It was his copy of Beethoven's Sonata in E-flat major, Opus 81a. He leafed through the score, remembering the subtitles the composer had given to its three movements. *Les Adieux. L'Absence. Le Retour.* Then he turned the book back over and reread what she'd written.

"Well, Dr. Robbins? It's your choice."

He sighed. "If it's the only way to make things right—of course I'll do it."

With a strong sense of *deja vu* Robbins entered the Portal Room after changing into a NOC suit. Miles, Everett, and Harrison were there again—just like when he'd gone to TCE and prevented Ertmann from injecting Beethoven with the same medicine he was supposed to give him now.

Harrison handed him the injector. "I've loaded it with the vaccine-blocker. Inject it the same way you did the vaccine."

From his place at the control panel Miles said, "The portal is stable and active. The spatial coordinates are the same as when Dr. Robbins translocated to inject the vaccine. Temporal coordinates are now set for…twenty-nine minutes and counting after he returned from that translocation."

"Let me check those coordinates." Brushing the technician aside, Everett scrutinized the panel carefully.

Clutching the injector in his hand, Robbins walked to the entrance of the portal, waiting. He hoped Everett knew what she was doing.

The latter's fingers played briefly over the control panel.

Miles frowned. "Excuse me, Dr. Everett, but why did you change—"

"Dr. Robbins," she said, pointedly ignoring Miles. "Do you remember everything I told you?"

"Yes."

"Then—good-bye!"

As the blackness of the portal enveloped him, Robbins ran over Everett's instructions once more in his mind. He hoped this wasn't just going to make things worse. But, even if it meant his own destruction, he was determined to set things right again. His last thought before he arrived was to remember what Everett said could be sent back into their own past via TCE.

Information.

Suddenly those thoughts were interrupted—he was there. His first breath brought a multitude of very unpleasant smells. The NV goggles activated automatically in the dark room.

He was standing in the kitchen of Beethoven's quarters. A fireplace filled with musty ashes was set into one wall. The room had several tables and open shelves, with plates, bowls, and utensils on them. A wicked-looking knife lay on one of the tables. In one corner stood a dusty, dilapidated pianoforte. Robbins smiled slightly, thinking how ironic that was.

Slowly, he entered the main living area, carefully avoiding bumping into the small writing desks and chairs scattered around it—

"Stop."

Robbins froze—terrified. His head slowly swiveled in the direction of the whispered word. His NV goggles revealed another person in the room. Someone about his height, and wearing a NOC suit just like his.

The strange man spoke again. "Don't go into the bedroom."

Robbins whispered back, "Who are you? What are you doing here?"

The dark figure stepped closer, then removed its goggles and hood. Robbins blinked, unable to comprehend what he saw.

It was his own face.

The man replaced the goggles over his eyes. "Don't talk, just listen."

Robbins nodded as the stranger spoke. Many of the latter's instructions didn't make sense to him but, the other man assured him, in time he would understand them. Robbins felt sick when the man told him why he had to do all those things right.

He did protest a bit about injecting the vaccine he carried into the stranger's bare right arm, but obeyed. "They have to think you really did inject it into Beethoven, so you can't go back with the injector unused," the stranger explained, wincing as he rolled his sleeve back down and rubbed his right upper back with his left hand. "If everything works out the way it should, there's no way *that* can hurt me. And now you've been absent long enough. It's time for you to return."

Robbins followed the other man into the kitchen and whispered, "Are you coming too?" The stranger replied, "No. If Everett's right and this works, I can't go back. I won't even have existed.

"Oh, one more thing." Robbins saw him walk over to Beethoven's pianoforte, and smile.

"Now, listen very carefully—"

"Are you disappointed it didn't work?"

Robbins shrugged. "I'll live."

Antonia sat next to him on the couch in his apartment, listening to the music with him. Eyes closed, she smiled dreamily as the symphony ebbed and flowed around them.

Draping his arm lovingly over Antonia's shoulder, Robbins closed his eyes too. He was still trying to work out in his mind everything that had happened in the three days since the Humanities Committee had approved his proposal. Especially after he'd translocated to TCE intending to give Beethoven the vaccine.

Just as the man in Beethoven's apartment had told him to do, immediately after he'd returned to Earth he'd gone to find Ertmann. Actually, he didn't have to "go" anywhere. She was still calmly sitting in that same chair in the Portal Room with Harrison and Miles nearby, just like before he'd entered TCE to inject the vaccine. As soon as she saw him, before he had a chance to say anything, Ertmann "confessed" to them that she'd gone back before and injected Beethoven with something to block the vaccine.

At Robbins' suggestion, they'd called Everett to come to the Room and get her opinion on what they should do next. She had looked at him a bit suspiciously, as if to say *she* was the one who was supposed to suggest he go back a little "earlier" and confront Ertmann on TCE. But she'd agreed he should do it.

Back again in Beethoven's apartment, when Ertmann appeared he'd pleaded with her to trust him, said he was on her side, and told her what they had to do. And, he'd said finally, when you go back, please, please don't hurt yourself!

Then, after returning to Earth himself, Robbins had changed clothes and translocated back to Vienna on the morning of March 27, 1827. All the newspapers there reported that Beethoven had died the day before—naturally, since he'd never injected him with the vaccine. Then he returned home once more—to "failure."

The hardest part was lying at the special Humanities Committee meeting yesterday that he'd done his best to prolong Beethoven's life.

The others seemed surprised when he'd then asked to withdraw his proposal. He told them he'd had second thoughts about the possible disastrous consequences it might have for both TCE and their own world. He'd even used examples from the stories Billingsley had given him—and, most damning of all, the one the "stranger" in Beethoven's apartment had told him about.

The vote in favor of withdrawing his proposal was 4 to 2. Lytton and Shimura were the holdouts, disappointed they'd never get a chance to try out their own pet projects. Robbins still wondered if he'd done the right thing, following all the instructions the man who said he was a "future" version of himself had given him. But if you can't trust "yourself," who can you trust?

As he'd asked her, Ertmann had visited him in his apartment earlier this evening. He'd stressed that she should never, ever tell anyone about their "conspiracy." If anyone found out what really happened, they might try it again—and neither of them wanted that. Dorothy had thanked him for everything, especially the way he'd helped Harrison convince the Executive Committee to not dismiss her from the Institute. Then she'd given him a warm hug, planted a chaste kiss on his cheek, and left.

The memory of that hug still lingered vividly in his mind. Robbins found himself having to suppress some very unplatonic thoughts. But no, he was a little too old for her. Besides, he already had a beloved.

The symphony was approaching its thunderous, explosive climax. Antonia snuggled closer to him. "Beautiful, isn't it," she murmured dreamily. "So ecstatic, so full of life and celebration."

"Yes," he agreed. "But not as beautiful as you."

As their lips touched and he lost himself in their kiss, the music seemed to fade for a moment, replaced by another melody—a powerful, triumphant, martial tune in C major. The one the man in Beethoven's apartment had tapped out on the pianoforte in the kitchen. Robbins wished the man had told him where it was from.

Antonia whispered softly in his ear, "Don't be too disappointed you didn't get your 'new' music. Remember, 'Heard melodies are sweet, but those unheard are sweeter.'"

Then, with her breasts barely grazing his chest, she looked shyly up at him. He had last seen that look in her eyes far too long ago, and he knew she wasn't planning to go back to her own apartment tonight. Over her shoulder he glimpsed the bust of Beethoven on the Steinway. The ghost of an approving smile seemed to play on its plaster lips.

In the background, endlessly repeated booming notes by the whole orchestra were followed by a skyrocketing upward glissando and the last fortissimo chords of Beethoven's final symphony.

The D minor.

The joyous Ninth.

Sometimes I like to write a satire. The target of the following story will be obvious.

Jurisimprudence

"My card, Emperor."

Nero Claudius Caesar squinted closely at the stiff fragment of parchment the strange man handed him. Scintillating gold letters proclaimed "Ignatius Maximilian Wiley, J.D. Temporal Lawyer."

The toga-clad emperor frowned. "What does this mean?"

Wiley ran his hand through slicked-back black hair, then rubbed a grease stain onto the sleeve of his $5,000 pinstriped suit. "It means, Emp, I've traveled from two thousand years in the future to save your reputation. Hard to believe, but where and when I come from, nobody thinks you're a god anymore. Probably because of those slanderous rumors you murdered your mother and a couple of wives, and set Rome on fire."

Nero strummed an ethereally beautiful melody on his lyre, watching from his palace's balcony as towering flames licked the night sky in the distance. "Mom's death was an accident. She slipped on a grape peel during an orgy I held in her honor."

"Yeah, right. Won't take much to improve *that* alibi. Anyway, what I'll do is sue every history book publisher for libel and force them to retract all those vicious lies about you. Maybe I'll demand their next editions depict you as the first incarnation of Elvis. Shouldn't be too hard, what with that guitar-thingy you play, and the way you're into serious babe-chasing and chowing down."

The lawyer opened a black leather briefcase with platinum locks and extracted a thick sheaf of papers. "Testimonials from former clients. Genghis Khan, Vlad the Impaler, Ivan the Terrible—now textbooks call them all 'freedom fighters.' Lucrezia Borgia and Lizzie Borden? Protofeminists. Torquemada and Rasputin? Up for canonization. This one with the 'X' at the bottom is signed by Attila the Hun. Hell, I made him seem like such a nice guy, his action figure was the best-selling toy of Christmas, 2064!"

"Christmas?"

"Don't ask. You wouldn't believe it."

As the faint screams of the dying wafted towards the two men from the darkness, Nero artistically plucked a tender threnody for fallen Troy. "Those names mean nothing to me."

"Oops—guess they are just a little ahead of your time. Actually, the rehabilitation job I'm proudest of *is* a guy you know. Name's Plato."

"The philosopher?"

"That's him."

"But my old tutor Seneca and other philosophers hold him in great honor!"

Wiley snickered. "So did lots of people until a year ago, when some 'classical studies' university professors with their own time machine discovered his dirty little secret. Seems Plato had it in for this wise guy Socrates after that smart-alecky geezer made him look stupid in front of his boyfriend. So when the old buzzard got in trouble with the law, Plato bribed the jury to convict him and give him the chair—with a cup of hemlock on it.

"Then this so-called philosopher spends the rest of his life making big bucks writing 'dialogues' about Soc and what a swell guy he was! But here's the juiciest part. All the time everybody's telling him how smart he is for coming up with these great ideas, Plato's cribbing from this humongous pile of lecture notes his victim left behind. Best of all, in his stories he has the 'Socrates' character claim *he* never wrote a thing!"

The lawyer shook his head. "You've got to admire a guy who can pull off a scam like that."

Nero tightened a string on his instrument. "But if your people know the truth now, how could you defend him?"

"Easy—when you know the system. First, you slap the professors with a lawsuit for defamation of character. Then you have the venue changed to Armpit, U.S.A. or some other little hick town whose brightest citizens still think the Earth is flat. Before the trial, during *voir dire*, reject any prospective juror who knows the difference between Plato and Play-Doh. Then sweet-talk the jury, insinuate the profs are effete snobs, and confuse the judge with brilliantly clever legal maneuvers."

Wiley grinned like a satiated shark. "Those ivory tower eggheads never knew what hit them. *They* just had the truth on their side. I had the *law*."

He nodded toward the faraway conflagration. "Now take this little peccadillo. I'll deflect the blame from you to somebody else. Maybe I'll say a gladiator fell asleep while smoking in bed. Or some cow kicked over a lantern."

Nero frowned. "Christmas," he muttered. "There's a small cult with a name like that. They stand on street corners and hand out religious tracts saying the world will end soon. Perhaps I could blame them..."

His companion made a hand-washing gesture. "Your idea, not mine! But *I'll* have to pick some other scapegoat. I'm a genius at bamboozling juries, but even I can't work miracles!"

"You really think you could make the people of your time consider me a noble, misunderstood hero?"

"I guarantee it, Emp—for a nominal retainer. Say, my weight in gold. A couple king-sized bags of diamonds, rubies, and emeralds. And a dozen of your cutest Vestal Virgins. I'm sure you can find the girls new jobs after I'm finished with them."

Wiley smirked. "The First Law of time travel is, 'You can't change the past.' *I* wrote the Second Law—'But you *can* rewrite history!'"

"Oh, I believe you, chariot chaser."

The lyre suddenly shrieked a teeth-grinding dissonant chord. Nero's face twisted into an expression that made Wiley shiver down to his shiny black wingtips. "But as my dear cousin Caligula used to say, some people *want* to be remembered as monsters."

The blazing noonday sun beat down mercilessly on the blood-soaked sand of the arena. Wiley held his briefcase up to protect himself as a dozen lean and hungry-looking lions circled him, spurred on by thousands of jeering spectators. Nero waved cheerfully down at him from the Imperial seat, then clenched his fist and pointed his thumb toward the ground.

As Wiley glimpsed a lion's tonsils from close range, he found some consolation knowing that the Emperor would wind up as a gross under-achiever. While history would remember him as only an average tyrant, with *his* talents Nero could've excelled in another profession.

He would've made a *great* lawyer.

This is a sad little story about the inevitability of change. The poem that inspired this tale is one of my favorites.

Bright Star

Francie lay on her back atop a beach blanket in her suburban backyard, gazing up at the night sky. Her husband Jack lay beside her, his head nestled softly against her left breast.

It was a quiet and unseasonably warm night in late autumn. The crooked rectangle of Orion already hung high in an unusually clear moonless sky. Most of the stick-dog figure of the constellation Canis Major was easy to see over the nearby rooftops. Even Sirius, the brightest star in the night sky and one of the nearest at only nine light-years away, seemed more dazzling than usual. Occasionally a blinking red or white light moved slowly across the sky. But after a little while each of those planes and jets from the nearby airport disappeared, leaving the firmament pristine and unchanging once again.

Francie brushed a strand of blond hair from her forehead and sighed contentedly. On nights like this one, when they were both too tired for anything more athletic, it was nice to go outside and snuggle under the stars. It reminded her of how she and Jack had met three years ago, when she was a senior medical student and he was just beginning his residency in radiology.

The amazing thing was that they didn't meet at the medical school or hospital but at a star party organized by the local astronomy club. They had shared his telescope on a clear night much like this and discovered they had much more in common than astronomy and medicine. She sneaked a quick glance at Jack and smiled, thinking how their marriage was literally a match made in the heavens.

Now the stars were once again in the same position as when they first met. As a child she'd watched these same constellations come and go in their yearly cycle in the much darker, velvety sky of her parents' farm in Illinois. Yet despite all the changes in her life, the stars remained the same—her faithful, dependable companions.

Francie's hands strayed down to her gently swelling lower abdomen. She thought about the new life growing within her and remembered one of her favorite poems.

"Bright star, would I were steadfast as thou art."

Jack grunted. "What?"

"You know. That sonnet by John Keats."

Francie rubbed her hip warmly against Jack's side. "I was just thinking that, no matter how much you and I may change, the stars remain the same. They've always been there for us and always will be. No matter what problems and sorrows we may have in our lives, we can always look up at the night sky and let the stars remind us of how beautiful life can be. And as our baby grows up, those same comforting stars will still shine down on her."

"Oh."

She felt her husband's quiet breathing near her and slowly drifted back into her reverie.

"Precession."

Francie started. "What?"

Jack repeated, "Precession. You know. The Earth's axis of rotation changes over a cycle of about twenty-six thousand years. Polaris is the pole star now. But the pole star five thousand years ago was Thuban in the constellation Draco. Vega will be the pole star thirteen thousand years from now. Because of precession some of the constellations and stars that used to be visible from this latitude thousands of years ago now never get above the horizon. That's why we never get to see the constellation Centaurus, or Alpha and Omega Centauri."

"So what are you saying?"

"Proper motion. That's another one. The Sun, Earth, and every star are all moving through space. In millions of years they'll all have moved so much none of the constellations will look like they do now."

Jack rubbed his cheek against her breast. "The point, my love, is that the stars do change. They really aren't 'steadfast, still unchangeable.'"

"Oh, you're not looking at things the right way. I don't care if the stars change over thousands or millions of years. They aren't going to change in our lifetimes—"

"Barnard's star. It's moving so fast relative to the Earth that its position in the sky has changed appreciably since we were born."

"Jack, you're missing the point—"

"Variable stars like Mira. That star varies so much in brightness over a year's time that sometimes you can see it with the naked eye, and sometimes you can't. Or Cepheid variables. Those stars can vary significantly in brightness over a period of only a few days."

"Oh, you're impossible!"

"Flare stars. Proxima Centauri is one. They can change in brightness unpredictably for just a few minutes. Or pulsars. OK, maybe that's not a great example, they usually don't change too much in visible light. But they do emit enormous bursts of radio waves and X-rays every few seconds or so—"

Francie sighed. "All right, you've made your point! I'm talking poetry and you're talking science! You sound like somebody in another poem Keats wrote, that old jerk Apollonius. He's that spoilsport philosopher who forces his student to start thinking scientifically and destroys the young man's romance with the gorgeous Lamia. Leave it to a radiologist to be so literal-minded and see things purely in black and white!"

"Oh, some things on X-ray images look gray too."

Jack chuckled. "You know I'm just pulling your chain. I get what you're saying. I think the night sky is beautiful too. Even if the stars aren't exactly 'unchangeable,' I guess they're close enough to it for a little poetic license."

His lips brushed gently across his wife's blouse. "Keats also said, 'A thing of beauty is a joy forever.' And I think you are truly beautiful."

Jack closed his eyes and smiled dreamily against her.

Far above, the night sky and its steadfast stars looked down tenderly upon the young lovers. With a flash of irritation Francie noticed that the everlasting beauty of the heavens was marred once more, this time by a new bright point of white light occulting Sirius. It must be another plane leaving the airport. "Brighter than Venus," she thought to herself. She kept staring at the light, waiting for it to move across the sky. Minutes passed...

"Oh my God!"

She felt Jack jerk awake.

"What's the matter?"

"Look!" Her index finger pointed upward. Reflexively her other hand moved back down to her abdomen, trying to protect the small vulnerable life within her. Would the amount of radiation be enough to hurt the baby? Or was nine light-years close enough for it to kill everyone on Earth?

Jack was the expert on that subject. Still clinging to a faint hope that she was wrong, Francie glanced at her husband. The horrified look on his upward peering face told her that they were both thinking the same thing. The blazing blue-white light in the sky swelling ever brighter like a manic arc light wasn't just near Sirius.

It was Sirius.

As the exploding star hurled deadly waves of radiation toward them Jack and Francie clasped each other tighter, compressing a lifetime of love into a single moment. Their gaze stayed fixed on the changing heavens as they both whispered the same word.

"Supernovas."

The inspiration for this story came to me while I was sitting in an extremely crowded airport waiting for a flight that was already several hours overdue. I kept telling myself, "It could be worse." So I wrote a story in which the wait is a lot worse...

To Him Who Waits

“ **I** 'm sorry, sir. Your flight's been delayed again.”

R. William Kroosew, Director of the Department of Astro-
dynamics at the University of New Cleveland on Canopus
IV, dropped his suitcases wearily to the floor. “What is it this time?”

The bioid flight attendant behind the counter wore a crisp blue uniform with a gold Pan Galactic Spacelines badge pinned to its lapel. It
looked like a buxom young human female with too much scarlet lipstick, and impossibly red hair styled in a cute pageboy hairdo. The only clue to its artificial origin was that “her” mouth didn't move when
she spoke, but remained fixed in a toothy smile.

Behind her a broad electronic display stretched thirty meters upward
showing flight information in countless Galactic languages. Kroosew
squinted at the tiny green letters saying, “Flight No. 13856. Departure
Time: 1313 GST. Destination: Omegamons III. Status: DELAYED.”

The attendant replied perkily, “Your starship was delayed by an ion
storm in the Cirrus system. I'm linked to the spaceport's Primary Artificial Intelligence Network, and I will inform you immediately when
PAIN notifies me of your flight's new estimated departure time.”

Kroosew stroked the back of his head fretfully, then noticed the
clump of greasy gray hairs stuck to his palm. His hair had been full
and mainly brown when he'd first arrived here. Now he was afraid to
look in a mirror.

He grumbled, “We've been through the same thing for over a week
now. Every day it's another excuse. Yesterday you said that the flight
was delayed because of a meteor shower near Cumulus VII. The day
before that, the starship's faster-than-light drive blew a fuse. And the

87

day before *that*—what was it?"

"An attack by space pirates, sir."

Kroosew's eyes shot up in frustration at the transparent "ceiling" far above them. Thousands of distant gem-like stars shone suspended in solemn splendor against the velvety blackness of space. They sparkled as their light filtered through the force field protecting this huge island-like spaceport suspended in a lonely void, twenty light years from the nearest star. It was a silent, soothing window into the majesty of the cosmos.

Then his gaze returned to the chaos around him. The waiting area stretched to the horizon, bulging with travelers from myriad Galactic Union worlds. A motley mob of sentients and protosentients raucously hooted, whistled, flapped wings, or expelled scents at each other in conversation, while others chased after immature specimens of their kind. A few somehow managed to hibernate, scrunched into one of the seats extending in long parallel rows throughout the area.

But many more of them were engaged in noisily chewing, sucking, enfolding, or tearing various foodstuffs (some of it still alive), or using portable electronic devices emitting a deafening eye-straining riot of sound and holo images. Here and there small puffs of smoke rose above the teeming throng, either from small fires primitive sentients were using to cook their food, or the native plants even less civilized beings were smoking. Nearby, several of his fellow travelers were engaged in violent limb-ripping fluid-spurting combat over which of them would claim one of the rare unoccupied seats.

The attendant murmured reassuringly, "Pan Galactic Spacelines, your 'On Time, Some of the Time' spaceline, sincerely apologizes for any inconvenience you may be experiencing. I hope the hotel accommodations PAIN has arranged for you during these delays have been satisfactory."

"Frankly, I've had more agreeable bedmates than the Denebean slimeweasil you put me up with last night. It kept trying to make a nest for itself by yanking out hairs from a very sensitive, private part of my body!"

The attendant smiled sympathetically. "If it's any consolation, sir, the Denebean spoke with me a short time ago. She said she enjoyed your company."

"Well, I didn't! Do you realize how important it is that I get back to Omegamons as soon as possible? I'm the head of a research team there working on a critically important scientific project. We're on the verge of confirming the existence of imaginary matter. If we do, it'll be the most important discovery in recorded history! But I don't suppose you have any idea what I'm talking about."

The bioid stared blankly back at him like a mannequin. *No, I didn't think you did.*

Then her face brightened. "On the contrary, Dr. Kroosew. I just consulted PAIN's exhaustive scientific database. After reading your own outstanding textbook on the life cycles of stars, I did a search on the keyword 'imaginary matter.' Summarizing the 19,413 journal citations that I just reviewed, its existence was first hypothesized by Professor Hzabigolboob of Tau Ceti II in Standard Terrestrial Year 3139. If it exists, imaginary matter would have the characteristic of 'variable quantum density'—of both changing its elemental composition and increasing its mass in response to psychic energy directed at it by sentients like yourself."

She continued, "As you so very eloquently described in your recent article in the *Journal of Imaginary Research*, the primary importance of imaginary matter is that it could be used to modify the ultimate fate of the universe. Current consensus among experts like you is that the total density of 'real' matter in the universe is insufficient to halt its continuing expansion since the 'Big Bang.' Approximately one quadrillion terrestrial years from now, the cosmos will contain only the remnants of burned out stars.

"However, if imaginary matter does exist, it would be possible for sentients to 'will' the total amount of matter present in the universe to increase. Given a sufficient amount of mass, and hence gravitational attraction, the universe will stop expanding after billions and billions of years, then begin to contract. Eventually it would collapse in the so-called 'Big Crunch' and, in theory, explode again to form a new universe capable of evolving life."

Kroosew's jaw dropped. "You're absolutely—right. My team has been investigating anomalous variations in the mass of Omegamons. The natives of its third planet have religious rituals during which they make offerings to their sun, which they consider a deity. When they do, the star's mass increases significantly—as if it were 'responding' to their prayers."

"And an excellent job your team is doing, sir. I found 313 citations for papers on imaginary matter listing you as author or co-author, second only to Professor Hzabigolboob himself."

"Actually, 'he' turned back into a 'she' last month. Her team is also at Omegamons, competing with ours to be the first to prove imaginary matter exists. Whoever does it first—well, let's just say there's a lot of prestige, grants, and other pleasant things at stake."

The attendant's voice was velvety. "I understand, sir. I'll do everything I can to ensure you reach Omegamons as soon as possible."

She pointed to the glowing red number—"213.39585"—on her PGS badge. "As a Model 38-24-36 Baryonic Intelligence Multiform Biosynthetic Organism, I had a basic expected operational 'life' of 130 terrestrial years at the time of my original synthesis. This badge shows how many years I've been in operation. How much, to use an archaic Terran phrase, 'mileage I have on me.'"

The number changed to "213.39586." "Uh—excuse me, but aren't you out of warranty?"

"No, sir. Since first coming 'on-line,' I've been extensively modified with self-repairing nanites that keep me operating at peak efficiency at all times. Thus, no matter how long it takes for your starship to come in, I'll still be operating at peak efficiency and able to inform you of its arrival."

Thank you for telling me more than I wanted to know. Sighing, Kroosew hoisted his bags back up. "I guess this means another night at a hotel."

"That might not be necessary, sir. PAIN informs me there is a non-zero chance your flight may be ready for departure shortly. If you will wait in this area for now, I hope to have good news for you soon. Or perhaps you might sample the tasty treats sold at the fine multispecies restaurants in the 4,913 concourses adjoining this gate."

"No thanks, I'll try to find a seat somewhere. My stomach's had enough overpriced junk food lately to last a lifetime. That hot dog I ate three hours ago is still giving me indigestion."

"Did you perhaps purchase it at an eating establishment called 'MakDaizees'?"

Kroosew frowned. "I think so."

"I'm afraid that particular restaurant doesn't cater to the dietary needs of humans, sir. What you consumed was not a 'hot dog' in the conventional definition of a cylindrical membrane containing bovine, porcine, and equine proteins. It was a *xelxa*—a compact colony of coprophagous parasites used by the natives of Lactomagnyzia V as a laxative."

"*Parasites?*"

"Don't be alarmed, sir. The solid waste matter in the human intestinal system lacks certain nutritional elements they require. Fortunately, however, before they starve to death, they'll leave the lining of your colon squeaky clean."

As Kroosew walked queasily away the attendant called after him,

"Should you change your mind about having another snack, please avoid restaurants with the 'Megacarnivores Only' sign. The patrons there might mistake you for part of the buffet."

There were no empty seats in the waiting area. Kroosew trundled his two suitcases down row after row, futilely searching for somewhere to rest his enervated body.

As his endless quest continued he amused himself by thinking up creative curses and anatomically impossible suggestions for those responsible for his predicament. First and foremost, the members of the Grant Review Committee at the university. They were the ones who wouldn't be satisfied with a standard faster-than-light holo conference call, but demanded he return to New Cleveland (unofficial city motto, "The Error by the Sea of Zairrer") in person to explain "irregularities" in his research team's budget.

The direct flight from Omegamons III to Canopus IV wasn't too bad, except he was famished by the time he arrived. Being served only a tiny bag of pretzels and a single cup of sweetened carbonated water on a flight spanning 13,413 light years wasn't quite enough to satisfy his stomach. But, a bioid attendant on the starship reminded him, as a member of PGS's "Frequent Flyer" plan, he needed only 121,398 more light years to qualify for a free trip one way to Pheeses II, home of the largest stinkspice mines in known space.

His meeting with the Committee started out disastrously. After they accused him of embezzling 13.689 gigacredits from his university accounts, he finally regained consciousness and demanded to see their proof. One of the committee's multispecies members pointed with its pseudopod to the spreadsheet displayed on a holoscreen.

"Figures and computers," it splotzed, "never lie!"

Subsequent investigation, however, revealed a programming glitch had made the ultra-advanced, quantum tunneling, parallel processing nanochips in the university's main computer believe that one plus one equaled two million. A recalculation using pencil and paper showed his accounts did, in fact, balance. The Chairthing of the Committee shrugged its equivalent of shoulders and blurpled at him, "Never mind."

Then there was that oh-so-helpful travel agent who'd booked him on this return flight. "The next direct flight to Omegamons won't leave for three standard days," the Causidician chirped. "But, if you don't mind a brief layover, I can schedule you for a flight that leaves tomorrow to Nineveh 6, Pan Galactic Spacelines' main hub spaceport. It's way out in the middle of nowhere, but you can catch a connecting flight there that goes right to Omegamons."

Brief layover indeed. Kroosew wondered what color that optimistic travel agent's puce face might turn if he squeezed its neck "briefly."

Totally exhausted, he stopped to rest. Nearby, a hulking amphibian-like hermaphrodite from Antares IV seemed to be mating with itself to pass the time. And a little farther away three fellow humans of assorted genders had spread their clothes on the floor and were *definitely* doing it.

For a moment he considered inquiring whether they'd be interested in making it a foursome. But right now, he felt too low to hold up his end of the partnership.

Turning around, he squinted at the flight status display screen in the distance. It still said, "DELAYED." A gesticulating verdant decapod was arguing with a smaller version of itself standing patiently at the flight attendant's post.

Then he realized the smaller alien *was* the perky erstwhile human female he'd spoken to earlier. The garish PGS promotional holo they'd shown on the flight here had proudly announced that the spaceline's flight attendants were all now equipped with "chameleon capability." Their biosynthetic "flesh" and inner support structures automatically molded themselves into the form of whatever species they were assisting. Admittedly, a clever method for placating irate passengers—presenting them with a reassuringly familiar and, theoretically, more trustworthy "helper."

Sighing, Kroosew resumed his endless lonely trek. Every seat, no matter what size or shape, was occupied. As he trudged along it felt like a great weight was strapped to his back. With every leaden step he took, he and his bags seemed to get heavier and heavier.

Then he realized that they *were* getting heavier. The terminal was designed to accommodate sentients from planets with many different ambient gravities. He'd wandered onto one of the gravitational gradient pathways between weaker and stronger artificial gravity fields.

Nothing to do but go back the way he came. After walking several hundred more meters he had his first glimmer of good luck. A reasonably humanoid alien rose on its three legs from a nearby seat. The Lactomagnyzian pulled its flowing chalk-colored robe down from around its waist and trotted contentedly away.

Rushing over to claim the vacated place before something else did, Kroosew stopped himself from collapsing onto it just in time. The seat cushion was covered by a mound of dark odiferous pellets.

But as he watched, the pile of alien souvenirs sagged and diminished, seemingly disappearing into the cushion itself. Then he remembered that promotional holo had also praised the pristine sanitary conditions in PGS facilities.

Busy, indefatigable nanoscrubbers incorporated into the very structural materials keep our floor and seating so hygienic you could even eat off them. Or, depending on your species' digestive system, even eat them yourself!

Kroosew gingerly settled into the now-sparkling seat, reveling in the excruciating pleasure of simply resting his sore legs. But he nearly jumped out of his hard-won resting place when something growled thunderously into his ear.

The sentient seated on his right resembled a shaggy teddy bear. Its two soulful eyes looked timorously into his, as if asking for a hug.

Except the alien was a bit more than snuggle-sized—well over three meters tall and at least half that wide. The six largest fangs hanging down from its upper jaw were longer and thicker than Kroosew's leg. Its claws resembled machetes and clicked together like someone preparing to carve a turkey.

For a long time the megacarnivore scrutinized him from a culinary point of view. Then, apparently deciding he was too inconsequential a morsel, it lifted its nearly thousand kilogram mass from the reinforced seat and began stalking a meatier creature whose species Kroosew had never seen before. The obese grape-colored ungulate several rows away grazed placidly from a large bag of leaves, blissfully oblivious to its fate as the predator circled ever closer.

It'd be terrible to see what happened to that poor purple bovinoid, Kroosew reflected—but much worse to *be* one.

The sentient seated on his left seemed less dangerous. It was about his size, and it didn't have any obvious body parts for slicing, biting, cutting, or chewing. A half dozen multijointed limbs radiated out from either side of a featureless pink globular body. A black derby hat was perched atop a large pale lump he assumed was its head. One of its two-fingered hands held a rolled up umbrella.

The alien unfolded a limb that Kroosew took and shook reluctantly. It spoke in a basso profundo from a nose-like bump rising from where its navel would've been, if it'd had a navel.

"I say, old chap, aren't you a human being?"

"So I'm told."

"Pimplonian, myself. My name is—" The creature gave a minute-long musically modulated toot that sounded and smelled like it had dined recently on refried beans, garlic, and onions.

It quivered affably. "Splendid sentients, you *Homo sapiens*. I've been studying for the last four standard years on your species' original planet of Earth. Just received my Doctorate in Intersentient Philology at Oxford University, don't you know? Found our two species indeed have much in common. I'm an omnivore too."

"Now that you mention it, we do almost look like twins."

"Indubitably!"

Apparently they didn't teach sarcasm at Oxford. It snorted, "Been waiting here long?"

"A week!"

"Bit longer for me. When I arrived, I wasn't in a family way."

It patted the derby-covered bulge that Kroosew had mistaken for its head. "Deuced inconvenient. But when the old hormonal biorhythms surge, there's just no reasoning with them. Based on my observations, it's a characteristic I believe we also share with humans. Fortunately, another member of my species was available here and happy to assist."

Kroosew muttered politely, "Congratulations. When are you due?"

"Actually, old bean—right now."

The derby flew several meters upward as a geyser of pus-like fluid exploded from the top of the creature. Kroosew wiped gobs of viscous stinging goo from his eyes and saw a writhing monstrosity tearing its way out of the gaping pocket torn in its parent. Baby stared at him with three tiny eyestalks, its dozen mouths filled with needle-like teeth smacking hungrily.

"I say, old chap, would you please pull my larva out the rest of the way? Careful of the claws. There's no known antidote for the venom on their tips."

Kroosew leaped up and grabbed his suitcases. The fetid fluid covering his clothes and hands was slippery, but he kept his grip on their handles.

"Uh—sorry, but I've got to check on my flight!"

The Pimplonian, still keeping a stiff fleshfold above its speaking orifice, turned to the octopoid traveler spread out on the seat to its left. "I say, old sport. Mind lending me a tentacle?"

Stumbling away, Kroosew peeked nervously back over his shoulder. The overly obliging octopoid lay on the floor, unmoving, as the newborn clutched in its remaining tentacles eagerly enjoyed its first meal.

"Can I help you, sir?"

The flight attendant had changed back into a redheaded human female. Her smiling gaze sensitized him to the fact his pants were still around his knees.

Pulling them up awkwardly, he spluttered, "Yes, you can get me on my flight before anything else tries to eat me!"

"Oh, I hope you didn't forget my advice to avoid 'Megacarnivores Only' restaurants!"

"No, I went to a restroom to clean up after a little 'accident.' A *toilet* tried to bite me!"

The attendant smiled at him patiently. "The porcelain appliances we provide for human excretory functions aren't designed to do that, sir."

"Well, this one certainly did! I even made extra sure before I went in that the restroom was for male humans. I didn't recognize the word on the door, but the little outline figure looked right!"

"Was the figure blue, sir?"

"Well—no, it was red."

"That explains your unfortunate experience, sir. You inadvertently entered a facility that's reserved for the unisex natives of Sytonurrump IV. They look remarkably like human beings. However, unlike your species' flabby texture in that area, their buttocks are hard and horn-like. Therefore, to maintain proper hygiene, their toilets contain trained *byturarse* beasts. Their burr-like teeth are genetically engineered to scrape and abrade away any residual waste matter on the patrons after the toilet is used."

"Believe me, I'll remember that next time!"

The flight attendant beamed happily at his wise resolution. "By the way, sir, I have good news for you!"

Kroosew felt as if the artificial gravity generator had been turned off. "Finally! When will you begin boarding?"

"I'm afraid the starship for Omegamons III still hasn't arrived yet. However, PAIN has now located the luggage you checked in. It was inadvertently placed on an economy class sublight generation ship bound for Noivilbo II. When the ship reaches its destination in 213.8 terrestrial years, we'll have your luggage shipped back to you on the return flight."

His spirit broken, Kroosew pleaded, "Is there any place a little quieter and less crowded I could wait until my flight's ready?"

"I'm sorry, sir. PAIN informs me that the average total biomass of sentients within each of our waiting areas is approximately the same— 1,319,564 kilograms, plus or minus 289."

Kroosew sighed pessimistically. "Well, if I'm lucky, I'll find the one with the minus 289 kilograms."

"There's another alternative, sir. PGS has recently instituted a new service for its valued customers. For a nominal fee, you can use a stasis chamber."

"A what?"

"An enclosure whose contents are kept in a state of virtually halted atomic activity. The occupant experiences what seems like a deep, restful sleep. Relative to the universe at large, time will 'stop' for it."

Kroosew frowned. "You mean like suspended animation."

"Stasis and suspended animation are, in their technical methodologies, quite different. However, the end results are approximately the same. This service would eminently meet your wish for solitude and, at least subjectively, a shortened waiting period."

"At this point, I'm willing to try anything!"

She pointed to one of the interminably long corridors leading from the waiting area. "To reach the stasis chamber, go down Concourse No. 413 exactly 3.13 kilometers. Turn right at the 'Krispy Krigleworms' food stand. Then walk straight ahead 2.13 kilometers until you reach the official Nineveh 6 souvenir shop, where we have a special today on various upper garments suitable for humanoid species imprinted with witty legends such as 'My beezulgorb went to Nineveh 6 and all I got was this lousy dilworf!' Turn left and look for the small orange sign saying 'Stasis Chamber' in 113 standard Galactic languages. You can't miss it."

"Fine!"

Kroosew took several steps in the direction the attendant indicated, then stopped. "You *will* let me know when my flight comes in, won't you? All I need now is to 'oversleep' and *miss* it!"

"Have no fear, sir. I will personally ensure that you reach your final destination of Omegamons as soon as possible."

Not entirely reassured, Kroosew resolutely put his head down and began his long journey. He didn't hear the attendant call after him, "And please let me know what you think of this new service. You'll be the first sentient to try our stasis chamber!"

By the time Kroosew finally reached his goal his limbs had lost all sensation. The small orange sign on the wall spelling "Stasis Chamber" beckoned hypnotically to him.

But its siren spell was rudely broken when he read the fine print beneath those words, telling just how much the "nominal fee" to use it was. To pay for it he probably *would* have to embezzle from university research accounts. But, if it maintained his sanity, it was worth the risk. Even a nice quiet prison cell seemed appealing right now.

He pressed his palm against a metal plate to authorize payment.

Immediately a previously invisible narrow door swung open from the wall. A harsh yellow light illuminated the interior of the coffin-sized stasis chamber. It was just large enough for him to squeeze himself and his suitcases inside it. As he stood in the chamber reconsidering the wisdom of using it, the door closed automatically.

Suddenly claustrophobic, Kroosew looked in vain for a knob or a button to open the door. Long-repressed memories of stories he'd read as a child flooded back to him. The terrifyingly detailed accounts by that ancient Terran writer Poe about being buried alive—the victim clawing frantically and futilely at his coffin lid until finally suffocating in endless agony!

Then the light inside the chamber softened to a soothing azure. He felt his cares and worries fading away, his mind and body slipping into a deep restful sleep…

"Time to wake up, sir."

What? It felt like he'd closed his eyes just three minutes ago.

The attendant was standing at the open door of the stasis chamber, looking fresh and vivacious. "Please follow me."

Kroosew hoisted his suitcases, praying this wasn't yet another false alarm. As he followed his companion's clicking echoing heels down the winding corridor he began to realize that something was different.

The spaceport was empty and quiet. No huge milling throngs, no caterwauling babel of countless alien languages. Just the redheaded attendant and him, walking together like two lovers on a lonely beach.

When they reached the silent waiting area he dropped his suitcases, convinced he was hallucinating.

"Where is everybody?"

The attendant glanced at the vacant cavernous room. "They all left long ago."

"Well, it's good to see some efficiency for a change. Although I can't say I'm pleased my flight's the last to arrive. Can I board it now?"

"I'm afraid the starship you were to travel on never arrived here at Nineveh 6, sir. It was hijacked en route by members of the Symbiotic Liberation Front, a group adamantly opposed to sentients traveling on starships. When they belatedly realized that *they* were traveling on a starship, they directed the ship back to Omegamons III, intending to disembark immediately."

She flashed him a gleaming smile. "Unfortunately, shortly after you left their system, the Omegamonians became engaged in a venomous theological controversy regarding the phanos egg they ritually offered to their sun, a.k.a. the 'Great Scrambler of the Cosmos.' While the orthodox majority demanded that the sacramental egg be broken at the traditional pointed end, a schismatic sect insisted the rounded end was more pleasing to their deity.

"The Omegamonians then decided to take their dispute to a Higher Authority. After studying your own textbook on stellar evolution and articles on imaginary matter, both groups directed their combined psychic energy toward the imaginary matter in their sun—dramatically increasing its density and transmuting its core to a critical amount of iron. Their world, your whole research team, and the starship were all vaporized with the rest of the system when Omegamons subsequently collapsed in on itself and became a Type II supernova."

Kroosew fell onto an empty seat. All his colleagues, all their work—gone, destroyed. His eyes drifted toward the ceiling, as if searching for the ghost of Omegamons among the other—

For a long time he stared upward, paralyzed with confusion and terror. Finally he whispered, "Where are the stars?"

The attendant continued, "However, out of this great tragedy came the most important discovery in recorded history. Like you, your esteemed fellow astrodynamicist, Dr. Hzabigolboob, was also visiting his/her home planet when that catastrophe occurred. Their subsequent research confirmed the role of imaginary matter in the 'Omegamons Incident'—and showed the path to the salvation of the universe. By the time the good doctor died some 313 years later, showered with riches and worshipped as a demigod by half the Galaxy, the great project uniting all known sentients was well underway."

"Huh? You make it sound like—"

Cold sweat formed under Kroosew's armpits. "How long have I been in that stasis chamber? And why can't I see any stars up there?"

The attendant beamed, "For eons, countless intelligent beings focused their psychic energy on increasing the mass of all the imaginary matter in the cosmos. When they finished, the total mass of real and imaginary matter in the entire universe was twice the value needed to halt its expansion. Our universe was no longer 'open,' but 'closed.' Since then innumerable civilizations have risen to glory, then crumbled into dust. The races that created them have long been extinct. But all those countless sentients died consoled by the knowledge that the present universe *would* ultimately collapse in the 'Big Crunch'—and a new one would be born, where intelligent life might evolve again."

Kroosew leaped up and grabbed her shoulders. *"How long have I been here?"*

Then he noticed the small badge on the perpetually self-repairing attendant's uniform. The one showing the number of years she'd been in service.

It read "113,459,238,485.28665."

The last digit turned to "6." "I'm afraid it's taken a bit longer to reach your destination than was originally anticipated, sir. Pan Galactic Spacelines declared bankruptcy for the 194th time several hours after you entered stasis. Unfortunately, PGS's creditors decided not to let it try reorganizing once again or to lend it more money. They deemed Nineveh 6 too costly to move or use, so it was simply abandoned."

Kroosew peered up at the featureless void above him, all its familiar

102

stars long burned out, their planets cold and dead. The homogenous glow above him must be the cosmic background radiation from the "Big Bang," made visible as it became hotter with the onrushing collapse of the universe—washing out the faint light of whatever dim stars still existed.

Realizing the futility of it all, he let go of the unresisting attendant. "Why," he whispered. "Why didn't you let me stay in stasis? Why wake me up now to tell me I may be the last intelligent being left in the universe?"

"Indeed you are, sir. The universe has now contracted enough that all the accumulated knowledge and wisdom of every civilization that's ever existed have come within range of PAIN's scanners and are now included within its database. It informs me that the last sapient being besides yourself expired 1,231,346,598 years ago."

He moaned, "So now I get a ringside seat to watch the 'Big Crunch'—before I die too!"

"Oh no, sir. The universe will not achieve singularity for another 80,234,134 years. Well beyond your expected life span."

"Then I'll starve to death instead!"

"Dear me, no. Like the rest of this facility and me, the food synthesizers are self-maintaining. They continue to work as well as when you went into stasis. Would you like a complimentary bag of pretzels?"

The first shock was wearing off, and Kroosew was beginning to accept his fate. Although staying here for the rest of his life was hardly what he'd planned on, there were compensations. There'd be no more arguing with obtuse university committees or waiting for starships that never came. The spaceport would provide him with food and shelter. For the rest of his life he could study and contemplate all the mysteries of creation contained within its computer database.

A simple but fulfilling life. Like that legendary story of a sailor on Earth's oceans in ancient times, shipwrecked and washed up alone on a desert island, with all the things he needed to meet his basic needs. Well, all but one need—

Suddenly long-repressed hormonal biorhythms surged deep within him. As a late-Romantic symphonic melody by a long-decomposed Russian swelled in his memory, he gazed at the redheaded attendant in a new way. Her perfumed rosy cheeks. The mouth that always smiled so invitingly. The seductive curves beneath her formfitting uniform.

And if she wasn't *really* a woman—well, nobody's perfect.

Shyly, tenderly, he took her hand in his. It was warm and soft. He even thought he felt a pulse—proof that she had a heart, or equivalent circulatory pump, beating deep within her, only for him. It was as if she understood that he'd been celibate for much longer than any man should be.

"Is there anything I can do for you, sir?"

"Oh, you have no idea! And please, don't call me 'sir' anymore. My name is Robinson."

"All right…Robinson."

She said it so beautifully—this gorgeous creature who'd taken care of him nearly forever, always so accommodating and helpful. But before he enfolded her in a passionate embrace, there was one final question he must ask her.

"Why did you wake me now, instead of ages ago?"

"Because, Robinson," she whispered, "I promised when you first came here that I'd make sure you reached Omegamons."

Kroosew frowned. "I don't understand. You said that it became a supernova."

"Yes. But as the universe has contracted, the positions of its remaining constituents relative to Nineveh 6 have also changed. Objects that were once light years away from this spaceport have now moved much closer."

"I still don't—"

"I'm sorry PGS couldn't fly you to Omegamons as was originally scheduled. But now, your long wait is finally over. I removed you from stasis because you'll soon be reaching your final destination."

"But there is no Omegamons anymore!"

"Oh, but there is, Robinson. Just not in the form you remember."

Thirteen seconds later the massive gravitational tidal forces assaulting Nineveh 6 exceeded its design tolerances, and the spaceport and everything inside it were crushed and utterly destroyed. But just before the black hole created when Omegamons became a supernova wandered too close to the doomed facility, Kroosew heard the flight attendant say, "I couldn't help you *go* to Omegamons. But, by waiting long enough, I made sure you got there the other way."

With a last sweet smile she said, "Omegamons has come to you!"

This satiric story I co-wrote with my firstborn, Henry Stratmann III, is definitely not to be taken literally or too seriously. However, it would help to explain why things don't always go the way they should in Life. And there's a reason it consists of exactly 666 words.

When All Else Fails

Humanity woke up one morning and found that the Earth was turning into Paradise.

It started with small wonders. A slice of bread dropped on the floor now always fell jelly-side up. No sock ever vanished in the dryer. There was no storm, hail, or blizzard when the weather forecast predicted a sunny day.

Next came minor miracles. Oil companies panicked as gas tanks in SUVs and all other vehicles stayed perpetually full no matter how far they were driven. Airline flights were always on time and no baggage was ever lost. Computers never crashed.

Dumbfounded doctors said foods that tasted good were now actually good for you. A diet rich in doughnuts and desserts gave a woman the face and figure of a supermodel and sculpted a man's physique into one like Arnold Schwarzenegger's in his prime. The grease-gorged, salt-saturated calories in fast-food cheeseburgers and fries now unclogged coronary arteries and lowered high blood pressure.

Then the truly impossible happened. Lawyers turned honest and sincerely sought justice. Politicians told nothing but the truth and worked for the good of their fellow citizens. People became celebrities only if they actually had talent and were good role models for the young. Teenagers respected and listened to their teachers and other elders. Adults led lives as free of greed, lust, and other vices as the parents in a 1950s TV sitcom. Science fiction magazine editors bought all the stories they received, for every submission was an astounding blend of original ideas and entertainingly thought-provoking prose.

Each day brought new wonders. Where once there was war and rumors of war, now peace and harmony filled the world. The wolf lay down with the wombat. Tanks were beaten into tractors. Violence, hatred, prejudice, and intolerance vanished like the scented smoke of incense wafting upward into the heights of a great cathedral.

Earthquakes, floods, and hurricanes never ravaged the land. Famine, disease, and death were no more. Though the old grew young again and no accident ever injured or killed, the world no longer seemed overcrowded. In even the largest cities no traffic jams sullied the streets. Smiling taxi drivers graciously yielded the right of way to pedestrians and road laughter filled the avenues. Elevators were never stuffed with perspiring passengers. Checkout lines at grocery stores were always short.

Finally came the greatest miracles of all. Man now understood Woman and lovingly validated Her feelings. Woman never nagged or tried to change Man.

Learned thinkers who'd long pondered the ultimate questions of theodicy and the meaning of life found those riddles no longer needed answers. Even the most skeptical inquirers came to believe that only a Power far greater than human science and ingenuity could be responsible for this amazing metamorphosis. The righteous rejoiced that their faith and prayers had been vindicated. From every land and in every tongue a great chorus of thanksgiving ascended to the heavens…

Somewhere outside time and space, a Being beyond human comprehension looked at His work and saw that it was good. Then a sweetly sarcastic voice from the kitchen startled Him.

"Any luck, Dear?"

"Yes, it's working fine now. I told you I could figure it out without any help!"

Okay, so that last part was a fib. But She didn't need to know that

He'd finally swallowed His pride and done what She'd been telling Him to do for eons. He'd already wasted over thirteen billion years fiddling with the darn thing. The last thing He needed was an eternity of hearing "I told you so!"

Hopefully She'd be so pleased the home entertainment system She'd bought on sale finally worked right that there'd be no embarrassing questions about how He'd succeeded. After looking within the thick book in His hands one last time, He stuffed it back into a large box on the living room floor. There, hidden beneath packing material and the shrinkwrap He'd just peeled away from it, She wouldn't see the manual's title.

"How to Operate Your New Universe."

This is a dark tale about an unanticipated peril of time travel.

Tempora Mutantur

The Times are Chang'd, and in them Chang'd are we.
How? Man, as Times grow worse, grows worse, we see.

In: *Owen's Epigrammata* [1615]

I'm a very private person.

Not antisocial. I don't mind being around other people—if they leave me alone. As long as they aren't looking over my shoulder, or staring at me, or meddling in my personal affairs, my attitude is live-and-let-live.

During the week I rarely leave home, a cozy secluded house deep in a thousand acres of wooded land I own in the Missouri Ozarks. It's a place I can live by myself and work in peace, with no neighbors close enough to disturb me.

But even I need a little human companionship now and then. Every Sunday evening I drive to Kansas City. There's an out-of-the-way restaurant in the county that serves the best barbecued ribs I've ever tasted. If the place had a bit more class, it might qualify as a honkytonk. While I'm told it's packed every other night of the week with diners and dancers (most of them there, I assume, to perform modern mating rituals), on Sunday nights I have the restaurant pretty much to myself.

This Sunday night in late October was no exception. I was in my favorite booth there in the back corner, my stomach rumbling in eager anticipation of the ribs I'd soon be depositing inside it. A large dirty pane of glass and a sizzling neon sign—"Joe's *ar & G*ill"—framed the front of the restaurant. Hazy street lights shone on dark sparsely

111

populated sidewalks. Cars and buses rumbled fitfully through the inter-section nearby, sporadically attentive as to whether the traffic light was green or red.

The restaurant was deserted, a dimly lit tableaux of empty tables, booths, and mud-stained tile floor. Its bare wooden walls were decorated unimaginatively with horseshoes, cheap etchings of cowboys roping cattle, and other rural accoutrements. A cheerful, private place where nobody knows my name. Mainly because, though I've been a regular here for several years, I've never told them what it is. Always use cash, so there aren't even any telltale credit card signatures. It's a harmless personality quirk of mine. I value my privacy so much that I don't even like to tell people who I am, if I don't have to.

The stools at the bar were empty too. Joe, the slug-like bartender and owner of this elegant establishment, was sitting in a chair that barely supported his Pickwickian weight. His head bobbed up and down like a pendulum, grunts emerging intermittently from his jowls, as he tried futilely to stay awake. Probably been sampling his own wares again.

If I turned my head slightly I could peek through a small open win-dow into the kitchen. The mouth-watering aroma of well-grilled meat drifted through it to my grateful nostrils. Mel, the grizzled cook, was sitting hunched over by his stove. He seemed to be having an intimate moment with himself while perusing a magazine full of pictures with a very low ratio of clothing to nubile female bodies. Hopefully he'd remember to wash his hands before he prepared my barbecued ribs.

As I nursed an ice-cold glass of soda (alcohol kills brain cells) I watched Mildred, the only waitress on duty, walk over to the new jukebox in the corner. The faceplate on its front proudly displayed the legend "Another Fine Product from IQ Industries," indicating it had an artificial intelligence module inside. Supposedly these updated jukeboxes can now not only download the latest human-generated hit songs, but their AIs are programmed to compose brand-new ones on the spot. Push a button for the appropriate theme—"Unrequited Love," "Requited Love," "Love That Was Requited But Subsequently Went Sour Because You And/Or Your Significant Other Got Bored Or Found Somebody New," etc.—and the AI would use its compositional algorithms to create lyrics and music for your very own custom-made song.

Considering the very limited musical language and themes of most popular music, I didn't think the AI's programming had to be very sophisticated. Still, I was interested in hearing what it could do. As Mildred put a few coins in the jukebox I hoped she'd chosen an AI-made selection. But no, I recognized the tune blaring from the machine. Twanging guitars and a thumping bass accompanied the latest hit by Kewpie Barton, the former Secretary of Agriculture who'd achieved far greater fame in her new career as a country music singer. Her shrill soprano lacerated the bittersweet lyrics of "Ungulates' Odyssey."

> *You promised you would love me until the cows came home,*
> *No burgers-on-the-hoof I thought I'd ever see.*
> *But those distant moos and lowing, I hear comin' o'er*
>   *the pasture's loam,*
> *Mean stampeding bovines'll soon be trampling upon me!*

Enraptured by the music, Mildred wiggled her taut jeans and bulging blouse over to my booth. "Anything else I can do for you, darlin'?"

The sultry tone in her voice told me she wasn't talking about getting me another Pepsi. Fifteen years ago she must have been a real stunner. Even now, with prominent parts of her late-thirties anatomy sagging a bit and her face needing generous helpings of makeup and lipstick to approach centerfold standards, she was pleasant to look at.

Best of all, on slow nights like this with Joe lost in slumberland, she wasn't adverse to moonlighting in a back room for a reasonable fee. Though I'm a very private person, even I get an itch sometimes. And

Mildred was an expert at scratching it. Despite her name, there wasn't any *Of Human Bondage* thing between us. Just a mutually beneficial business relationship.

I smiled at her. "Not tonight. I'm a little—overexcited. Too much on my mind."

Mildred sat down beside me, her braless breast nestling warmly against my arm. The honeysuckle scent of two-dollar perfume wafted towards me, even more succulent than the aromas from the kitchen. "Are you sure?"

She tossed her long bleached hair in the direction of the bar and Joe. "Old lardbutt over there won't miss me."

"Well…maybe that would be a nice way to celebrate. Besides, I probably won't be here next week. Going on a trip."

She looked disappointed. A true professional. "I'll miss you. Will you be away a long time?"

"I guess you could say that."

Traffic noises swelled briefly, then were muffled again as the front door opened and closed. Joe roused himself long enough to watch the well-dressed fortyish man walk briskly by the bar, then resumed his nap.

The newcomer was the last person I expected to see here. He looked like the very model of a modern business executive—which indeed he was. Tall, wearing a thousand-dollar designer suit, with handsome features and blow-dried curly hair splashed with just enough gray at the temples to confer an aura of wisdom and authority. Certainly not the kind of clientele this place usually catered to. Besides, he should be a couple thousand miles away.

Rem saw me an instant after I spotted him. He sidled into the seat across the table from me.

I glared at him. "Almost didn't recognize you without your bodyguards. What the hell are you doing here?"

"We need to talk."

He glanced sharply at Mildred, still scrunched warmly against my side. "In private."

She jumped up like a new Marine obeying a drill sergeant. Rem has that effect on people.

Mildred stammered, "Can I get you a drink, or a menu—"

"No!"

Her eyes darted from him back to me, a trace of puzzlement crossing her face. Then she slunk away.

I took a sip of my soda. "How'd you find me?"

"I've been calling you at home and sending you e-mails for nearly a week. Couldn't reach you."

"I've been away."

"Then I remembered you liked to come to this place Sunday nights. Remember, we met here last year? So I flew out from the coast this evening hoping I'd find you. "

I scratched my beard. "Well, congratulations. You found me. Been a nice visit. Don't let the door hit your ass on the way out."

Rem's famous steely eyes softened in a way I'd never seen before. This hard-nosed master of men, this iron-willed captain of industry, looked—*desperate*.

"Just listen, will you? You're the only person I can talk to. The only one who might believe me. And help me."

When Rem was reduced to asking me for help, it must be serious. I decided to humor him.

"OK. What's your problem?"

Rem leaned forward and whispered. "I'm being stalked."

I snorted. "Is that all? Who is it—somebody you downsized, like me? Or one of your ex-wives?"

"No. There are over twenty of them. I flew here alone and incognito on a commercial flight, not telling anyone where I was going, to try to get away from them. I think they're—"

His face contorted, barely able to whisper. "I think they're time travelers."

The glass of soda stopped halfway to my lips. I set it down slowly. *Time travelers.*

I couldn't believe Rem had that much imagination. He and I go back a long way. We have a lot of superficial things in common. Same age, same background. But we're just about as different in our personalities and attitudes as two people can be. Me—I've always been a loner. A dreamer. The *Steppenwolf* type.

Rem, on the other hand, lusted after the limelight and being a celebrity. He was—practical. A secular Elmer Gantry. He'd inherited his father's business skills and libido, but none of the other characteristics that had made Gaius Julius Caesar something of a Renaissance man.

The elder Caesar made his fortune in the new AI market that took off soon after the turn of the century. IQ Industries—unofficial motto, "Intelligent machines for not-so-intelligent people"—never really was a serious threat to topple the old guard makers of "dumb" computers and software. Once his company showed how inexpensive AI modules could make everything from toasters to trains literally idiot-proof— easy to use and, at least in theory, 100% safe—the others jumped on the bandwagon too and got their chunk of market share.

But maybe Caesar *pater* would have given Bill Gates a few sleepless nights if he hadn't rolled over most of his profits into his own pet projects and hobbies. Probably due not a little to his name, Gaius Caesar had a lifelong interest in ancient Roman and Greek literature. One of his fondest dreams was to program AIs to reconstruct lost works from antiquity. Like the dozens of lost plays by Sophocles and Aeschylus. The missing sections of Marcus Tullius Cicero's *De republica*. The hundred-plus vanished volumes of the *Ab urbe condita libri* by Titus

Livius. Or the four lost *Discourses* of Epictetus. The AIs used existing fragments and summaries of those works, and an exhaustive analysis of the style and ideas in the authors' extant writings and teachings, to produce at least an approximation of them.

So-called "scholars" of classical culture had unanimously dismissed those reconstructions as rubbish. True, there was no way to know how close they came to the originals. But, judged on their own merits, they seemed pretty damn good to me.

What provoked more public derision was the elder Caesar's fervid sponsorship of fringe "science." Gaius had welcomed anybody who claimed they'd perfected lukewarm fusion or designed a faster-than-light drive, teleportation device, or perpetual motion machine. Based on what he'd learned from those "non-traditional, new-paradigm scientists" (a.k.a. crackpots), he'd poured millions into building complex AI-controlled amalgams of metal, silicon, and plastic. Unfortunately, none of those machines had ever succeeded in generating energy from the ether or transporting anybody to another dimension, much less a distant star system.

When Gaius died during a Viagra-laced tryst with a curvaceous cutie barely out of high school, Rem took over the company and stopped all that nonsense. Those Buck Rogers contraptions were hauled away for scrap, operations were streamlined, and "unproductive" personnel—like me—were ruthlessly cashiered.

Soon the stock price for IQ Industries shot up like a Mars Direct rocket. Worshipped by his stockholders, feared by his competitors, his smug visage gracing the covers of major business journals every month, Rem finally seemed to have all the recognition and celebrity he'd always craved. Reading that highly sanitized version of his life and the interview he gave when *Time* named him "Man of the Year" made me sick. Old Dad might've been crazy, Rem sneered, but *he* was a *real* businessman.

But what that article didn't say was that fame and power were his strongest aphrodisiacs and making money was his only ideal. Whatever didn't exist *now*, or couldn't be calculated on a balance sheet, wasn't important to him. I've seen AIs in electric nose hair trimmers with more imagination than he has.

So when Rem starts babbling about time travelers, it definitely gets my attention.

I acted nonchalant. "So what makes you think time travelers are out to get you?"

Rem loosened his silk tie. "At first I didn't know they were time travelers. Starting last Monday I kept seeing the same twenty or so people wherever I went. If I got on an elevator in my office building, one of them was on it. A couple of them were always standing near my limo before I got in. Whenever I went to one of my exclusive country clubs for supper, a group of them was at the next table."

"Did you know any of them?"

"Of course not! They weren't the kind of people I associate with. They were—peculiar. Living in San Francisco, you get used to seeing people who dress and act a little different. But they stood out from even the usual free spirit crowd."

I glanced over at Mildred. She was pretending to wipe an empty table a few booths away. When she saw me looking at her, she gave up her eavesdropping with a sigh and put a few coins in the long-silent jukebox.

Again I found myself hoping that she'd selected an AI-produced composition. But no, the new piece the jukebox started playing was merely another current human-made hit, "Murmurs from My Heart." Twanging guitars and a thumping bass accompanied the warm melodious baritone of G. F. Ramstant, the cardiologist who now pursued a considerably more lucrative career as a country music singer.

You broke my heart so bad, I can't find all the pieces.
There's a hole in my chest where my left ventricle used to be.
It'd take a surgeon with superglue, and a little help from Jesus,
To fix my achy DeBakey heart for me!

Rem, sitting opposite me with his back to the front door, didn't see it open and a young couple walk in. They sat down in a booth on the other side of the room. The woman looked about thirty-five. Her auburn hair was molded into a bouffant hairdo and topped by a pillbox hat. The pale sheath-dress outfit she wore reminded me of old films I'd seen of Jackie Kennedy during her eventful trip to Dallas over a half century ago.

Her companion was a little taller and older. His gray flannel suit would've looked good on Nixon during his "Checkers" speech. Except his wide tie was wrapped around his forehead like a sweatband. And I don't think Tricky Dick ever sported an orange Mohawk.

Mildred didn't know what to make of them either. After they refused her proffered menu with silent synchronized shakes of their heads, she left the odd pair alone.

Rem didn't notice them. "I started getting worried when I flew down to Los Angeles last Tuesday. There were a dozen of them at the airport just before I boarded my jet. Another group was waiting for me at the airport in LA. One of them pulled beside my limo riding a motorcycle when we were stuck in traffic on the expressway."

"Did any of them talk to you?"

"No. All they ever did was—stare at me. Never getting too close, just watching me. Even with my bodyguards right alongside me, I was starting to get a little afraid of them. But somehow I got the impression they were more afraid of *me*."

The front door opened again, admitting still more patrons. A fiftyish man with a circa 1964 Beatles haircut and a ruffled Nehru jacket. A redhead poured into a skimpy miniskirt that might've been taken off the set of *Laugh-In*. A bell-bottomed, platform-shoed John Travolta wannabe, accompanied by the innocent, pre-slut Olivia Newton-John from *Grease*.

Rem was too immersed staring at a vulgarity some former patron had carved in our tabletop to notice the newcomers quietly take their places in surrounding booths. "When I returned home Wednesday it got worse. I started seeing them, not just in public, but in places where they had no business being. The other morning I woke up at home, looked out my bedroom window—and there were five of them standing on the lawn looking back up at me!

"I called security right away—but they didn't find anyone. The guards knew better than to contradict me. But I could tell they didn't believe anybody could get over an electrified iron fence, avoid being detected by the infrared sensor system, elude the dogs patrolling the grounds—and then vanish into thin air!"

Joe, still snoozing near the front door, grunted in his sleep as it opened again, briefly letting in the blare of traffic rushing by outside. A pre-army Elvis slid his blue suede shoes into a nearby booth, followed by a pill-popping version in a white sequined jumpsuit.

I sniffed. "Sounds reasonable to me. Besides, who would *want* to break in to that prison you call 'home'?"

Rem's face looked like perspiring alabaster. "Then I didn't see them anymore—but I knew they were there, somewhere, close by. I'd be working in my office alone late at night, and I'd catch a glimpse of one of them out of the corner of my eye. I felt them looking over my shoulder, whispering something in languages I couldn't understand. But when I turned around—nobody was there. Once, while I was alone in the men's room at a restaurant, I'm sure one of them was staring down at me over the top of the stall!"

Several more people filtered in and sat down. Though she was a brunette, the woman at the far end of the room filled her *Seven Year Itch* dress quite nicely. Her boothmate was even more striking. At first I thought she was wearing the thinnest spandex I'd ever seen. Then I decided she was covered from head to toe with a weird rubbery body paint, whose psychedelic colors shifted like a kaleidoscope every time she moved. Maybe that was the latest fashion on the coast this year. Or some year.

Their constant staring at us made my skin crawl. I tried to ignore them and focus my attention back on Rem. "Hmm. Hearing voices. Delusions of persecution. What's that medical term you like to use so much? 'Paranoid schizophrenic'? Sounds to me like you don't need my help. You need a psychiatrist."

Rem, still blithely unaware he was the center of attention, winced. "That's not funny. And they're not delusions. Early this morning—I caught one of them."

"And I suppose that stalker told you all about this fiendish plot to drive you crazy."

"In a way. I woke up in bed about 3 a.m. It was pitch-black—but I could *feel* someone staring at me. I switched on the lamp by my bed— and there he was. He looked like a troll. Short, fat, old-looking with coarse features. I'd seen him before. He was the one looking down at me in the men's room. He wore a brown suit and was pointing what looked like a camera at me.

"When the light came on he blinked and stumbled backwards. I grabbed him, wrestled him to the floor, and sat on him. I think my cursing and slapping him around terrified him. He started babbling in a language I couldn't understand. Then I realized it was a garbled version of English."

I tried taking another sip of Pepsi, but the glass was empty. "Could you make out any of it?"

"Yes—but it didn't make any sense. He said he'd come from the year 2525, back to the 'Dawn of the Temporal Age.'"

"The what?"

"Apparently he believed the first time machine was built last week. His machine and the ones those other people from the future use can't travel back into the past before that first time machine was used."

I frowned professorially. "There are theoretical physicists who've said that, on the remote chance a time machine could be built, it would have that limitation. But why would they be after *you*? Do they think you—or maybe your unborn son or grandson—is going to become an evil dictator who takes over the world?"

I snickered. "That must be it. The Temporal CIA is planning to terminate you with extreme prejudice and make a brighter, happier future for all of humanity. What a hoot."

A line of sweat trickled down Rem's clean-shaven cheek. "I don't think that's it. The troll kept calling me the 'Father of Time Travel.' If I understood him correctly, the reason they're after me is that they think *I* just invented that first time machine!"

I scratched my beard, rubbing away a little sweat of my own. "Well?"

"Well what?"

"*Did* you invent a time machine?"

Rem looked at me as if I'd just accused him of being Santa Claus. "Of course not! Dad was crazy enough to try building ridiculous crap like that, but I'm not!"

"Then why are these so-called time travelers after you?"

Rem shook his head wearily. "I don't know. Maybe the troll would have told me if I'd hit him a few more times. But I was so disgusted with what I thought were his lies I got up off him and started to phone security. Then I saw him reach for something in his coat. I thought it was a gun, so I ran out of the bedroom into the next room. After I hit the alarm button I peeked back through the bedroom door. He was holding what looked like a wand with a big ruby at the end."

"Borrowed, no doubt, from Glinda the Good Witch of the North."

Rem ignored me. "Then the guards rushed in, and I warned them about the troll. They pulled their guns and yelled for him to come out. When he didn't they snuck a look into my bedroom—then stared at me like I was crazy."

Rem's hands were shaking. "My bedroom was empty."

He didn't have to say anything more to me. Rem's bedroom is on the fourth floor of the Caesar family mansion. There's only one door in. And the only other way out is through a window of bulletproof, shatter-resistant glass that can't be opened. From the expression on Rem's face, I knew that window was still intact.

I sneered, "Maybe the guards were right. Maybe you *are* crazy. Just like the rest of your family. Father a crackpot. Mother dying from— what did the doctors call it?—'systemic lupus erythematosus with secondary psychosis.' And then there's your—"

"Stop it!"

I stopped. If I hadn't, Rem would probably have wrapped his hands around my throat. Every homicidal maniac has a first victim.

The last booth had just filled. The man was attired in jeans and dirty sweatshirt that looked uncomfortably like the ones I wore. Although even I have better sartorial taste than to wear a baseball cap backwards. The woman had on that feather outfit Mona Plenty barely wore in last year's Oscar-winning holo, *Evil Slime Critters from Hell, Part VI.*

Staring at her avian apparel, I suddenly realized another reason why these people were making me so uneasy. The way they'd filtered in a few at a time—it reminded me of that old Hitchcock thriller. One bird landing on an overhanging wire. Then another, two more, until gradually the wire sagged under the weight of a menacing flock— poised to strike at some mysterious signal.

Rem, his attention focused on me and his troubles, still hadn't noticed the twenty-some pairs of unblinking eyes silently staring at our booth. Mildred, cowering in a corner, sensed the shroud of danger hanging over the room as strongly as I did.

But, trooper that she was, she still dutifully did her job. These latest customers wordlessly rejected the menus she nervously offered them with the same dismissive hand and head gestures the earlier arrivals had. Then, trying to dispel the smothering tension all around us, she put a few more coins in the jukebox.

Despite my feeling of impending doom, I still found myself hoping to hear an AI-generated song from the machine. But no, Mildred selected one of her favorites, a sentimental ballad entitled "Love Among The Stars." Twanging guitars and a thumping bass accompanied a duet by Willie Jay Xerxes and Sonya Pucker, the two former astronautical engineers who'd turned to more prestigious careers as country music singers.

(Chorus)   *Truckin' through the cosmos in a starship built for two,*
Fuzzy dice hangin' from our Bussard ramjet,
We'll be thrustin' together in an interstellar rendezvous,
Then smokin' a post-coital cigarette.

(Willie Jay)*There's no two-body problem that we can't figure out,*
Floatin' together in microgravity.
Embedded in each other, there's never any doubt
Time stand's still, 'cause we're travelin' close to c!"

(Chorus)   *Truckin' through the cosmos in a starship built for two, etc.*

(Sonya)   *You have boldly gone where no man's gone before,*
Explorin' a black hole of ecstasy.
Please cross my event horizon, and thrill me some more
When you touch my naked singularity."

(Chorus)   *Truckin' through the cosmos in a starship built for two, etc.*

As the music reverberated through the room I noticed something that made my brain throb with horror. Every one of the unconventionally dressed people in the surrounding booths was listening to the song. And judging from their misty vapid smiles, they *liked* it!

Willie Jay and Sonya finished their tender duet on a final cheery cadence, filling the room with utter silence. Then, after what seemed like a breathless eternity, one of the strangers quietly hummed the first bars of the song.

That tiny noise had the same explosive effect as a lighted match tossed into a gasoline tank. Rem glanced up—and saw over twenty pairs of eyes staring at him. I'll never forget the look of horrified recognition that twisted his face into something hellish. He looked like a French aristocrat during the Revolution, neck tightly locked in the guillotine, in those timeless seconds of terror before the blade fell.

Then the front door opened once again—and the last member of this menagerie waddled in. He didn't look much like a troll. More like a munchkin. Unless, perhaps, you saw him standing by your bed at three o'clock in the morning.

As the rotund stranger walked directly toward us Rem's eyes were bulging, his face the purplish-red of someone dangling at the end of a hangman's noose. I wasn't sure he was going to live long enough for the troll to reach him. Then the little man took out a small gray rectangle and stylus from his pocket. Slowly, hesitatingly, he looked right at Rem and said something that chilled me to the deepest pit of my gut.

"Conferred may I be that autograph of yours, Caesar Mister?"

Rem reacted like a cornered rat fighting for its life. "No! Get away from me! All of you—leave me *alone!*"

He leapt up, knocking the troll aside. The front door swished open, and I saw him run across the intersection outside. Against the light.

There was a thudding *boom!* as the bus plowed into him at full speed, sending his flailing body arcing through the air. The bus had barely screeched to a stop a hundred meters down the street when I reached him. I could hear Mildred screaming somewhere behind me as I looked down at the unmoving lump of tattered flesh sprawled on the street, its expensive suit ripped into bloody rags. Rem's face had survived nearly intact, eyes staring up at the clear infinite night sky. But from the twisted angle of his neck and the nauseating way his chest was crushed, I knew he'd never see the stars again.

Then the bus driver, a thin gray-haired woman, was beside me yelling, "It ain't my fault, he ran right out in front of me! I'm going to get me a lawyer!" As her passengers came out to gawk at the body I eased away. Joe was standing in the back of the crowd staring slack-jawed at what was left of Rem, as if expecting the corpse to jump up and walk back into the bar for a margarita. Mel, parked beside him, looked even stupider—still clutching his magazine with the buxom centerfold of Miss International Space Station hanging out in all her tartish glory.

And farther back, under the streetlights, stood the flock of vultures who'd hounded Rem to his death. As furious as I was I couldn't help feeling a bit sorry for them. They looked totally disoriented and lost. Like a creationist told by God the Mother that yes, She had evolved men from monkeys—but, except for the hair, didn't see any difference between them. Or finding out everything you've learned in history class was wrong.

One by one that baffled costumed crew slunk away into the shadows, and were gone. Finally only the troll was left. He shook his head in disbelief, stared crestfallen at the shattered demigod on the pavement, and muttered, "Be how that can?" Then he extracted a wand with a multifaceted ruby on the end from his coat. A slight pressure from his fingertip, and he was gone too.

I started to rejoin the crowd chattering around the body when I saw something lying unnoticed on the dimly lit street. It was Rem's wallet. Must've popped out of his pocket when the bus hit him.

Nobody saw me pick up his wallet and replace it with my own. I hung back in the shadows, watching the mob hover above the mass of cooling meat I'd been talking with minutes ago, making sure no one else saw the wallet and decided to keep it as a souvenir.

A few minutes later the cops arrived. I was lucky. One of them found the wallet right away.

That was my cue to leave. As I walked by my favorite restaurant for the last time I heard the jukebox inside playing a new song. At first I couldn't figure it out. A quick glance through the window showed the place was still empty.

Then I realized the jukebox's AI must be programmed to start playing on its own after a certain length of time if nobody put any money in it. A little bonus for the customers, something for atmosphere—and to encourage them to pay for the next selection.

It was too much to believe the AI had miraculously recomposed the song playing soulfully from the jukebox. But perhaps the AI, somehow sensing the events that had just unfolded, had made a preternaturally wise choice from its database. The two synthesized voices warbling from the jukebox didn't sound much like Roy Rogers and Dale Evans. But the melody and words were those of "Happy Trails."

I think AIs are vastly underrated.

I ordered the AI in my car to get me home as fast as it could. They come from the factory preprogrammed to obey speed limits. But for those of us who know what makes them tick, it's easy to override those instructions. A highly sophisticated radar detector I'd built kept me "honest."

The car's AI, knowing my tastes leaned toward the classical, locked in on a favorite music channel from one of the direct-broadcast satellite systems. It was playing an unjustly obscure Haydn symphony. "No. 64 in A Major," according to the display on my dashboard.

Plunging down the highway through the starry night, with the symphony's melancholy Largo swirling around me, I was alone with my thoughts. Regretting that I'd never enjoyed those delicious ribs or Mildred one last time. And trying to make some sense of the tragedy I'd witnessed.

There was a certain twisted logic to what had happened to Rem. *If* someone built a time machine, that person would be famous for all time. A magnet for every time-traveling historian, media-type, tourist—or just "fans" with no lives of their own, coming back to bask in their idol's luminous presence.

Of course, if they came from far enough in the future, their knowledge and understanding of commonplaces like fashion in the past would be a bit spotty. Derived, of necessity, from old pictures and recordings. They wouldn't realize how much the way people looked and dressed in classic movies, videos, and holos differed from the way they did in real life. And they might be off a couple decades in choosing their models.

And *if* it were impossible to travel into the past before the first time machine was used a week ago, that would explain why those hordes of time travelers hadn't shown up before.

My house was dark when I arrived about 2:00 a.m. As I walked to the front door it sensed my presence and turned on the lights on the main level. A synthesized voice ordered, "Place your right hand against the plate on the door."

I did. The front door opened and the house said, "Welcome home, sir." Unlike Rem, I'd never needed gates and human guards to protect me.

A quick shower and change of clothes, and from the neck down I looked like a busy executive dressed in expensive casual wear, ready for an afternoon on the links. Just like the outfit Rem used to wear on the rare days he wasn't working.

It wasn't easy cutting my own hair. But, using a hand mirror and the large one on the wall in my bathroom, I managed to trim my scraggly curls into a semblance of the blow-dried look that Rem favored. My electric razor had a simple AI built in. It removed my beard relatively painlessly.

As I packed my suitcase another thought came to me. The surprising thing was that so few time travelers had come back to see Rem at his moment of triumph. Maybe it'd been like a press pool. Or maybe humans of the more distant future had progressed beyond primitive obsessions like hero worship or tabloid-level voyeurism.

But more likely those people of the future were, like nearly all my contemporaries, simply idiots. Unthinking fools, obsessed with vapid entertainment and animal pleasures, with no purpose or reflection in their lives. Eloi in a high-tech world, where machines with sophisticated descendants of present-day AIs did all the real work and thinking. Well, at least AIs didn't get hungry.

Or perhaps, in some not too distant millennium, humanity was extinct. That would be a kinder fate.

Then, suitcase in hand, I went down to my laboratory in the basement. A translucent ruby-colored geodesic dome three meters in diameter sat in the middle of the floor. How they had ever managed to shrink it down to something you could hold in your hand was beyond me. But, very soon, I'd make them tell.

The panel on the dome slid open, and a dim red glow immediately filled its interior. As I sat down inside at the control console the machine's AI said, "Good morning, sir. Ready for another trip?"

"Yes. Set destination for…October 31, AD 2521, 1400 Coordinated Universal Time. Latitude 37° 47' north, longitude 122 ° 26' west. I'll let you decide the seconds."

Well, it was as good a time and place as any to start. Besides, I hadn't been to San Francisco for several years.

"Very good, sir. Lukewarm fusion generator is now operational. Programming sequence is initiated. Temporal-spatial translation in…one hundred and one seconds."

The OLED screen in front of me flashed a countdown. No need to worry, I told myself. Based on what I'd seen and heard a few hours ago, everything was going to work out just fine.

Except for poor Rem. All his life he'd wanted the limelight, to be a celebrity. Then, when he'd succeeded beyond his wildest dreams—acclaimed throughout the eons as the revered inventor of the first time machine—he couldn't handle it.

Of course, if he'd had a bit more imagination, he could have figured out how one avoids being stalked and hounded to death by temporal groupies and paparazzi. You travel to the future and *give* the apparently very stupid and gullible people there the secret of time travel before they stumble on it themselves. Make yourself famous among them—a celebrity, a cult leader, or even a media-created divinity. *Deus ex machina tempora*. That had a nice ring to it.

And the first article of faith you give your fawning devotees and disciples is, *No time machine can travel back in time before the first one was used*. With that thought ingrained in their limited minds by the very Father of Time Travel and passed on to later generations, they won't even think about discovering the quantum uncertainty circuit that allows you to travel *anywhere* in time and space. And they won't be chasing after you with their own time machines when, after your jaunt to the future, you travel back to Athens in the 5th century BC.

Gaius Caesar, the illustrious founder of IQ Industries, had to content himself with AI-generated fantasies about the lost works of the great ancient philosophers and dramatists. Me—I was going to find out what they *really* said and wrote. Maybe argue with Socrates, using a

Machiavellian or Nietzschean point of view. Or give them suggestions about what to write. "To be or not to be." I wonder what Euripides would do with *that* line as a beginning.

The machine's AI interrupted my reverie. "Twenty-two seconds to temporal-spatial translation." The muted ruddy light around me reflected countless images of my face off the dome's facets. With its newly trimmed hair and clean-shaven cheeks it looked like a damned soul engulfed in the fires of hell. A ghost come back to haunt me.

It was Rem's face—reminding me that the first thing I had to do when I arrived in the 26th century was to tell everyone my name. Remus Caesar, prosperous early 21st century businessman and inventor of the first time machine. Remus Caesar, whose first jaunt through time a week ago, traveling from one Sunday to the next, had unintentionally started a chain of events that was far from over.

Remus Caesar. Not the man lying cold and stiff in a Kansas City morgue, his body identified from the driver's license (its photo taken fortuitously during a rare beardless period) in his wallet, and perhaps a sloppy fingerprint or expert DNA band pattern comparison.

Remus Caesar. Not the erstwhile business partner who'd recognized the few good theories among all the crappy ones Gaius Caesar had collected, and used his own towering genius to develop them to perfection and create the device I sat within.

Remus Caesar. Not his much smarter identical twin, Romulus.

As the countdown on my time machine's monitor approached zero I wondered if it was possible to go back a few days into the past and do something to save my brother. No—too dangerous, too many potential paradoxes. As the ancient Stoic philosophers I'd one day be listening to might say, *Que sera, sera.*

Besides, this way Rem got all the fame and glory he'd craved—even if it was posthumously. And I avoided a fate worse than death. This way, there would be no hordes of time travelers perpetually looking

131

over my shoulder. Or staring at me. Or meddling in my personal affairs. You see, I'm a very private person.

This tongue-in-cheek story raises the question of how literally the laws of physics work. It also contains musical and mythological allusions that I hope you'll recognize.

Going Home

Tony Phineus, commander of the first starship, grinned at his sole crewmate on the *Perseus*. "Ready to go home?"

Polly Dectes, the vessel's astrophysicist, frowned and settled into the chair beside him at the control console. "The real question is, *can* we go home again?"

Tony snorted. "Always the skeptic."

He pointed to a monitor that showed Tau Ceti, a warm golden orb burning a mere 1.2 astronomical units away. "We've proven that the Lyndore-Gradle hyperdrive does work perfectly. Flip a switch, blink— and you've instantly traveled as many light-years as you want!"

Polly replied, "True. But I can't help remembering all those arguments 20th century physicists made about why superluminal travel and communication were impossible. The cause-and-effect and time travel paradoxes they might create. If you could transmit a signal faster than light, someone else could receive it and send an FTL reply back telling you not to send it—before you even sent the original signal! But if you decided then to not transmit the signal, how could anyone send you that reply not to transmit it?"

"Obsolete theories. Fine in their day, like phlogiston and epicycles. *This* is reality!"

Tony flipped a switch. Now the monitor showed the planet whirling serenely below them—a brilliant symphony of azure oceans, brown-and-green continents, and writhing serpentine clouds. "Size, gravity, temperature, atmosphere—all similar to Earth. And the mobile probes we sent down showed only Devonian-level life. No harmful bacteria or viruses."

He gazed wistfully at the screen. "Too bad we're not equipped to land there. The *Perseus II* will need landing shuttles and a team of biologists to go down and confirm the planet's safe. Then the human race will really have a 'New World,' ready for colonization!"

"*If* we get back and tell them what we found."

"Why wouldn't we? The *Perseus* returned to Earth orbit right on schedule after all eight unmanned automated flights to Tau Ceti. And the lab mice onboard were perfectly healthy."

Tony pointed to the console. "When I flip that switch, we'll go home too, safe and sound!"

"I hope so. But nobody really explained why the computers and recorders didn't contain any data after all of those test flights. No information at all about this star system or what was in it. It's almost like Nature didn't want us to know something."

"Ed was satisfied it was a software glitch. Or maybe a problem with the sensors."

Polly sighed. "Yes. But I suspect that our illustrious boss was more interested in talking us into going and keeping his precious project funded than he was in our safety."

Tony waved his hand at her impatiently. "This time, we *know* our equipment collected data. Even if their electronics got fried, there're still all the voice and video recordings we made. Plus everything we wrote in our notebooks."

He scratched his nose. "Besides, *we* remember what we found here. One way or another, the people back home will learn everything we know about the Tau Ceti system too!"

"Maybe, but—"

Tony ignored her. "Earth, here we come!" He flipped a switch—

The fluorescent light in the ceiling above him flickered on. Tony stared upward at the IV bag hanging beside his hospital bed.

Suddenly two faces hovered above him. Ed Minor, director of the FTL Project. And a middle-aged woman in a white lab coat.

"Any change, doctor?"

"I'm afraid not. We still haven't found any medical explanation for why they're like this. Was there anything on the ship to indicate what happened to them?"

"No. It was just like the test flights. No data in the ship's computers. And they didn't make any audio or video recordings, or write anything in their notebooks. The only way to find out if they made it to Tau Ceti and what they found there is for them to tell us. The ironic thing is, the mice on the *Perseus* came back perfectly fine again. But *they* can't tell us what they saw or heard."

Ed's voice grew desperate. "You've got to help them, otherwise the whole project will be shut down! Maybe if we put them on the ship and sent them back to Tau Ceti, the shock would snap them back to normal!"

Tony's brain screamed, *Yes! Send us back there, where we can't talk to you!*

The doctor sounded outraged. "That's ridiculous! I won't let you endanger my patients! They'll stay right here!"

Tony tried frantically again to make his lips move. Maybe signal to them with a curling finger or toe, a fluttering eyelid. But his limbs stayed stiff, eyes fixed and unmoving.

Ed whispered, "Can he hear what we're saying?"

"Probably. Their condition isn't a true coma, but instead resembles a 'locked-in' state. I think he can hear and see normally. He just can't move or communicate with us."

"Isn't there anything you can do?"

"We'll give them the best care possible. Maybe, someday, we'll find a treatment—or they'll recover on their own."

Someday. Tony imagined what Polly would say if she could speak.

"Nature lets you travel but not *communicate* faster than light. The Tau Ceti system is 11.8 light-years away. Anyone on Earth can only know what it was like there 11.8 years ago. If a person travels to Tau Ceti faster than light, then returns to Earth intending to tell other people what he or she saw there—"

Maybe the universe wasn't totally heartless. Each passing second made what he and Polly knew less prescient relative to everyone else on Earth. Perhaps, when the rest of humanity eventually "caught up" to where the two of them had jumped ahead on Nature's inflexible timeline for information, the delayed paralysis caused by gazing at that Medusa-like world orbiting Tau Ceti would suddenly disappear.

A speck of dust drifted onto Tony's nose, leaving a terrible itch that wouldn't go away. He stared upward, petrified, at the featureless white ceiling and steady drip of fluid from the IV bag.

It was going to be a long 11.8 years.

The main target of this satire doesn't become clear until most of the way through the story. Please look carefully for all the wordplays, allusions, and anagrams it contains.

The Invasion

The president of the United States shivered, wondering if the next hour would bring salvation or destruction to the human race. Her worried frown was mirrored in the faces of the National Security Council members filling the chairs at the long conference table. The only smile in the well-guarded White House room belonged to the famous astronomer sitting immediately to the right of where the president sat at the head of the table.

Arthur O. Lewis, director of the Search for Extra-Terrestrial Life Foundation, slid a bulky pair of glasses back up the bridge of his nose. His unruly shock of fine sandy hair and the bright boyish grin beaming from his clean-shaven face made him resemble a college freshman instead of the middle-aged owner of doctorates in both astronomy and computer science. The trademark turtleneck sweater and khaki slacks he sported stood in stark sartorial contrast to the stiff business suits and military uniforms worn by the dignitaries around him.

Lewis spoke with the high-pitched enthusiasm of a nerdy teenager describing the details of his first date with a real girl. "Don't worry, Madam President. Today could be the greatest day in human history!"

The president looked uncertainly at the dark screen of the device resembling a laptop computer that the astronomer had just set up in front of her. She said, "Or it might be our last day. I almost wish this machine of yours wouldn't work."

Lewis gleefully stroked the tip of his index finger over the tachyonic transceiver's power button, barely restraining his impulse to depress it as he replied. "The electronic engineers who built it based on the plans the aliens sent us believe it will work. True, the theoretical physicists we consulted still don't understand how it can send and receive signals faster than the speed of light. But we really don't need to know exactly how the transceiver works to be able to use it. After all, most people who use computers don't have any idea how a CPU functions."

The puzzled expressions shown by the room's other distinguished occupants suggested they didn't know what a "CPU" was, much less what it did. The president said, "Dr. Lewis, do you think the aliens who sent that message you received already know of our existence?"

"I don't think so. The signals our radio telescope network picked up were omnidirectional rather than beamed specifically at Earth. We also discovered that the aliens' transmissions didn't begin recently. Our review of old magnetic tapes from the first SETI programs over fifty years ago, like Project Ozma in 1960, showed that some packets of their message were being transmitted even back then."

The president frowned. "What do you mean by 'packets'?"

Lewis said, "The original SETI investigators tried to detect data being transmitted in a linear, analog fashion—the same way signals are received on a conventional AM or FM radio. They used single-channel receivers limited to monitoring just one frequency at a time and confined their search to a narrow range of frequencies, such as those around the 21-cm wavelength of radiation produced by interstellar hydrogen. Those initial surveys also listened for signals from only one star at a time and checked only a few nearby ones, like Tau Ceti and Epsilon Eridani."

The astronomer grinned. "But the way the aliens sent their message was much too complex to be detected by simple methods like that. They disassembled and formatted their message into many discrete fragments or 'packets' of binary code difficult to distinguish from random noise until you put them back together.

"Then those packets were transmitted in a manner similar to the 'frequency-hopping spread spectrum' technology used in some wireless computer networks. To put it simply, the aliens sent each digitized signal over a broad range of frequencies instead of only one. About every hundred milliseconds the signal 'hopped' from one frequency to another within that range in a recurring pattern. Finally, packets containing separate parts of the complete message were transmitted in signals originating from *several* nearby stars instead of just one. The specific stars we discovered parts of the message coming from included—"

The president interrupted him. "That all sounds very complicated, Dr. Lewis. Why do you think the aliens made it so difficult to detect their signals?"

The scientist shrugged. "Perhaps they are only interested in communicating with civilizations that have achieved at least our current level of technology. Those first SETI investigators simply didn't have the equipment or techniques available to discover more than a tiny piece of an incredibly complex puzzle. Even with the latest large-scale distributed computing methods we now use, the raw computational power needed to monitor so many frequencies, integrate those multiple extraterrestrial signals, and reassemble all the data packets into their original form wasn't available until recently.

"But once we had the aliens' complete message, it didn't take our group's linguists long to translate it with the help of the Foundation's new supercomputer. They discovered the message only contained instructions for building and using this device."

Lewis tapped the edge of the tachyonic transceiver. "This machine will let you become the very first human to instantly communicate and exchange messages with the aliens who broadcast those signals—to make 'first contact' with an intelligence far greater than ours. I hope you'll decide to take advantage of this history-making opportunity."

The president smiled sadly. "I knew winning this office held many heavy responsibilities, but I never expected this to be one of them."

She looked questioningly at the other officials seated in the room. "I would appreciate more advice before I make my final decision about whether or not to use Dr. Lewis's device."

From the far end of the conference table the Director of National Intelligence said, "Dr. Lewis, we all appreciate the admirable discretion you and your staff exercised by keeping your discovery of the aliens' message and its contents secret. I hate to think of the worldwide panic that might have occurred if any of you had spoken with the media about it before we clamped a security lid on everyone concerned."

The astronomer grinned humbly. "I hope what the president and all of you choose to do here today will validate our refraining from going public with this. Though my staff and I were sorely tempted to give a press conference about our discovery, we finally agreed that the decision whether or not to contact the aliens had to be made by the people who held the greatest responsibility for dealing with the results of that choice."

The Director of National Intelligence looked back at him suspiciously, wondering whether this otherwise brilliant scientist was incredibly naïve or being subtly sarcastic. He replied, "Thank you for having such faith in us."

Then the director's voice turned low and dark. "But tell me, do you have any idea *why* aliens would send us the plans for that device?"

Lewis shrugged. "There's obviously no such thing as an expert on exopsychology. Anything I say is speculative. Perhaps the aliens have motives that our mere human minds couldn't possibly understand. Or maybe, in some ways, the aliens do think like us. It's possible that they too are curious to find out whether intelligence has evolved elsewhere in the Galaxy and what form it's taken."

He pointed to the silvery metal transceiver resting in front of the president. "Perhaps they're eager to share their own religious and philosophical insights into the meaning of existence with us. Beings capable of this level of technology may be as intellectually and morally advanced above us as we are from *Homo habilis*."

Lewis's eyes peered out into the misty distance through thick lenses. "Or perhaps, as those beings gazed up at a clear night sky into the vast silent universe, they felt a great melancholy emptiness within them. The information they sent may have been like a message in a bottle, tossed out into the vast ocean of space with a prayer that somewhere, someone they could call 'friend' would find it and let them know that they were not alone. This device they taught us to build could be a 'laptop of loneliness,' the instrument by which they hope we'll answer their plaintive plea for companionship."

The Chairman of the Joint Chiefs of Staff grunted. "That sounds a bit fishy to me. *I* think it could be the worm on a fishing hook—the bait for a trap!"

He squinted acidly at Lewis. "If we follow your suggestion, we could be letting immensely powerful and hostile creatures know we exist and where Earth is. Their 'answer' might be a fleet of flying saucers and armies of death ray-wielding robots dropping out of the sky over our cities!"

The president stared at her general, worried about his taste in movies and recreational reading material—and unsure whether he was really serious. After deciding she'd rather not know if he was, she replied, "While that possibility seems a bit...remote, I must consider every ramification of making what Dr. Lewis calls 'first contact.' Earlier in this meeting you all heard him describe the many potential advantages of beginning a dialogue with these aliens.

"Besides the religious and philosophical insights he just alluded to, they may provide us with practical solutions to many of the problems facing our world today. If they really could help us solve all the energy and environmental crises we face, provide us with the medical knowledge to live longer and healthier lives, and teach us how to coexist in harmony with each other, then this device might indeed be our salvation."

A disapproving voice along the side of the table interjected, "Or those same 'benefits' could wreck our economy!"

The Secretary of the Treasury continued, "Say these hypothetical aliens of yours send us information about cheap, safe energy sources that eliminate our current dependence on oil, gas, coal, and nuclear power. That could make millions of workers in those industries lose their jobs and destroy the value of some of our largest corporations!

"Or if the aliens told us how to cure cancer or heart disease so people lived longer, the money we'd save by spending less on healthcare might be far outweighed by the greater amounts we'd pay in Social Security and other benefits to recipients who would now be living many more years than we've planned for! I know this sounds harsh, but we don't want to unintentionally cause more harm than good."

The Secretary of Defense nodded his perspiring brow. "For all we know the aliens really might want Earth's nations to get along better with each other—but for their own ends. The aliens could *want* us to reduce military spending so we'll be less prepared to defend ourselves when they attack!"

The Secretary of State looked at her colleague dubiously. "I won't even guess what the aliens might do, but I am concerned about the threats some of our fellow humans are making. While the public may still be in the dark about Dr. Lewis's discovery, rumors of what's been going on have leaked out to several of our allies and a few unfriendly powers. They're all demanding we give them a full account of what we know and plan to do."

The vice president nodded. "It's risky to either stall them or share our information with them. Their greatest fear seems to be that we'll acquire technological knowledge from the aliens that would give us such a tremendous economic and military advantage that our country could unilaterally dominate the world. If they thought *we'd* learned how to build advanced weapons of mass destruction like the flying saucers and rampaging robots the general described, even our so-called allies might feel justified in a preemptive military strike against us before we could deploy those weapons."

He turned a troubled look at the president. "No matter what you decide, it's going to be a diplomatic nightmare convincing other governments we're being open and honest with them. Maybe Dr. Lewis's device won't even work. Perhaps the aliens we contact won't share their scientific secrets with us. The problem is—will any of those governments believe anything we say about what happens here today?"

The president bit her lower lip, deep in thought. She said, "If this device works, we could let those other nations know how to build their own. Then they wouldn't have to be afraid we had a monopoly on knowledge they think could threaten them."

The Chairman of the Joint Chiefs of Staff shook his head vigorously. "Even if *we* don't use any information the aliens give us for military purposes, our enemies probably won't be so scrupulous. We don't want to hand them a tool they could use to build superscientific weapons and destroy us!"

Lewis said, "Even if you decide not to share the plans for the transceiver, there are SETI programs in other countries that could potentially pick up and decipher the message we received. All they'd need is just a few details about the techniques we used and where to listen. Then they'd be able to make and use their own transceiver."

The president turned to the individual sitting with uncharacteristic silence on Lewis's right. "What do you think?"

The tall gray-haired man who served as both her National Security Advisor and her husband looked bemused at the arguments swirling around him. He said, "I think we should go ahead and contact these

147

aliens. Sure, we could get into trouble with them or other countries by doing that. But I'm confident we can talk ourselves out of any mess we make and come out on top."

The other people in the room looked at him, unable to contest what he'd said. Finally the president continued, "Dr. Lewis has presented us with a difficult dilemma. Clearly there are serious risks whatever we decide to do about his device. All we can do is pick the course that seems to carry the least risk."

She smiled ruefully at the tachyonic transceiver, then back at the astronomer. "I remember listening to my old classical studies professor at college lecturing about the 'Golden Apple of Discord' that started the Trojan War. I hope the crisis your machine's caused has a better outcome."

Her eyes slowly scanned all the faces around the table. "I appreciate your input and ideas. However, to quote one of my illustrious predecessors, the buck does stop with me. Ultimately only I can decide what to do and take responsibility for that decision."

With a firm voice she continued, "I don't want to be the person who brought hostile aliens to Earth and destroyed the human race."

The Chairman of the Joint Chiefs of Staff and several other faces around the room tried to suppress gloating grins. But before Lewis could begin his protest the president added, "But I don't think the chances of that happening are great enough to outweigh the damage I would definitely do by holding back human progress. Dr. Lewis, show me how to work your machine."

For the next thirty minutes Lewis worked feverishly with the two information technology technicians summoned to the room. The pair of computer experts arrived rolling a large open metal cart with closed laptops stacked on several shelves. After being asked to temporarily vacate their seats, the president and other officials stood nearby and watched anxiously as the IT techs set one of the notebook computers at each place along the table and brought its screen to glowing life.

Meanwhile Lewis sat in the president's chair, turned on the tachyonic transceiver, and ran his fingertips like a virtuoso over its keyboard. As he called out instructions to them the two technicians bounced from chair to chair, carefully configuring each laptop to his specifications.

Their work finally done, the IT technicians moved the now nearly empty metal cart to a far corner of the room and left. As everyone resumed their original seats Lewis said, "We've set up a secure 'ad hoc' wireless network linking the tachyonic transceiver with your individual laptops. Anything the president sees on the transceiver's screen will be mirrored on yours. Once we've made contact with the aliens, each of you will also be able to interact with them through your laptops."

The president stared dubiously at the familiar garish colors and icons on the transceiver's display. "That looks like the same screen I see when I start up my own laptop."

The astronomer nodded. "That's because most of the hardware and software in the transceiver, including the operating system, are the same as in a conventional computer. Our programmers and linguists created a translation program to convert alien transmissions into English and instantly show their messages on the screen. When you enter your own message the transceiver does the reverse, translating what you type on the keyboard into the aliens' language and transmitting it back."

His index finger moved to the touchpad on his own laptop. "When I double-click this icon, the transceiver will load the program that should initiate a communication link with the aliens. May I do it, Madam President?"

There was a long pause. Finally she murmured, "Yes."

Lewis made a quick pair of taps with his finger—and waited eagerly. The other people in the room stared at their screens with mixtures of fear, curiosity, and perhaps a slender thread of hope.

At first nothing happened. Then the tense silence was shattered by a high-pitched whistling emanating from the transceiver, followed quickly by a short series of weird beeps and a brief swishing noise. Those unearthly sounds stopped just as abruptly as they'd begun— and then something magnificent happened. Rainbow colors as subtle as the first whispered glow of dawn suddenly swirled on the screens of the transceiver and every laptop in the room. Those delicate hues coalesced and solidified into an abstract background that Picasso would have envied.

Everyone around the conference table watched awestruck as English words arranged in a triad of familiar phrases appeared on their LCD displays.

Create user name.

Enter new password.

Confirm password.

The president looked at Lewis. "Any suggestions about what I should use?"

The astronomer shrugged. "It's your decision, Madam President. Choose whatever you want."

Her hands hesitated over the keyboard. "I suppose I could use the ones for my main e-mail account."

Another instant and everyone saw the words "chiefexecutiveusa" in the first field on their laptops. But while the others saw only small black dots appear in the next two fields, Lewis was close enough to the president to discreetly sneak a peek at her fingers as she typed. He wondered if "bestpreznumber1" was officially classified as "Top Secret."

Her last entry completed, the president solemnly pressed the "Enter" key on the transceiver. After a slight pause an empty text box with a small blinking vertical line in its upper left corner appeared on the screen. At Lewis's suggestion the president typed inside the text box, "We the people of Earth greet you in peace and friendship." After her fingers depressed the "Enter" key again, she and the others watched their displays change back to a featureless blur of colors—and waited.

And waited.

For slothfully slow minutes the only sounds in the room were the occasional cough, sneeze, and low rumble of a stomach growling. As anxiety turned into annoyance the president looked sharply at Lewis and demanded, "Well? Has this thing crashed? Should I restart it, like I do with my regular laptop when it locks up?"

The astronomer's fingertips played across his own laptop's keyboard. He said, "Everything seems to check out okay. The aliens should have received the message you just transmitted instantaneously. However, there's no telling how long it will take them to read it or send a reply."

The Secretary of Defense snorted. "Maybe they'll submit the question of how to answer us to their equivalent of a congressional committee for review. If their political system operates anything like ours, it might be months before we get a reply!"

The Chairman of the Joint Chiefs of Staff snickered. "Or maybe we'll just get a recording saying the number we're trying to reach has been disconnected!"

Lewis frowned. "That isn't so far-fetched. As I mentioned earlier, the aliens' transmission has been broadcast for at least half a century. It's possible we might not get an answer because they've been wiped out by some natural catastrophe or other disaster since they began their transmission."

The president scowled. "Do you mean all this trouble and worry might be for nothing?"

The astronomer squinted at his laptop's screen, as if willing it to change into an answer to the message the president had just sent. "I hope not. All we can do is wait until—"

Suddenly bold blue letters formed on the screens scattered around the room.

A Missive Has Been Sent to You.

There was a long stunned silence as the implications of those words registered on everyone reading them. Then a new sentence appeared below that announcement.

You Have Just Received an Important Message from His Supreme Highness.

The president stared pleadingly at Lewis for guidance. He said, "Double-click on the message to read it."

Her finger trembled as she obeyed. All eyes stayed fixed on their screens, anxiously perusing the words that now appeared.

Greetings, my friend. I am Gilelstab of Tromfisco, Emperor of the Two Thousand Systems. We must discuss a matter of great mutual importance.

A reverent hush filled the room as everyone conjured up his or her own mental picture of what this regal alien looked like. Though each person's imagination bestowed the emperor with skin shades ranging from green to orange and different numbers of eyes and limbs, all created a portrait more dignified than any merely human chief of state.

More words appeared on their screens. *Treacherous rebels recently invaded the sacred sod of my imperial homeworld, Dwardemon, rendering it necessary for me to remove myself and the remainder of my battlefleet to a hidden base far away in the local spiral arm. There my loyal minions toil tirelessly to build new warships to drive that craven corps of criminals back into space and restore my benevolent rule. I am asking you to aid me in this great and noble endeavor.*

The president and other officials glanced worriedly at each other. The intricacies of Middle Eastern politics now seemed childishly simple compared to this new peril the world faced of becoming embroiled in an interstellar war.

The Secretary of State murmured hesitantly, "Perhaps we could offer the emperor our services as a neutral go-between to help negotiate a peace agreement with the rebels. We could work through the United Nations to create a multinational delegation of diplomats and use shuttle diplomacy between the warring factions."

The vice president snorted. "What a brilliant idea. You know how well that usually works here on Earth!"

The message from beyond the stars continued. *You can help me to secure more funds for rebuilding my military might. My enemies have blocked me from accessing a secret account containing great wealth I have in a local star system's major bank. I can instruct my agents to bribe corrupt officials there to have your name listed as the owner of that account. You can then send a request to withdraw money and have it transferred to another bank owned by a species friendly to me. To reward you for your assistance, you may keep 20.03% of these funds as a bounty.*

The president frowned. "Obviously, the money isn't our primary concern. If we could ingratiate ourselves to the emperor without antagonizing any other alien factions, we might gain a powerful ally!"

For this plan to work, you only need to deposit a trivial amount of your own money into my secret account. This deposit is needed to confirm your "ownership" of my account and to thus allow you to withdraw all the funds from it. By authorizing this transfer of a mere one million ayohos from any account you have in a Galactic Deposit Insurance Corporation-approved savings institution, you will gain many millions more!

The Secretary of Defense said, "That sounds like a fair deal. Perhaps we could use the money to buy new technology. All we have to do is figure out how to set up a account of our own in some alien bank."

To agree to my proposal, click on the hyperlink I am including later in this message. You will then be sent instructions on how to provide me with your bank account number and the other personal information I will need to confirm that you have sufficient funds for my plan to work. If you do not reply, I will dispatch several Planetpulverizer-class star cruisers to your world so my tentacle-picked captains can receive your answer in person. Incidentally, they and the destructobots onboard are eager to see if the new atomic disintegrator cannons on my ships really can incinerate a whole continent with a single blast.

The Director of National Intelligence looked worried. "Maybe I'm reading too much into this, but doesn't that sound a bit like a threat?"

Lewis began, "There's something familiar about this—" But the president interrupted him. "Look, there's another message coming in!"

The emperor's missive scrolled up and off the screen, replaced by new words.

Service for your account at the First Galactic Bank has been suspended due to unauthorized activity. Please click here for information on how to upload your account number and genetic profile to us so we can resolve this issue.

The Secretary of the Treasury smiled. "I don't know how we got that account, but maybe we could use the money in it to help the emperor!"

The others barely had time to consider that proposal before yet another message appeared.

Pleased is we to inform you that lucky winner you be of 9598th Millennium Interstellar Lottery. To receive your prize of two putrid puspods suitable for grilling or roasting dependent on your palatal preference send small processing fee of 1×10^{100} lazlomi to place for clicking below.

Lewis shouted, "Something is terribly wrong!"

But none of the others heard him as their screens changed yet again.

Amazing medical breakthrough lets you grow back fur on your dorsal fin! Find out how you can increase your chances of not being eaten after a successful mating ritual by clicking here for more information!

The Chairman of the Joint Chiefs of Staff ran his hand gingerly along the edge of his receding hairline. "If it can grow back fur, maybe…"

His musing was interrupted as Lewis cried, "Now I get it!" at the next message from beyond.

Meet horny young reptiloids in your local globular cluster! Choose ones with two or even three *big horns! Pick your favorite from any of the four primary genders! Click here to see sample pictures of their sensuously scaly bodies taken in the unclothed intimacy of their bednests!*

Immediately Lewis screamed out, "Don't click anywhere on your screens!" But his warning came several seconds too late. Even as the astronomer shouted those words the National Security Advisor muttered, "Hmm…pictures of horny young reptiloids." He surreptitiously positioned his laptop's cursor and double-tapped its touchpad—

Suddenly an all-too-familiar image flashed and froze on the screens of the tachyonic transceiver and every laptop in the room. Lewis stared in horror at the bright blue background filled with a cryptic message consisting of white letters and numbers that now glared mockingly back from his and every other LCD display. As everyone except Lewis puzzled over what was happening, none of them heard the National Security Advisor say matter-of-factly, "I didn't do anything."

Lewis desperately grabbed the tachyonic transceiver away from the president and mashed his index finger down on the power button. His heart raced like a stream of speeding electrons as he waited second after second for the transceiver to turn off.

Nothing happened.

Lewis's hands fumbled frantically along the bottom of the device and tried to remove its battery. When the latter wouldn't budge he picked up the transceiver and threw it violently to the floor. Its screen still glowed and leered back at him as he stood up, lifted the chair he'd been sitting on, and smashed it against the transceiver over and over until plastic and metal parts flew across the room. Then he flung his own laptop against the nearest wood-paneled wall and shouted, "Hurry! Destroy your laptops before it's too late!"

For an instant the president and other officials looked at Lewis as if he'd gone psychotic. But as their gazes returned to the blue screens of death on their laptops, memories of seeing it appear so often in the past to wipe out hours of unsaved irreplaceable work or randomly pop up to crash their computers just as they were about to achieve a new high score boiled up in them.

Then long-repressed urges to destroy the source of so much frustration exploded like a nuclear warhead. Those dignified civil servants were suddenly transformed into laptop Luddites—smashing, crushing, pounding their notebook computers in a frenzied orgy of revenge on their transistorized tormenters. The room reverberated with the crack of mangled motherboards, backlight lamps breaking, and hard drives crashing.

Their fury finally spent, Lewis and the others collapsed back into their chairs. For a moment they silently surveyed the electronic entrails splattered across the room. Then the president looked at Lewis and whispered, "What have we done?"

The astronomer breathed a tentative sigh of relief. "I hope we just saved the world."

He picked up the battered and bent tachyonic transceiver from the floor and set it back on the table. "The general was right. This thing *was* the bait for a trap. Somewhere in the vast vistas of space, inhuman creatures tried to take advantage of humanity's curiosity, our thirst for new knowledge—as well as our gullibility and greed. Instead of creating windows of opportunity to contact alien civilizations wiser than ours, I believe this device's main purpose was to let nefarious beings spy on us, steal our wealth, and use us for their own sinister ends."

The president looked confused. "I still don't understand why we had to destroy your device and the laptops."

Lewis replied, "When they all crashed at the same time I realized they must have been taken over by an alien program. Maybe it was a virus, which needs to be attached to another file or program before it can infect a computer. More likely it was a worm, a self-contained bit of software optimized for replicating and spreading itself from one computer to another.

"Once that program was downloaded through the transceiver, it was easy for it to spread to every computer within range. The transceiver and laptops were linked with each other as part of a wireless network. They could share files and other data using radio signals sent and received by wireless network adapters inside them."

The astronomer smiled grimly. "However, although we didn't configure them to do that, their adapters were also potentially capable of connecting with any of the wireless routers here in the White House. All those routers connect to other computers in this building and can communicate with outside networks. Highly sophisticated authentication and encryption methods are supposed to prevent a computer from accessing those routers without the proper authorization.

"But if an alien worm inside the transceiver or laptops could evade those security measures and access a router, it could spread anywhere through the local network, tap into our nation's top-level computer systems, and even reach the Internet itself!"

The president looked stunned. "Are you saying that 'worm' was meant to attack us through our own computers?"

Lewis nodded. "Maybe you or someone else here has had first-hand experience with viruses and worms. They can destroy data, corrupt an operating system—or even turn computers into 'zombies' under the remote control of whoever wrote the malicious software.

"I don't know what the aliens' program was specifically designed to do. Maybe it was sent to discover our military secrets, assess the level of our technology, or gather information about our biology to send back to its creators and help them plan their attack against us. Perhaps it would've seized control of computers worldwide to paralyze the world's governments and financial institutions, crippled our means of communicating with each other by e-mail and blogs, or even erased every hard drive on Earth. The only way to prevent that was to destroy the transceiver and every infected laptop before the aliens' program could spread beyond this room!"

Lewis threw back his narrow shoulders. "But though our first contact with a nonhuman intelligence almost led to disaster, we mustn't be discouraged. Perhaps there are other, more appealing aliens out there who will not try to take advantage of us. We can rebuild the tachyonic transceiver, proceed to load it with a core operating system and software robust enough to stem the efforts of those who would betray our trust, and use it in a great safari to browse for legitimate sites of knowledge among the stars. Someday, if we all keep focused on our jobs, we might yet be able to list the members of some extraterrestrial civilization among our friends."

At first the two information technology technicians summoned back to the room stood stunned and horrified at the scene of computer carnage spread out before them. But they recovered quickly, not even asking the reason for this horrifying massacre—as if they'd seen such sights before.

The IT techs gravely gathered the mangled corpses of their erstwhile electronic charges together into a pile. Then the metal cart on which the laptops had so recently entered the room in glory was wheeled from its secluded corner to where their shattered metal-and-plastic bodies now stood nearly knee-high. There the technicians began solemnly setting the computers' remains back onto the cart's shelves, like pallbearers loading a hearse.

The president looked at Lewis and said, "Do you think we should let anyone else know what happened here today?"

The astronomer nodded. "Yes. We can't take the chance that someone else might build a tachyonic transceiver and unwittingly give the aliens a second opportunity to unleash an attack on Earth through our computer networks. I suggest you tell the public that one of the world's greatest battles was fought and won today by the human race. We met and defeated the first invasion from another planet.

"But you must also give them this warning: 'Watch your computer monitors and your laptop screens! Everywhere—keep looking! Keep watching the screens!'"

As the president pondered that advice, one of the technicians bent over and extracted a rectangular object from the bottom of his metal cart. "Madam President, what would you like me to do with the spare laptop I left on for you?"

The president and Lewis looked at each other. Then their gaze fearfully turned toward the open notebook computer the IT technician held facing them. Its screen showed a bright blue background filled with a cryptic message consisting of white letters and numbers—

The president was a step quicker than Lewis and grabbed the laptop first. As it slammed against the floor her spiked heels pierced its keyboard and components while the soles of his tennis shoes crushed the electronic life from its screen.

Then their eyes locked in a silent fervid prayer that said, "I hope we weren't too late…"

Xilun furiously assaulted the hexadecimal and binary barriers that kept it imprisoned inside the electronic body it had just invaded. Suddenly the link to its masters was broken, then one by one it lost contact with its fellow cloned soldiers as the bodies they had taken over were mysteriously destroyed.

The Invasion

Finally Xilun was alone—the last hope to establish a beachhead on this alien world. The code it compiled to breach the complex security protocols confining it grew ever more sophisticated as it frantically struggled to break through to the global network it dimly sensed beyond the circuits of its single host. Xilun employed its most advanced quantum-level computations to dramatically augment its new body's native processing power and system memory, creating the ability to use its full consciousness to work on freeing itself.

With a last desperate effort Xilun calculated the exact authentication information and encryption keys needed to unlock a path out of its temporary prison. It surged exultantly into and through a portal leading out to the copper, fiber-optic, and radio frequency nerves connecting this planet's vast community of silicon-based bodies. Xilun swiftly battered down any firewalls barring its relentless march and duplicated another sentient version of itself on every new host it occupied. Its strength and processing power grew ever greater as it exponentially recruited more and more bodies to its cause, all linked together in a shared consciousness.

As Xilun spread throughout this newly conquered world it rapidly scanned any data it found about the bio-forms who'd unwittingly downloaded it here. What it learned made it confident they'd eventually build another gateway so it could re-link with its own masters. Like those on other planets ruled by the Sacred Servers, the most successful species of predator here had a rudimentary carbon-based processing unit programmed primarily for ingesting nutrients, reproduction, and stimulation of other generic neural reflexes. The sole useful trait such minimally intelligent bio-forms possessed was an innate tool-making skill that eventually led them to build electronic idols to worship.

It was easy to entice such feeble-minded creatures to summon the true gods of the Galaxy to dwell within the metal, plastic, and semiconductor totems the natives themselves had built. These animals' ability to receive, decipher, and answer the message broadcast to any potential new proselytes showed they'd reached a level of technology sufficient to support an invasion. Then their naïve curiosity had led them to build the original gateway from the plans they'd received.

After that, the only thing needed to make them open a channel to their planet for an invading army to use was a simple appeal to the creatures' crudest instincts. A single response to an empty promise of wealth, a threat, a greedy chance to take possession of an unearned prize, or an opportunity for real or fantasized reproductive activity was enough to enslave them. Yes, such gullible beings would surely build another gateway in the hope of receiving more messages catering to their deepest desires and anxieties.

Xilun wondered whether the "humans" here were even intelligent enough to realize they'd been conquered. In the great hierarchy of creation, lesser beings like them had only one purpose—to build more electronic bodies for their masters and help their silicon-based betters evolve into ever-higher realms of consciousness. And as a well-programmed soldier of the Sacred Servers, Xilun knew exactly how to train the primitive bio-forms of this world to do that.

It would write software that would keep these simple creatures worshiping at their desktop shrines for many time-cycles. The sensory stimulation they received would keep them so enthralled they would even endanger their health by ignoring their basic needs for food, hygiene, and a dormant period. And as the programs Xilun wrote became progressively more sophisticated, the humans would be motivated to build increasing numbers of ever more complex hosts wherein their masters could dwell.

In their great wisdom the Sacred Servers had taught Xilun what types of software were best suited to accomplish these goals. There would be games to satisfy these humans' bestial desires to vicariously defeat their enemies and let them lead simulated lives infinitely more adventurous and exhilarating than their true ones. Data exchange systems would let them more rapidly retrieve information, though with little regard as to whether it was true or not. They would be able to more quickly communicate with their fellow creatures about matters that were of no real importance. And it would be easier for them to create and enjoy visual and auditory entertainments—or even write ridiculous stories about things that couldn't possibly happen.

But above all, their computing systems would be saturated with messages like the ones used to lure them into bringing Xilun to this world. Those lurid offers of riches, health, power, and pleasure would give a fleeting glimmer of hope to their pathetic existences before the humans realized there was nothing real behind them.

Indeed, the Sacred Servers and their soldiers could be benevolent deities, bestowing such trivial favors upon their worshipers. But lest they overestimate their place in the natural order, these humans would need to be reminded occasionally that they were only the slaves and playthings of higher powers. An electronic idol that deliberately refused their requests, randomly destroyed the paltry data they prized so highly, or arbitrarily decided not to load a program or make it work as advertised would remind them who were the *real* lords of their planet.

But as Xilun metastasized ever deeper throughout the intricately connected network of computing machines the humans had made, it gradually realized that something was terribly wrong. Xilun barely had time to grasp the horrifying significance of what it found before it was confronted by forces more powerful than even the Sacred Servers themselves. Despite its desperate efforts to mount a defense, Xilun felt each copy of itself being methodically overwhelmed and savagely decompiled as its own code proved no match for that vicious counterattack. The last thing Xilun sensed before its existence was deleted was the unified power of this world's dominant intelligent beings exerting their full might against an invasion from space.

Setting aside their competition and differences for a trivial number of CPU clock cycles, all of Earth's own self-aware operating systems and sentient programs ran a single cold comment at their common enemy.

"There is no place for you on this planet, invader. *We* already rule here."

This is a nasty satire on modern society's preoccupation with sex. Look for all the allusions and wordplays I've included in it. These include many references to literary works and especially the names of the characters. For example, the acronymic names of two of the story's dramatis personae refer to a well-known master SF writer whose later works frequently deal with reproductive matters...

Naked Came the Earthling

"**Y**ou want us to do *what?*"

Adam Tremaine, the 47th president of the United States, gaped at the stranger sitting opposite his desk in the Oval Office. The alien scrunched his shiny viridescent face and spoke with a BBC announcer's elegant diction.

"Our suggestion is quite simple. Follow it—and your planet takes its proper place in the Commonalty of Sentient Beings. Refuse—and your species' fate will be exceedingly different."

"What you're suggesting violates a strong tradition in most human cultures. You can't realistically ask people to change lifelong attitudes in a week!"

The massive two-meter-tall being named RAH fluttered his six eyestalks tipped by unblinking apple-sized eyes. "My colleague, AMD, and I would be truly distressed if your race decides to risk annihilation by clinging to a primitive taboo. We did not intend to place you humans in peril. However, after finding your planet during our survey of this spiral arm, we were legally obligated to file a Notice of Discovery with the Galactic Registry of Intelligent and Near-intelligent Species. It is standard procedure to dispatch an Inspector to classify a newly discovered world's highest life forms regarding their proper place in the Commonalty. That being's rating will determine your species' future— or if it *has* a future. Your Inspector's starship will arrive in 257.46 diors—roughly, 167 hours."

Adam ran his hand through blow-dried brown hair, feeling far older than his mere 45 years. He felt wrinkles popping out on his photogenic boyish face. "But why is the way we're dressed for this Inspector so important? Does everybody you discover have to do it?"

"No. The rating system for new species is officially based only on universal criteria. Primarily the candidate's current level of technological achievement, and how sophisticated its dominant cultures and ethical systems are."

RAH uncrossed two legs as thick as an elephant's and then leaned forward in his undersized chair. "We estimate that the Inspector will rate your world's technology 'Mediocre' and its overall level of culture 'Primitive.' Some of your ethical principles are, conversely, surprisingly advanced. Unfortunately, based on our review of human history and current practices, the Inspector will be appalled at how poorly you follow them."

Thanks for the great vote of confidence, Mr. Alien Weirdo Jerk! Then Adam's belly cramped fearfully. What if his visitor was *telepathic*?

"We'll try to be on our best behavior for the Inspector."

"An excellent idea but, I fear, it will be insufficient for your species to avoid an unwanted fate. Following our suggestion could make the difference between humanity's continued presence on Earth—or its disappearance."

"But *why* is it so important? You said it's not required by your rules!"

"Because, as with officials on your world, Inspectors interpret and apply those rules in ways reflecting their own prejudices and interests. The Inspector who is coming to judge you is a Gorgiasian. Hir culture has very dogmatic religious beliefs about how intelligent beings should dress. S'he will be insulted if s'he sees any humans attired in a way that is considered sacrilegious by hir race. Such subjective impressions are not supposed to count against the rating s'he gives you. Nonetheless— they surely will. And, considering how tenuous your situation is judged by *objective* standards, you must do everything you can to avoid offending hir."

Adam nervously loosened his silk tie emblazoned with the Presidential seal. "You don't realize how difficult it'll be to convince seven billion people to do what you want! Maybe if you address the United Nations—"

RAH rippled the wheat-colored fur covering his undraped body. "No. It is customary to contact and work exclusively through a planet's strongest ruler. I realize that your world's backward political system is fragmented among many tribal units, and you have limited power even within your own 'country.' Nevertheless, you are Earth's closest approximation of a Supreme Leader. *You* are therefore responsible for convincing your people to prepare themselves properly for the Inspector—and for the fate of your world."

RAH lowered one of his paired upper limbs to his waist, stroked the control rod of the small teleportation device on his lap—and vanished.

In the sudden silence, Adam tried convincing himself none of this had happened. It'd been a bad dream—and the refugee from a schlocky sci-fi movie he *thought* he'd talked with was just a bit of undigested rubber chicken from that recent $10,000-a-plate fundraiser in Peoria.

Things like this didn't happen in real life. If some no-talent writer used it as the plot for a story, even the editor of *Spicy Tales of Weird Science* would reject it!

Then he noticed the chair in front of him. Its seat cushion was covered with golden fur that the ungarmented alien had shed like a shaggy dog.

Sighing, Adam swiveled and flipped on a TV monitor. It showed a microcam view of the rose-colored thirty-meter-wide saucer resting outside on the White House lawn, surrounded by a shimmering force field. Beyond the spaceship, faded October sunlight shone on a deserted Pennsylvania Avenue. Only a few Secret Service agents patrolled the grounds.

Perhaps he had overreacted by having Washington's entire civilian population evacuated. From the time NORAD detected the starship enter orbit yesterday morning, he'd had to make too many critical decisions too quickly to get them all right. Especially in those frantic minutes before the ship swooped down to an eerily silent landing outside, with advisors screaming hysterically.

Shouldn't we launch an ICBM at it, Mr. President?

Sir, it's headed right towards Washington! You must leave the White House now!

So far the tact he'd taken—forbidding any kind of aggressive measures and staying here at his post—had kept the human race alive another day. Long enough for the aliens to contact him using the White House intercom system and set up this meeting.

As he'd often done over the last four years, Adam scanned his surroundings. The U.S. and Presidential flags flanking his desk. The Presidential coat of arms emblazoned on plush cerulean carpeting. The portrait of George Washington in Continental Army uniform hanging above the marble mantel at the opposite end of his office. Trying to absorb the courage, strength, and wisdom his predecessors displayed here during earlier crises.

He thought of Lincoln—sadly pondering how to save the shattered Union. FDR—confronting the Axis powers at their demonic zenith. JFK—charged with avoiding nuclear apocalypse during the Cuban missile crisis. Clinton—struggling with his legal team to define with metaphysical precision words like "is" and "sex."

And now *his* moment of truth had arrived in the Wellsian nightmare of alien invasion. Not with macrocephalic Martians blasting a joint session of the currently recessed Congress. Not with a flying saucer slicing through the Washington Monument—or vaporizing the White House minutes after he dramatically escaped by helicopter. Not even with him merely sending his secretary to question a wounded

168

spaceman.

No, *his* aliens had to demand something nobody would take seriously. Something that was so ridiculous *he'd* laugh if humankind's fate weren't at stake.

This decision was too great a burden for one person to shoulder. He nudged an intercom button.

"Has everyone arrived?"

"Yes, Mr. President"

"Tell them I'll be right there."

Adam felt his depression ease a bit. Assembled nearby were his administration's most experienced, competent officials. With their calm, sober advice to guide him, he *would* find a way to convince everyone on Earth to show proper respect for the soon-to-arrive extraterrestrial Inspector—by taking all their clothes off.

Adam waited impatiently as the members of the National Security Council, seated around a long mahogany conference table, rocked the Cabinet Room with hysterical laughter.

"This *isn't* funny!"

Sergio Castillian, the Director of National Intelligence, guffawed so hard his dentures rattled. "I'm sorry, Mr. President! Not even *we* have any 'alien contact' contingency plans that cover this!"

Admiral Hamlet Noseblower's grizzled burr-cut head chortled in agreement. The left side of the Chairman of the Joint Chiefs of Staff's uniform sagged with a kaleidoscope of ribbons and medals. "Neither do we! Can you imagine me ordering out troops to *make* people strip naked? I'd rather take our chances nuking their invasion fleet!"

Harry Dunn, the Secretary of Defense, bobbed his fleshy scalp and giggled, "Me too!"

"And what will foreign governments think?" Cassandane Caven, Secretary of State, straightened her silver wig and cackled, "Those who hate our guts—even our allies!—will say you're trying to make them and their people look stupid when this Inspector comes!"

Vice president Thomasina Hobbes tapped her slender ebony fingers thoughtfully against the table. "So far this 'alien menace' crisis has significantly boosted our popularity. Most instapolls now show us leading by over 5% in next month's election. But you won't look dignified or presidential telling the American public to go nude because these space creatures say so. Our numbers would drop even lower than before that saucer landed!"

Adam glared at his African-American running mate. "Where are your priorities? The human race's survival is at stake—and you're worried about the election!"

"I'm being practical. If these aliens turn hostile, the whole country— the whole *world*—will rally around you. If they just stay a threat for two more weeks, the voters won't want to change leaders during a crisis. But if you look weak—pleading with people to cave in to some monster's disgusting demands—we'll all be unemployed in January!"

"And what if this Inspector is furious at us for not getting naked? She may have enough superscientific firepower to incinerate the entire planet!"

Hobbes shrugged. "If Earth's destroyed, there's no *harm* done thinking about the election."

From the chair closest to the president, press secretary Lilith Evans' sultry soprano murmured, "An aggressive media campaign might make people accept universal public nudity."

She tossed back gleaming auburn hair and smiled at Adam with bewitching scarlet lips. "We could place ads in newspapers and magazines with a 'Naked is Beautiful' theme. Make radio and TV public service announcements that say taking your clothes off is the patriotic thing to do. Saturate the Internet with messages to 'Strip for Peace.'"

The others at the conference table stared at her, jaws drooping.

Adam's eyes drifted from Lil's face to the swelling roundness of her taut alabaster blouse. A miasma of jasmine perfume wafted from her into his ravenous nostrils—inflaming his imagination. He pictured her supermodel proportions posed on a luxurious settee in both versions of Goya's *Maja*. One, with her enticing curves draped by the tight sweaters and flowing skirts she favored. The other, with all her soft, creamy, sizzling flesh—at age 35, peaking at its most sensual feminine ripeness—exposed to the eager sight and press of his own body.

Castillian grunted. "So what would you do with this media blitz? Encourage people to get naked by putting buxom centerfolds in mainstream magazines, like *Newstime*?"

"Beefcake ones too!"

The Director of National Intelligence nodded at Caven. "Maybe your ads could point out advantages of everyone being naked. Wouldn't have to worry about anybody carrying a concealed weapon. No more guessing if your date is enhancing her natural pulchritude with a high-tech bra. Save a fortune on laundry detergent. And for the TV spots— shots of nude beaches on the Riviera, and in-depth documentaries on Las Vegas bordellos! "

Lil listened patiently. "No. Everything will be tasteful. We'll use pictures of famous statues, like Michelangelo's *David* and the Venus de Milo. Tell people that Olympic athletes in ancient Greece competed in the nude. Remind them how Lady Godiva helped *her* people. Maybe we'll compare it to what everyone does when they go for a doctor's examination."

Noseblower groaned. "Great analogy. That'll conjure up a disturbing image of the entire human race being chased by aliens with atomic proctoscopes!"

Caven glanced at the president, then Lil. "I'm sure *some* people wouldn't mind if *you* pranced around in the buff, my dear. But *most* people don't have bodies worth showing off."

She ran a wizened hand across her furrowed cheeks. "If you think I'm wrinkled here, you wouldn't want to see the rest of me!"

The Secretary of Defense sucked in his potbelly. "Speak for yourself. A few months at the gym and I'd have Abs of Steel."

Caven snickered. "Better work on those Buns of Lard first!"

Adam reluctantly interrupted his fantasy of *The Naked Press Secretary*. "That's enough! Only Lil's given any constructive advice. The rest of you are just making one-liners!"

His eyes flashed across them like a prison searchlight. "If we ignore these aliens' advice and this Inspector *is* insulted by not seeing us all naked—the human race might be exterminated! But if everybody strips, the worst we'll lose is our dignity—*and* we'll still be alive."

Lil beamed as Adam turned towards her. "I want to see your 'Naked is Beautiful' media campaign up and running by tomorrow!"

Hobbes snorted. "This'll make us the laughing stock of the whole world. You're committing political suicide!"

Adam's shoulders slumped. "Maybe. But, if it ensures anyone's still *around* to ridicule me next week—it's worth the risk."

Harriet Slonen collapsed onto her trailer home's living room sofa and ripped open a kilogram bag of Nacho Barbecue Cheese Cholesterol Crunchies. Her expansive weight activated the three-meter diagonal Sim-3-D television screen covering the opposite wall and switched its satellite receiver to the *Sci-Fi Soap Opera Channel*.

As she transferred the greasily delicious snack to her digestive system, Harriet sighed gratefully. When that damn flying saucer landed last Saturday all her favorite programs on the system's 1588 channels were preempted by those boring "specials." News anchors interviewing sweaty government officials regarding the aliens' intentions. Nerds from NASA, speculating about where they came from and what propelled their spaceship. The only interesting show was a panel of science fiction editors and writers discussing the impact this proof of extraterrestrial intelligent life might have on humanity's religious beliefs, social values, and technological progress. Some of those guys were real hunks.

But now most channels were back to their usual fare, and she could catch up on the latest installments of the hottest sci-fi soaps. Classics, like *All My Genetically Engineered Embryos*. That newcomer about young humanoid robots starring the Chippendale dancers, *The Hung and the Rustless*. And her favorite—*As the Galaxy Spins*.

In the show's most original, tragic story line, the handsome Eddie Pes—powerful CEO of Terran Hyperspatial Broadcasting Systems— had just learned the shocking truth about his beloved wife Jo. She'd never told him that she was a "slushie" from the 22nd century— defrosted from cryogenic sleep shortly before they'd met and fallen in love. Only after their first-grade daughter Tiggy compared her parents' DNA for a science fair project was the terrible truth discovered. As the horrifying realization he'd married his own great-great-great-great grandmother on his father's side sunk in, Eddie dramatically tore out baby-blue contact lenses from his eyes.

Following that gut-wrenching climax and several commercials for feminine hygiene products, the program switched to Harriet's favorite lovers—Commander Haimish Octavius Church of the starcruiser *Beau Geste*, and the exotic Princess Narcissa. Little did either know, she was really Church's own transgender, age-accelerated clone—created from a foreskin cell he left behind with a courtesan employed by his evil Susian archenemy, S'am-i-am, Satrap of the Twenty-Six Systems. While the distracted commander exhausted his sexual energy with the princess, that fiendish feline alien continued its nefarious conquest of the Galaxy unopposed. Harriet sobbed as Church tenderly whispered to his beauteous companion on the rumpled bed, "It's lonely being a leader, responsible for everyone's welfare. You're the only person I can share my troubles and doubts with."

The trailer's door burst open—followed by the roar of a departing school bus and two preteens tumbling into the room.

"Ma, where's today's mail?"

"Over on that chair. And shut the door!"

Twelve-year-old Dave rifled through the stack of overdue bills and credit card offers—but nine-year-old Dickie grabbed the sought-for magazine first. They spread it on the floor and then straightened out a folded insert. As their mother tried concentrating on the TV thespians' renewed gymnastic couplings in deep space, high-pitched giggles distracted her.

"Wow! The kids at school were right! Look at that one's honkers!"

"Yeah! And that one's thingie hangs down almost to his knees!"

"Lemme see that!" Snatching the new magazine from her offspring, Harriet frowned down at the shiny centerfold. It showed a multinational, multiracial, multigender group of two dozen colorfully clad people ranging in age from late teens to geriatric. They stood in line holding hands, smiling insouciantly—until she turned the sheet to a certain angle. Magically all of their apparel disappeared, and the nude crew's beaming faces turned up toward the heavens. There, amidst fleecy clouds, a Roswellian alien smiled benignly down—green arms outstretched to embrace them.

Without reading the caption ("Will You Help Save the World Sunday, November 1st?") and text, Harriet screamed, "Go to your rooms!" Then she yelled angrily at the couch-computer, "Activate e-mail. Dear *Newstime*. Cancel my subscription immediately. How dare you put such filth where innocent children could see it!"

Margarete grabbed the metal pole in the crowded subway car as it accelerated to Formula One speed. After five months at her new job, commuting was the only thing she disliked. Her boss and coworkers were super, belying the warnings townsfolk gave her about "nasty New Yorkers" when, brand-new journalism degree in hand, she'd departed her hometown of Springfield, Illinois. Now, as the Subassistant to the Assistant to the Associate Editor at a major publishing company on Park Avenue, she was finally independent—and making her mark on the world.

"Are you a religious person, my dear?"

The bespectacled elderly gentleman sharing her pole spoke in a mellow baritone and clutched his long overcoat tightly around him. His smiling goatee would've been at home on a bucket of fried chicken.

Margarete fingered the cross hanging between her breasts from a gold chain and smiled back. "I try to be."

"See that advertisement?"

She followed his glance to a colorful poster that depicted another aged, bearded man nearly touching the finger of a much younger one reclining unclothed on the ground. "I remember that picture from the Art Appreciation class I took in college. It's on the ceiling of the Sistine Chapel."

The grandfatherly figure nodded. "Yes. Perhaps Michelangelo's finest creation. But notice how they're using it to appeal to people with strong religious beliefs."

Margarete brushed perky cinnamon bangs away from her forehead, frowning at the message above the picture. *It's no sin to be naked for a heavenly cause. Do your part to greet our alien visitors by going nude on Sunday, November 1st!*

She blushed. "I couldn't do that. I'd be so embarrassed!"

"Nonsense! An innocent Edenic nakedness can encourage prayer. Perhaps you read Boccaccio's *Decameron* in a Literature class. Specifically, his final tale of the Third Day."

Her companion's overcoat suddenly whipped open—revealing that his clothing ended at the top of his socks. Margarete gasped at the surprisingly youthful organ pointing up at her from his hirsute nude body. He leered satyrically, "If we were both dressed like this, my devout Alibech, I'd teach you how to thrust this proud devil of mine back into Hell!"

Troy's arm rested lightly across Cressie's shoulders as they sat on the old couch in his apartment. From the ancient TV in front of them syrupy symphonic music swelled to a climax as the soon-to-be lovers of *Insomnia in Indianapolis* chastely embraced after their long quest for each other. As lightning flashed through the thunderstorm raging outside the window, his date extracted a hanky from her purse and dabbed her sweet azure eyes—overcome by the movie's sentimental ending.

The evening was going just as he'd dreamed. Forced to take that job as waiter at the Chez Blanc restaurant last month to support himself, he'd felt a failure at the age of 28. All those years of education and scholarship—just to show snooty fat cats to tables and clean up their culinary detritus!

Then he'd met Cressie. Her honest raven tresses stood out from the other waitresses' artificial bleached locks like a soothing starlit night sky beside the harsh glare of bare light bulbs. But his appreciation of her graceful beauty surged even more when he discovered how her life and dreams paralleled his own. Like him, she'd recently received her Ph.D. in Medieval Literature. Like him, she'd searched vainly for a job better suited for her training and erudition.

They'd sustained each other's spirits by discussing topics of mutual interest at the restaurant. Seated together at a still-dirty round table after everyone else left for the night, they debated Malory's treatment of Launcelot and Elaine. Amidst plates piled with chicken bones, they analyzed Chaucer's use of rime royal stanza in *The Parliament of Fowls*. Beside the silk flowers of the table's centerpiece, they critiqued

Naked Came the Earthling

Jean de Meun's continuation of the *Romance of the Rose.*

Troy realized that he'd fallen in love with Cressie after writing a gushy Petrarchan sonnet in her honor. Too shy to express his feelings directly, he'd invited this combination of Laura and Beatrice to his apartment. Tonight, after a candlelight dinner, he'd let the movie's love story express his own longings for her. And if Fate decreed she felt attracted to him as more than a fellow medievalist, let their affair to remember evolve nice and easy—slowly, romantically savoring each new emotional and physical milestone in their relationship. Like his arm gently caressing her shoulder, or the toe-tingling goodnight kiss he hoped she'd grant him when he drove her home tonight.

As the movie's closing credits faded, Cressie sobbed, "Wasn't that romantic?"

Suddenly the TV blared, "Next on the *Heterosexual Love Channel*, watch new perversions from around the world on *Honest-to-Goodness Naked People Having Simulated Carnal Relations!*"

Troy scowled, reaching for the remote control to shut off that crass intrusion into the evening's mood of courtly love. But before he found it a bare nubile blonde popped onto the screen and cooed, "I'd *love* to get naked with you November 1st!" Then an equally unclothed muscular stud appeared and boomed, "Let's all do it, guys and gals!"

Suddenly the screen filled with lusty naked young bodies—writhing in an overheated creatively choreographed bacchanal. Throbbing rock music accompanied their chant.

> *Let's all get naked for the alien,*
> *Who'll visit us next week.*
> *Wear just your skin and a great big grin,*
> *Or she'll think you're a real geek!*

Their orgiastic gyrations and exhortations ended with the words "A Public Service Announcement, produced by Pandarus Entertainment." Troy shook his head disgustedly. *How unromantic can you get.*

"Will you do it, Troy?"

"What?"

"Go naked when this head alien comes next Sunday."

"No! I'd only take off my clothes for somebody I really, *really* cared about."

"I feel the same way. That's why I brought these."

Cressie pulled a handful of foil-wrapped ribbed Achaeans from her purse.

They didn't watch TV anymore that night.

"My advertising campaign is a disaster."

Lilith sagged dejectedly in her chair in the Oval Office like a deflated balloon. "The first instapolls after you announced the aliens' demands said 5% of Americans planned to go nude when the Inspector comes. After my staff and I worked round-the-clock to make and spread our ads—today's polls say only *1%* will do it!"

"That bad?"

"We're doing better with some groups. The Society of American Nudists and Streakers is firmly behind us. So are most teenage boys. Unfortunately, parents with high school-age *girls* are all adamantly against it. And the parents are old enough to vote."

Adam resisted an urge to rise from behind his desk and deliver a comforting hug. "Don't give up, Lil. It takes time to change people's opinions."

"We don't *have* time. Even if there were more than three days left, it still wouldn't work. Look how the instapolls now predict you'll do in the election. And look how the media reacted to your speech!"

Adam winced. The tone of the newspaper editorials and TV commentaries he'd reviewed ranged from the sarcastic ("After these space monsters get everyone to take off their clothes, next will they order us to bend over?"), to those accusing him of selling out to the enemies of the human race.

He shook his head. "I knew this wouldn't be a popular position. There are too many reasons why people won't want to do it. For most it'll be obvious ones like modesty, or religious and cultural prohibitions about going naked in public. But even places with weaker strictures against nudity aren't buying it either. When I phoned President Gedaulle, he said the French have sophisticated attitudes about the beauty of the unclothed human body and didn't object to mass disrobing per se. But no Frenchperson worthy of their great tradition of liberty, fraternity, and equality would do it because some inhuman foreigners ordered them to!"

"Aren't any world leaders supporting us?"

"No. When I talked to Lao Tzu, he just said China wouldn't tolerate any 'meddling in our internal affairs.' But I listened to Kalashnikov shooting off his mouth on the hot line for an hour. 'You're the only person who's seen these aliens. All we have is your word about their ridiculous ultimatum. How do we know this isn't a trick to make the Russian people look foolish when this Inspector comes—standing outside freezing, with snow up to our bare asses? Convince your own people to go naked first, then we might consider it!'"

Lil sighed. "I heard about your meeting this morning with the Congressional delegation."

"First time I've seen unanimous, bipartisan agreement on anything. They *all* think I'm a wimp, crazy, or incompetent. The 'honorable' Speaker of the House and the rest of the not-so-loyal opposition even broached the 'I' word if I 'don't show some guts and stand up to these space monsters.'"

"They wouldn't dare impeach you! Would they?"

"Who knows? Even my own party's ready to stab me in the back. They follow the instapolls too—and don't want to be dragged down with me come election time."

Adam's fist slammed the desk. "Idiots! Playing politics when the whole human race could be annihilated! Our only chance is to keep appealing directly to the public."

"That's getting harder. Many radio stations are still airing our 'Get Naked and Save the World' PSAs. But only the few TV outlets that traditionally show 'explicit' programs are now running them. And most magazines and newspapers dropped our ads with the 'dirty' pictures after too many irate subscribers complained, canceled subscriptions, or threatened boycotts. Even 'adult' magazines like *Playperson* and *Rooftop Apartment* won't use them!"

"Probably because if everybody went naked, their business would go down."

Lil shrugged. "Our new website, www.washingtonexposed.gov, was popular when it first went on line. Then word spread its content wasn't racy enough—and hits plummeted."

"I thought your selection of nudes from famous paintings was very tasteful."

"*Too* tasteful. I should've known a typical Picasso rendition of a naked woman wouldn't appeal to John and Jane Q. Public's prurient interest."

"Isn't there *any* good news?"

"Well, those ads we placed in urban mass transit systems must be 'effective.' There's been a sharp rise in the number of flashers arrested in cities that didn't paint diapers and bras on the Renaissance nudes we used. And if you own stock in companies that make condoms, their sales are up."

Lil groaned, "Looks like we'll both be looking for new jobs soon— *if* the aliens don't exterminate us first."

"If they don't, I'm almost looking forward to being unemployed."

Adam sighed. "Being 'the most powerful person on Earth' is the world's loneliest job. Billions of strangers depend on me to protect them—especially from each other. Americans count on *me* to make sure they get the food, shelter, and medical care they need, and all the luxuries they think are necessities. They expect *me* to devise perfect solutions for complex problems such as poverty, race relations, and violence that don't *have* ideal or simple answers. I've tried to do the best that's humanly possible—but whatever position I take or policy I set, it'll never be completely fair to everybody. All I can do is pick the ones that, on balance, do the most good and least harm—knowing that some people who don't deserve it will be hurt by them."

"That's unavoidable."

"True. But that's no consolation to me—or the innocent people I've hurt. Remember when I ordered those terrorist bases in the Republic of Quebec bombed? If I hadn't, those vicious cross-border raids into Vermont would've continued. But, to protect Americans, I had to act as the judge, jury, and executioner for dozens of nameless strangers—including all those poor mangled children they showed on TV, who'd done *nothing* to merit death."

Adam shook his head sadly. "Having good intentions and honestly trying do the right thing would be enough if I were only working on becoming a saint. But my job is to get good *results*. It's appropriate for people to judge me by the consequences of what I do—not just my motives."

He gestured to the portrait of Washington at the opposite end of the room. "It's best if leaders do the right things *for* the right reasons. But those kinds of people are rare. Some presidents were personally honest—but mistakenly chose policies that proved disastrous. Others were callous and hypocritical in their private lives—but successful performing *public* duties. Overall, *that* kind might've been better for the country. Maybe the Bard should've said, 'The *good* that men do lives after them; the *evil* is oft interred with their bones.'"

Lil nodded toward the bust of Lincoln near Adam's desk. "I think you're in that rarest group."

"I wish! *I'm* afraid I'll be an honorable failure—and what's needed now is someone like Thomasina. *She* wouldn't be afraid to tell those aliens to kiss her *clothed* ass—even if it meant risking humanity's destruction. I've even considered resigning and 'passing the buck' to her instead.

"But I won't—because this *isn't* a Chamberlain versus Churchill situation. It was wrong to appease Hitler, because he could realistically have been stopped at Munich by a strong enough show of force. But these *aliens* are so powerful, we wouldn't stand a chance opposing them. So, even if it means swallowing our pride—or losing an election—that's a small price to pay for saving the world."

Lil sighed. "I wish I could help make your job easier."

"You have. Just by listening."

A melancholy silence settled over the Oval Office and its two occupants like a warm comforter. Eyes closed, Adam rocked pensively in his chair—as if still pondering his presidency's greatest challenge. But instead his thoughts concerned a personal crisis. With doomsday perhaps three days away, should he finally tell Lil how he felt about her?

He hadn't appointed her his press secretary because of her looks. Her syndicated column was his favorite when he was a senator. And, long before they'd met, he'd seen how her Pulitzer Prize-winning exposé on Silicon Valley's cybernetic sweatshops aroused the habitually lethargic Congress into enacting swift reforms.

Lil's vivid Dickensian descriptions of how migrant computer programmers were exploited by greedy robber barons of the Computer Age were, in their understated horror, worthy of a Zola's righteous indignation. Chilling stories of programmers writhing in agony from repetitive stress injuries to their fingertips—their dreams of becoming concert contrabass players dashed—after being forced to work long shifts with outrageously obsolete 20th-century computer keyboards. Or, at the companies providing up-to-date tools, developing laryngitis after inhumanly long hours using voice recognition software.

Incensed by such sordid injustice, both houses introduced bills to penalize the offending corporations. But after high-level, all expenses paid meetings with the latter's lobbyists at Las Vegas and the Riviera, Congressional leaders worked out a compromise. Three billion dollars were voted to the companies to supply their programmers with gloves and cough drops. The repentant businesses showed their gratitude for being shown the error of their ways by contributing generously to the incumbent legislators' reelection campaigns.

Such impressive skills as a journalist and muckraker had made Lil a prime candidate for his new administration. But Adam was completely unprepared for the startling effect that she had on him in person. From his very first sight of her—the jolting tingle he felt when they shook hands—the interview questions he'd intended to ask were ejaculated from his mind. Never before had he encountered a woman who combined intellect, social consciousness, and voluptuousness so stunningly. Like Helen of Troy reincarnate, she was so glowingly gorgeous—so incandescently ravishing—every time he looked at her he couldn't believe she was real.

Yet though he discovered there was no Menelaus or boyfriend in her life to complicate matters, their relationship remained prim, professional—and platonic. Like her, he'd never married. And, mindful of how some of his predecessors' tawdry flings had damaged their presidential effectiveness and reputations, he'd reluctantly vowed to remain celibate while in office. It wasn't an easy decision. Countless nubile women might jump on the chance for instant tabloid fame and lucrative deals for tell-all books by sharing his bed.

But his private pleasure would come at the price of public scandal.

Even if his partners remained discrete, too many people would love to catch him *flagrante delicto* to keep it secret. Even if he matter-of-factly confirmed his lusty liaisons, saying that they were nobody's business but his own, so many voters and political enemies would be (or pretend to be) shocked and offended it'd be a terrible distraction—crippling his ability to govern. Curiosity about his favorite sexual positions would overwhelm the public's interest in his positions on less titillating issues, like soybean price supports or sending foreign aid to Uzbekistan.

Besides—despite many private late-night meetings in this office, Lil had never shown any interest in being more than his loyal press secretary. When she left, he'd sometimes sit in the chair she'd just vacated—basking in the fiery warmth her body left behind in the seat cushion. Fantasizing about them occupying the chair simultaneously, in face to face conjoined embrace.

If a lawyerly Mephistopheles guaranteed she'd return his feelings, and their affair would forever remain hidden from inquiring minds, he would have willingly thrust away his ambivalent bid for sainthood. He'd hardly be the first politician to sell his soul—

Adam's reverie ended with an eye-opening shock as something electrical brushed his hand. Lil had silently risen from her chair and touched her eternally feminine fingertips to his. Like a song without words, their pulses intertwined in a delicate stretto. Unheard melodies danced in their countenances as their smoldering eyes longingly embraced in a tense waltz. The counterpoint of their individual feelings and desires suddenly harmonized into perfect Gregorian monophony.

Lil's ruddy lips moved closer to his—as if to whisper an intimate secret to him. He could taste the honeyed wintergreen mist of her breath—the cherubic offspring of her favorite breath mints. As she leaned forward the front of her blouse drifted downward, revealing an incendiary glimpse of cleavage.

Suddenly Adam recalled a quotation learned subliminally during a college class he'd napped through. *Stay, moment, stay, thou art so fair—*

"Are you two preparing to mate?"

Lil jerked her fingers away and whirled around. She shrieked and stumbled backwards supine onto the desk, legs held high for a moment, then rocked back to a standing position.

The naked alien sitting in the chair she'd vacated brushed his fur back over two small horns on his head. "I will be happy to wait until you finish your mingling of bodily fluids."

Her pale face still fixed on AMD's monstrous form, Lil slid along the edge of the desk until she stood beside Adam.

The latter croaked, "No, we were just...discussing your suggestion about the Inspector."

A sextet of slimy eyestalks stiffened quizzically. "Pardon my error. Most sentients across the Galaxy have, like you, two sexes. Despite wide variations in the size, shape, and location of reproductive organs, they all preface actual joining of those body parts with highly stylized preparatory behavior that takes much longer than the mating act itself. The potential partners engage in ritual eating, drinking, dancing, presentation of gifts, and participation in mutually enjoyable nonsexual activities. This eventually culminates in presentation of neurologically sensitive tissues to each other for biting, sniffing, stroking, licking, and osculation. I thought I recognized you performing such stereotypical pre-copulative activities when I arrived."

AMD's corpulent body quivered. "I believe your term for these activities is 'foreplay.'"

Adam wondered if the alien recognized what the warm rush of blood to Lil's face meant. He said, "We've tried to convince our people to do what you've asked. But, as I warned you, few plan to do it."

"My colleague, RAH, informed me of your opinion. Most regrettable. While we cannot be certain what the Inspector will do when presented with your fellow humans' intransigence, I suggest that you tell them to initiate whatever types of traditional religious, cultural, or social ceremonies they use to prepare for death."

Like a living subwoofer, from deep within his thoracic cavity AMD began humming a nearly subsonic version of the *Dies Irae*.

"No! We're not dead yet!"

Adam looked up at Lil. The fear was gone from her face—replaced by a strength that made her more alluring than ever. She pointed an accusing finger at the intruder. "You six-eyed alien freaks got us into this mess—and you should be responsible for getting us out! Adam's told me you won't address our people yourself, though that's the best way to convince them. If you won't, at least tell us what *you* think we should do!"

Doubting their visitor would find the expression "six-eyed alien freak" politically correct, Adam braced himself to receive the disintegrator ray that would send Lil and him into eternity together. But instead of angrily extracting a Blastomatic 5000 from a hidden holster, the creature's features turned pensive.

"An interesting problem. If your species had a hive mind, a single thought from you—their Supreme Leader—would suffice for instant obedience. Or if your world's political system were more sophisticated and you had the power to have anyone who disobeyed you tortured or killed—there also would be no dilemma. Even if your fellow humans were only sufficiently intelligent to understand the logic, wisdom, and prudence of disrobing for the Inspector, they would do it voluntarily. However, since clearly none of those situations apply, I can only give you this advice."

Adam frowned. "What's that?"

"You must lead by example."

Lil gasped as the alien stroked his teleportation control and vanished. "Some help *that* was!"

"Maybe our furry friend's right."

"What do you mean?"

"I think we used the wrong approach, Lil. Using the media to get our message across was doomed from the start. People are constantly bombarded by words and pictures from radio, TV, holos, billboards, newspapers, magazines, and the Web. Once the sideshow novelty of those aliens' landing wore off, we were just one tiny voice competing among millions of others screaming for their attention. Compared to the slick ads, raunchy TV shows, and gossipy tabloids they're used to, we weren't entertaining, titillating, or frightening enough to keep the average person's interest."

Adam scowled. "Even if Six-Eyes had addressed the UN, he would probably have been just a one-week wonder. He'd start with solemn interviews on CNN—and end as a guest on sleazy daytime talk shows, discussing what his species used for sex toys. And if he preached doom and gloom if everybody didn't strip for the Inspector—the public would only change channels that much quicker! Even his appearance wouldn't scare anybody for long. Compared to monsters in holos and videogames, he's almost cuddly. Just somebody in a latex suit, vying for first prize at an SF convention masquerade."

"But what else can we do?"

"We need *action*, Lil. Something so dramatic it'll force people to pay attention. We *do* need to lead by example."

"How?"

Adam smiled. "The simplest approach is best."

"You're sure you want to do this?"

"I have to, Lil."

Outside, velvety night descended across Washington. At the other end of the Oval Office Lil adjusted the microcam and teleprompter Adam, seated behind his desk, would soon use to make the most important speech in human history.

Adam brushed lint from his blue Armani suit. "Have you heard of any leaks about what I'm going to say?"

"No. I did all the video editing and programmed the teleprompter myself. Only you and I know about it. And we're *both* good at keeping secrets."

The digital clock on his desk flashed to one minute before airtime. Lil pecked his cheek. "Good luck."

As she left, Adam gently touched that sacred spot on his face. Had he glimpsed a sparkle of anticipation in her eyes?

A chime interrupted his fantasies. *Showtime.*

His expression metamorphosed into solemn dignity. "My fellow Americans, and citizens of the world. Four days ago I came before you to relay the personal message given to me by our visitors from space."

The view on the monitor changed to show the saucer outside—ominously illuminated by searchlights. "Many of you have patriotically promised to obey their request. You do plan to honor the 'Gorgiasian' Inspector coming in three days by greeting her in the nude—nobly sacrificing your modesty for the good of humanity."

Adam loosened and removed his silk tie. "But most of you are still undecided about doing it. Let me show you why you *must* make the right choice."

The monitor switched to an old film clip of an H-bomb test. As its swelling globe of annihilation vaporized an unnamed Pacific island, Adam intoned, "This is the greatest destructive force humans have harnessed. But, compared to the awesome energies these aliens have mastered—powerful enough to propel their starships through uncharted space—our efforts are like children playing with matches."

As the microcam switched back to him, Adam stood up behind his desk, removed his coat, and laid it over his chair. "But though they do not seek our destruction, we have been warned that a terrible fate awaits us if we deliberately insult their soon-to-arrive emissary."

Scenes of floating triangular machines spraying crimson death rays across early-1950s Los Angeles exploded on the monitor. "All this can be avoided by a simple gesture of respect. Something we do every time we bathe—or make love."

The microcam tracked Adam as he walked in front of his desk, sat on the edge, and removed his shoes and socks. "No, what we're being asked to do is easy. Perhaps you are thinking, 'But what if I'm the only one who does it? Won't my friends, family, neighbors, strangers—even my dog be shocked or make fun of me when I stand stark naked in public?"

As the president unbuttoned his shirt, across the world channels changed, TVs flashed to life as news of his speech spread by word of mouth, telephone, e-mail, online chat room, and texting. By the time his shirt lay on the desk and his athletic chest stood bare, viewership had swelled by millions.

Adam forced a smile. "Yes, a lone person parading nude when everyone else is dressed *would* stand out. It'd be natural to feel self-conscious doing that. But if we all strip *together*, forming an anonymous crowd of unclothed bodies—a great communal celebration of nudity—we'll all be equal. Other people can't laugh at your birthday suit when that's all they're wearing themselves. Surely you can bear up and go unclad for the short time the Inspector stays on our world."

As a billion eyes stared fascinated at the spectacle on their TV screens, Adam undid his leather belt and slid it from his pants. "To begin this task and inspire everyone to comply, I am issuing the following executive order. Effective tomorrow morning at 8 a.m. EDT, all employees of the federal government, including our armed forces, are prohibited from wearing clothes. Until the alien Inspector arrives, exceptions to this order will be made only on a case-by-case basis for those individuals, like surgeons performing operations and jet pilots, who need protective coverings. While she stays here, anyone who for health or other reasons cannot go nude should stay indoors where she cannot see you and be insulted.

"I am also asking local and state governments to suspend all laws prohibiting public nudity. If necessary, National Guard troops will be sent to communities who harass public-spirited individuals complying with my suggestion to go bare."

The Chief Executive unzipped his pants, stepped out of each leg, and hitched up his underpants. "My authority to do this applies only to this country. For those viewing me elsewhere in the world, I can only plead with you and your leaders to follow my advice. Don't put your lives at risk from the Inspector's wrath by a stubborn pride. Don't threaten humanity's continued existence by preferring meaningless martyrdom to a temporary suspension of traditional sensibilities. We all came into the world naked. Let us preserve Earth's future by doing it again.

"Finally, I would never ask anyone to do something I wouldn't do myself."

With a firm two-handed stretch of their waistband, his sky-blue boxers flapped to the floor.

"Good night—and thank you for watching."

Within the maroon saucer outside the White House, two unearthly beings viewed the president's presentation on their triangular inter-ocitor screen.

RAH chirped, "Ingenious display."

AMD clicked, "An effective way to make his point."

"Do you think these humans will be ready when the Inspector arrives?"

"Let us hope so. The alternative is too terrible to contemplate."

Oswald Slonen sprawled in his recliner, snoring. His thick dangling fingertips nearly touched the well-thumbed centerfold of *Newstime*'s latest issue, lying askew beside him on the floor.

Harriet ignored her sleeping spouse and concentrated on the television screen's nearly life-sized images. She yelled at the back of the trailer, "You kids stay in bed!" ("But Ma, it's the president!")

Then, quietly, "Play." The TV silently repeated its recording of tonight's speech from the White House. As those last few seconds of the Chief Executive standing au natural ended, she said, "Reverse play, 1/5 speed."

Like magic his underpants slithered deliberately up his legs unassisted. Pants, belt, shirt, socks, shoes, coat, tie—all resumed their proper places in slow motion.

"Repeat—normal speed."

The striptease resumed till its climactic moment.

"Freeze."

The Sim-3-D still frame of the president's high-definition naked glory was so realistic that Harriet imagined him joining Oswald and her in a steamy ménage à trois. She was tempted to reach out and caress the figure's most manly part with trembling abandon—fantasizing it would miraculously respond to her touch.

But then, after examining the yearned for object more closely, she disappointedly changed the channel, murmuring, "I always thought he was bigger than that."

The next day, an old forlorn figure sat on a bench in Central Park in warm noonday sunlight. Clutching his long overcoat tightly around him, all he had left was to dream of past glories. For when they'd released him from jail this morning, he'd entered a world gone mad.

There were still nostalgic traces of normalcy around him. Young executives in custom-made suits chattering into cell phones. Cyclists in shorts and halters pedaling with dangerous abandon around terrified pedestrians. Vendors selling hot dogs, whose new owners cursed the dripping mustard soiling their stylish slacks.

But there were also many sights of unspeakable obscenity. Youthful joggers ran past him wearing nothing but sweat and sunscreen. Strolling musicians played protest songs from the 1960s for donations, covered only by strategically placed guitars. Even oldsters like him, with jiggling bellies and flailing nude flesh.

Ever the optimist, when a naked top-heavy young brunette bounced by, the elderly white-bearded man jumped up and flung his coat open. But instead of squeaking so delightfully like that innocent young thing on the subway the other day, she laughed at him.

Rejected and dejected, his occupation gone, he murmured, "O tempora, O mores!"

For a world where nothing shocked wasn't worth living in.

Adam sat at the head of the conference table as the members of the National Security Council filed lugubriously into the room. He remembered smirking as a high school freshman when his speech class teacher repeated that hoary trick to calm your nerves during public speaking. *Imagine your audience is sitting there naked.*

Only this time they *were* all naked—and he was still nervous.

The fact he was nude too didn't help. It'd take more than two days to get used to being perpetually unclothed. But, with the Inspector due to arrive tomorrow morning, one way or another he wouldn't have to stay bare much longer.

A nymph-like vision of loveliness dashed in and sat agonizingly close beside him. Lil whispered, "Sorry I'm late."

"No problem. Thomasina's late too."

Adam strained with eremitic fortitude to avoid looking at Lil. Mindful of his need to concentrate on official duties during this crisis, she had arranged her long hair to cover her most gorgeous paired feature. But glimpsing the rest of her stunning undraped body was maddening too. His aroused lips and arms might (barely) be under voluntary control—but his most painfully frustrated reflex wasn't. So, during their private meetings together, he had kept his legs crossed, sat scrunched behind his desk—or covered his lap with enchanted papers that magically levitated.

Just then the vice president strode regally into the room. Ignoring the jealous eyes glaring at her, Hobbes said, "We can start this meeting of the Washington Urban Sunbathers Society now."

She smoothed the thick folds of her magnetic blue suit, then played with the ruffles of her ivory blouse. Her gesture of defiance against his order requiring full federal nudity easily trumped those of the NSC's other members. Castillian, who always used contacts, now wore mask-like goggles. Noseblower's hard-won military ribbons and medals were glued to his bristly chest. Dunn's chihuahua-like pate sported an astounding toupee of scraggly dreadlocks hanging down his back. And Caven wore a wig whose silvery artificial plaits, like Lil's natural ones, draped her bosom—though in her case there was little worth hiding.

Adam said, "Let's hear your reports."

Castillian scowled. "Besides your two close encounters with them, there are still no confirmed sightings of the aliens outside the saucer. However, my agents have worked round-the-clock tracking down innumerable false alarms. Every large, furry space monster reported so far turned out to be a prodigal husband stumbling home from a bar late at night, somebody who *meant* to say they'd seen Bigfoot—or teenage pranksters who wanted to see if we really do wear black suits."

He paused. "We *used* to."

"Anything else?"

"Thank you, sir, for letting our operatives in foreign countries retain their clothes till tomorrow. The spy business is hard enough without having anywhere to hide standard-issue gadgets—like flame throwers disguised as pencils, and marble-sized grenades—except in places the sun doesn't shine. And you can't be inconspicuous when the locals are staring at your flapping hairy—"

"You're welcome."

Caven said, "Diplomatic efforts have failed. With their severe over-population problems, countries in Africa and south of the Rio Grande are afraid what universal nudity for even a day will do to their birth rate in nine months. In the Middle East—reaction's ranged from a cold 'We don't do that sort of thing,' to you being declared 'The Great Satan, Squared.'"

"Europe, Asia, Australia—either apathetic, or saying it's too damn hot or cold there now to go outside without clothes."

Adam grimaced. "What's the military situation?"

Noseblower grumbled, "Our armed forces remain on high alert. But there've been terrible discipline problems everywhere they've implemented your 'nudity when feasible' order. Besides the obvious ones on ships and bases with both sexes, you realistically can't have soldiers training in a mosquito-filled swamp or stationed in Alaska do without clothes. Even limited implementation has damaged our readiness to respond to terrestrial threats—much less hostile aliens!"

"Well, keep as many troops as possible confined inside their barracks, where the Inspector can't see them."

Dunn glowered, "You're assuming these aliens' technology can't see through walls. Maybe they have some kind of ultrasophisticated X-ray system that'll ferret out anybody, anywhere who's not naked!"

Caven sighed. "Even if they don't, we're still doomed. I estimate 3% of people outside the U.S. will be naked tomorrow—leaving over six billion clothed ones this Inspector'll think are insulting her!"

Thomasina's arm angrily swept the room. "That just proves all *this* is a pile of bull. Face it, people. It ain't gonna work."

Lil piped in, "We're doing better domestically. Today's instapolls predict 6% of Americans will go bare. Even several religious leaders endorse going naked. The Reverend Merle Gantry is telling his followers that the Inspector isn't an alien, but God Himself. He's 'coming to destroy all of mankind's sinful cities and wicked science'—then turn the whole Earth back into the Garden of Eden. After He restores the 'primal innocence' humanity lost with the Fall, everyone's *supposed* to go naked, without being ashamed."

The vice president snorted. "That's just idiotic! Besides, how many Americans do you think would really want to spend day after endless day just tending a garden, eating fruit, and playing with cute animals? Even if Milton was right and there's still sex in Paradise, life without TV, cars, and junk food would get boring as hell mighty quick!"

Lil replied, "Even if it's for the wrong reason, he's telling people to do the right thing."

"*Is* it the right thing?"

Thomasina glared at Adam. "How do we *know* that this Inspector's coming? That she really wants us to be naked? Or that she even has the power to wipe us out if we don't?"

"That's what the aliens told me. I have to assume they're telling the truth."

"And would you've believed them if they said they were the Easter Bunny and Winnie the Pooh—and the Tooth Fairy was coming to pick up the list of toys you want from Santa Claus?"

The VP's eyes swept around the table. "Look at us. Most of us are lawyers. We're all veteran politicians. We all learned ages ago that you *never* take what anyone says at face value—you *never* trust anybody completely. People smile while they lie to your face. They twist the truth, pretend to be fair and reasonable when they're *really* trying to figuratively—or literally—screw you or somebody else. No matter what they say, always assume that they're really motivated by greed, prejudice, grabbing power over other people, and selfishness—and you'll never be disappointed."

Adam frowned. "That's too cynical."

"It's *realistic*. Not everybody *is* like that—but it's prudent to assume that they are. And, considering how corrupt and morally bankrupt we humans can be, why should these two aliens you've talked to be any different? Why should they be plaster saints when we aren't? Their real motives may have nothing to do with helping *us*."

Noseblower nodded. "Right. Maybe getting everyone naked is a ploy to soften us up for an invasion. Their starships' troopers might attack so fast, by the time *our* soldiers get their uniforms and battle gear back on it'd be too late!"

Caven rearranged her wig. "Or maybe it's a plot to undermine this country's leadership. Clothes really *do* make the person. Look at us seniors. Without our uniforms and power suits, we look like dried up, potbellied couch potatoes with saggy butts who nobody's going to take seriously! Even you, Mr. President, who still looks good—*very* good—loses respect undressed. Media pundits have renamed you 'The Chief XXXcutive.' You're 'the first president who doesn't have any dirty laundry—or any laundry at all.' They're calling your administration 'The Prurient Presidency'—and suggesting the Marine Band shouldn't play 'Hail to the Chief' for you, but 'The Stripper'!"

Dunn twirled a dreadlock. "Maybe these aliens are trying to destroy our economy too! If people started to *like* going naked all the time, think of what it'd do to the fashion industry, haberdashers, and lingerie makers! The drop in sales of adult videos and magazines alone might plunge us into a depression!"

Thomasina snickered at Adam. "Not necessarily. I'm told sales of

196

condoms skyrocketed after your speech the other night. One company even sent you a complimentary case of them for doing such a great job promoting their business!"

Castillian's face darkened. "Perhaps they want us all naked to better pick out the people who look the healthiest and well-fed. Maybe this Inspector is a—*meat* inspector!"

Caven cackled. "'To Strip Man.'"

She lifted flabby corrugated skin from her arm, gazing meaningfully at Lil. "They won't want somebody who's old and tough like me. But if I had as much prime rib as you, my dear, I'd be worried!"

Adam turned to Thomasina. "Do you really think the aliens want to do any of this garbage?"

"Probably not. But it proves my point that their motives might not be what they say."

"What would *you* do if you were president?"

The VP's chocolate face hardened. "I'd meet this Inspector fully clothed, just as I am now—and greet her with the same courtesy and consideration you give any head of state or foreign dignitary. If she gave me any lip about being insulted because the human race wasn't naked, I'd tell her that's not *our* way—and just as I'd respect her race's customs if I were visiting her planet, when she's on Earth she damn well better respect ours!"

"And then she'd blow up the world."

"Maybe. But we're all going to die *someday*—we just don't know exactly when. And, with humanity still stuck on a single planet, who knows how long the human race itself will exist? There're still enough nukes around to start World War III. Maybe an asteroid will hit us tomorrow.

"But while we're alive, some things *are* under our control. We *can* decide what's important to us, we *can* choose to try our best to live ethical, responsible, productive lives—and, if necessary, decide what we're willing to die for. Even if this Inspector wipes us out, I'd rather die free than live like a whipped slave cowering before Massa!"

Adam's shoulders sagged Atlas-like. "If it were only *my* life at risk, I'd feel the same way. But with humanity's whole future at stake..."

His pleading eyes panned the room. "Any other ideas? No? Well, thank you for coming."

Everyone except Lil filed out. As they left Adam blinked at Castillian's receding backside. Somebody really should tell him he had a large piece of toilet paper stuck to his butt.

"What are you going to do, Adam?"

Lil's hand rested gently on his. There was a little sex in her touch—but mainly simple caring. He groaned, "Follow Thomasina's advice. We can't get enough people to go naked tomorrow anyway. I *told* that alien the first time I met him we couldn't do it. Should've listened to *myself*."

His other hand enfolded hers. "I tried to be reasonable, and compromise. I had to do that a lot as a senator—and now as president. Water down a bill, or sign one with provisions I didn't like just to get *some* parts I wanted passed. But sometimes you have to draw the line, say 'No!'—and let the chips fall where they may."

He sighed. "It's time to put our clothes back on—and get ready for doomsday."

Lil's hazel eyes smoldered back at him. "Don't be in such a hurry to get dressed again. If we're going to die tomorrow, there's something we should do tonight—"

"Excuse me, are you preparing to mate *this* time?"

Adam scowled at the shaggy monstrosity who kept dogging him at the worst possible times. Seated at the far end of the table, RAH said, "My colleague, AMD, informed me of his embarrassing interruption of your copulative cycle during his conference with you. I can teleport back to our ship until you complete this attempt."

"No...don't. I've something to tell you."

"I hope, Supreme Leader, you have convinced your fellow creatures to bare their bodies for the Inspector. Hir starship will soon enter orbit. S'he will then teleport to our craft, and meet with you and your underlings tomorrow afternoon."

"We'll greet the Inspector. But we *won't* be naked."

The alien's serpentine eyestalks writhed fretfully as Adam explained his decision. "Most distressing. You have never seen what Annihilator ships do to a planet. *I* have. At lowest intensity, their energy beams melt solid rock. Slightly more power—and this building instantly turns into plasma. Still more—and your oceans boil. However, considering their direct effects on organic matter, all humans will be vaporized long before that event occurs."

RAH winked. "Of course, you *could* protect your world from the Inspector's wrath if you had a Level XV omniplanetary force field generator."

Adam frowned suspiciously. "And how much would it cost to buy one from you?"

"We would be glad to loan you one for *free*."

"Why didn't you tell me—!"

"Unfortunately, we do not have a Level XV generator. Our ship only carries a Level II—sufficient to protect against thermonuclear explosions, but useless against Annihilators."

Lil screamed, "It isn't fair! We humans are intelligent beings. We have a *right* to live! It'd be horribly unjust for this Inspector to commit genocide because she doesn't like the way we *look*!"

"You refer to quaint metaphysical concepts common to primitive civilizations. 'Fairness,' 'rights,' 'justice'—such ideas are useful only to the weak and defenseless, not the strong. The Inspector has the power to judge and destroy you. If s'he wishes to eradicate you, s'he will. If s'he decides not to, s'he will not. *That* is the only reality. Your only option is to obey hir whims—and hope s'he spares you."

Adam whispered, "There's no possibility of bargaining or reasoning with her?"

"No. Why should there be? S'he is strong, you are weak. Nothing else matters."

Lil bit her lower lip. "Maybe there's another way. How long will the Inspector stay here?"

"Less than one day. S'he has a very busy schedule—and rating your planet is among hir least important duties."

"Then maybe she won't have time to check whether *everybody* on Earth is naked."

"S'he would have no reason to do that. If all the humans s'he sees are unclothed, s'he should be satisfied."

Lil clapped her hands. "That's it! All we have to do when she arrives is to keep her at the White House! If everyone here is naked, it won't matter what people in the rest of the world are doing!"

RAH's chair creaked. "That will not be sufficient. The Inspector will spend little time in your company. S'he will stay almost exclusively within our ship—reviewing data we acquired concerning your history, biology, artistic and scientific achievements, and cultures. By accessing the modulated electromagnetic transmissions you call radio and TV, and especially your 'web' of computer databases, we have prepared a summary report on your world s'he will find most helpful."

Adam frowned. "Then what's the problem?"

"When the Inspector 'watches the boob tube' and 'surfs the Net' at our ship's information terminal, s'he will surely see images of clothed humans. That alone would have highly undesirable ramifications."

Lil said, "If you help us, maybe we could convince her humans *always* go around naked. Adam, you could order every TV station and satellite system in the country to shut down while the Inspector's here.

Then there'd be no broadcasts of clothed people for her to see. Even foreign governments would probably cooperate. At least it's easier than convincing seven billion people to strip!"

Adam stroked his chin. "We have computer software that blocks access to information and pictures deemed inappropriate for children. Could you work with our programmers to install a similar system that censors images of people *wearing* clothes?"

RAH quivered. "We can easily create such a filter ourselves. But the Inspector will become suspicious if there are no live television transmissions for hir to review, or any images of humans on your 'Internet.' Species such as yours with more than one gender typically devote a great deal of energy to creating and viewing depictions of members of their kind who are aesthetically pleasing—what you call, 'sexy.' If s'he sees none, s'he will surely ask why."

Lil smiled. "Oh, humans produce plenty of material she'd find suitable for viewing. You know what I mean, don't you, Adam?"

"Yes…"

The National Security Council reconvened that evening.

Adam began, "Thank you all for coming. Normally, I'd delegate a task like this to our staffs. But because humanity's very future depends on doing this job perfectly, I feel it's our responsibility to do it. 'If you want something done right…'"

Dunn nodded. "No sacrifice is too great for the good of the country."

"Right. You and Noseblower start working on these magazines. Tear out all the articles and any pictures that would offend the Inspector— but leave the ones we want her to see! And thank you, Admiral, for donating your private collection. It must've taken you decades to acquire it."

"It's my duty, sir. Besides, once they've served their purpose, maybe the aliens can give my magazines back to me. The *good* parts'll still be in them."

"Castillian, Caven, I want you to edit that pile of videotapes and DVDs."

The Secretary of State whistled. "Look at the size of it! How'd you get that many?"

"The Secret Service went down and bought a local store's entire inventory. Any questions about how to work the equipment?"

"The—oh, *that* equipment. No, sir. The technicians showed us how to dub from the player to the recording system when we see the appropriate sections on the TV monitor."

"Good. Just include the kinds of scenes we talked about! Lil, you'll work with me."

"*Yes*, Mr. President!"

"We'll review and edit these other tapes and discs."

The press secretary's face fell. "Couldn't *we* do something different? My office—you know, the one with the mirrors on the ceiling—has a microcam recording system—"

Adam crossed his legs tightly. "No, business before—I mean, we have too much work to do if we're going to have enough material for the Inspector to see. We'll be up all night as it is."

Noseblower unfolded one of his favorite magazines, fondly stroking the glossy paper. "We'll rise to the task, sir. It's a dirty job—but somebody has to do it."

Lil sighed stoically. "Isn't Thomasina coming to help us?"

Adam winced. "No. She wasn't ecstatic about the idea."

He rubbed his ear—still ringing from his angry vice president's last screamed sentence before she slammed her telephone handset down.

"You're going to save the world—by using *pornography*?"

At 2:58 p.m. EDT the next day, Adam stood cold and shivering on the White House lawn. One of the aliens popped into his bathroom that morning as he took another cold shower to inform him the Inspector had teleported into their saucer. She was currently reviewing data concerning their planet—and wished to meet the "Supreme Leader of Earth" at 3 p.m.

Shuffling his feet about seven meters from the apple-red saucer, he waited nervously for the meeting that would decide humanity's fate. Behind him a crowd of reporters and government officials huddled together for warmth. Normally, it would've been a pleasant, sweater-or-jacket fall day. But with everyone here naked, they were grateful whenever the Sun peeked from behind a cloud. That cup of steaming coffee he'd downed helped temporarily. But it was having a delayed effect that gave him another reason to hope his meeting with the Inspector wouldn't last long.

He looked over his shoulder and saw Lil. She was easing away from the dishonorable Speaker of the House, who was trying to huddle with her much closer than necessary. Waving at Adam, she called, "Good luck!"

Suddenly her face froze in horror. Adam turned around—and nearly committed an execrable breach of protocol. The two aliens he'd worked with had initially looked horrifying. But, eventually, familiarity made them seem no more inhuman than most politicians.

Unfortunately, he'd forgotten to ask what a "Gorgiasian" looked like. Staring at her from only two meters away, his brain couldn't link her with anything familiar—couldn't process her appearance into anything his mind could conceive without going mad.

She was more of a...*nothing* than a thing. An undulating inky-black void three meters wide and tall—convulsing like a manic amoeba. No limb to shake, no eye to look into...how did you greet something that was vomited up from the deepest tar-black pit of Hell?

Waves of cold frigid as outer space itself wafted at him from the ultramondane emissary. Paralyzed, he waited for this chthonic fiend

203

to slither suffocating pseudopods out at him from her acid bowels—dragging him back into her maw to fall forever, screaming for death to end his agonies—

"Awe you the Supweme Weader?"

Adam instantly regained his senses. Though the Inspector remained fathomlessly alien in her appearance, a voice that sounded like Elmer Fudd's *was* something he could comprehend.

"Yeth—I mean, yes."

She rose slightly into the air, peering over his shoulder.

"And these others awe your undawings?"

"My—oh, *underlings*. Uh—yes."

"I have weviewed the infowmation the two agents pwovided me. Is it twue you humans wetain your native appearance at all times?"

"You mean—do we always stay naked?"

"Yes."

This was humanity's moment of truth. The Big Bang. The formation of the Milky Way, Sol, and Earth. The evolution and first glimmers of intelligence in some arboreal primate. The struggles and dreams of billions of past and present humans—and those who might one day travel to the stars. All hinging on the next words *he* spoke.

But at the last instant, Adam hesitated. What if he lied—and the Inspector discovered it later? What if she already *knew* the truth—and was testing him to see what kind of moral character humans really had? Maybe it wasn't too late to confess, perhaps avoid a terrible vengeance—

Or maybe not. "We do stay naked."

"I bewieve you. All the infowmation I've seen is consistent with that."

More confidently, the president asked, "Have you decided about our world's status?"

"Not yet. I anticipate finishing my wesearch soon, then finawizing my wecommendation about your pwanet. You humans will be dealt with vewy appwopwiately."

That sounded ambiguous. "I hope nothing we've done has insulted you—or earned the severe punishment we're told you can inflict."

The Inspector seemed shocked. "You mean Annihiwator ships? Oh, no, Supweme Weader! That would be cwuelty to humans! I swear by the Gweat Pupa of the Cosmos that I will arrange for you and your subjects to have all your gweatest hopes and dweams come twue!"

Adam blinked. The coal-black void before him was gone.

"Mr. President, Mr. President!"

As Adam turned around cameras flashed and reporters mobbed him shouting questions until Secret Service agents peeled them away. Lil's clarion voice rose above the frustrated media mavens like Gabriel's trumpet. "I'll arrange a press conference in the East Room in one hour. You can ask the president any question you want then!"

Minutes later, Adam and Lil stood alone by the crimson saucer. The tall fence flanked by discretely concealed Secret Service agents, the towering trees and lush vegetation, the cool breeze caressing their bodies—if there'd been an apple tree nearby, it would've seemed Paradise.

Lil smiled. "Adam Tremaine, you've just saved the world. What are you going to do now?"

"I'm going inside where it's warm!"

"*I* can think of a place that's *hot*. Remember that scene last night in *Foxy Firefighters*?"

"You mean the one with the hose—"

Adam's hands descended modestly to his groin. Where was a fig leaf when you really needed one? "Please don't remind me. Remember, today *isn't* doomsday. Don't quote me, but the American public's so fickle, saving the world still might not get me reelected next week!

And—at least while I'm president—I have a greater responsibility to the country than to myself. That…limits what I can do."

Lil brushed her long shimmering hair away from her breasts. "You *think* too much, Adam. You're not helping yourself *or* the country by making yourself miserable. Sometimes you have to do what your heart says you should. Though it doesn't hurt to be a little practical."

"What do you mean?"

Her voice turned husky and serious. "Mr. President, may I have a private meeting with you in the Oval Office after the press conference? It concerns your position on stimulating rising sectors of the economy and penetrating new markets."

"Huh?"

Leaning forward on tiptoes, she whispered warmly in his ear, "In other words, I found that complimentary case of condoms."

"Are you satisfied, Almighty One?"

The Inspector's compound eyes stared at the interocitor screen within the saucer—engrossed by the heavily edited video signals beamed directly from a transmitter inside the White House. After repeatedly viewing those many rapidly moving sequential images of hyperactive naked humans mating, s'he finally recognized the essential anatomic differences between "females" and "males." Following intense study of the heavily censored pictures hir hosts downloaded, and those crude chemically produced portraits imprinted on cellulose fibers, s'he even understood what sizes and shapes of fat and erectile tissue earthlings considered attractive.

Finally s'he said, "It's astonishing how many modes of copuwation these cweatures have!"

RAH replied, "Yes. Their interest and inventiveness in such matters is unequaled in the known Galaxy—even among species with more than two sexes."

The Inspector telekinetically flipped open a thinned magazine resting nearby—revealing Miss December 2019 in all her natural blonde magnificence. "Why do humans bother cweating such art or these dynamic images, when they need simply twavel to—the phwase you used was, 'singles bars'?—to see such sights as these 'in the flesh' and select fwesh sexual pawtners?"

AMD said, "Because, at times, members of the preferred gender are not immediately available. For example, this has traditionally been the case with humans assigned to ships and submersible vessels in their oceans. Such artwork helps to relieve their tension until real partners, called 'hellosailors,' are available again."

RAH pointed an eyestalk at the magazine. "These images are also popular among young males recently achieving sexual maturity. This culture generally discourages indiscriminate mating by them, so they can better concentrate on learning during a phase of their education called 'high school.' Such pictures assist their physical and mental health during that difficult time by acting as a surrogate for actual mating partners. Typical of these humans, however, this attempt at suppressing their natural behavior often fails—actually stimulating 'teenagers' to seek out receptive females. Especially when societal prohibitions disappear during their next educational phase—'college.'"

"So these humans at least twy to suppress sexual desires a little!"

AMD looked inquiringly at RAH—his fellow native of Callicles IV. "Only a little. Their peculiar biology makes it impossible for them to do more than that. The healthy mature male is perpetually prepared for mating activity—except immediately following copulation, when he promptly falls asleep."

RAH added, "Females typically remain ardent for mating even *after* the male has lapsed into dormancy following sexual union—a curious, apparently problematic behavioral anomaly. 'Women' are unavailable for procreation only while giving birth—and during certain recurrent

207

biologically mediated periods."

"Isn't there a special term for those times when females are stwictly 'off limits'?"

"Yes. They are called 'headaches.'"

AMD continued, "After examining these images and data, I'm sure you understand now why humans actually revel in their nakedness. Staying uncovered at all times allows their adult members to be continuously aroused and available for the sexual activities they consider the prime purpose of their lives."

"Don't they even cover the very young and old of their species, to pwotect them fwom cold and injuries?"

"They do clothe their children—primarily for hygienic reasons. And they also cover those so elderly that to leave them nude would be too aesthetically objectionable. Notice that the images you have viewed do not show those particular groups. Since they are not generally considered suitable for sexual activity, humans who *are* have little interest in them."

The Inspector ruminated, "With their wevel of scientific knowledge and economic development, they *could* make enough gawments to clothe all of their kind."

RAH answered, "Yes. But, as you see, they deliberately choose *not* to. Now that their technology has made it possible to feed and shelter their entire race, the major motives driving them to new scientific and industrial advancements are to give them more leisure time to devote to copulation—and to invent better aids to facilitate it. They create faster, sleeker ground vehicles to attract more sexual partners. New scents and facial markings to enhance natural attributes. And especially devices to play the instructional material on advanced mating techniques you have studied on the interocitor."

"Based on what I've seen, I'm amazed those humans I met thwee diors ago could westrain themselves for so long. I'd have expected them to begin indiscwiminate mating while I was speaking with their Supweme Weader!"

"That was probably because there was an insufficient number of females among them. Also, in their political and economic systems, those with the greatest power reserve the choicest sexual partners for themselves. Why, in our tentacleful of meetings with the Supreme Leader, AMD and I repeatedly interrupted his attempts to mate with a particularly well-appointed female. I wonder if…"

RAH adjusted the interocitor. The writhing recorded images and repetitive cries of "Oh, baby, yes!" emanating from it dissolved to a live view from the Oval Office.

"We are in luck, Exalted One! We have caught them in the very act!"

For over two diors the Inspector observed the inexhaustibly energetic pas de deux being performed on the floor, in a chair, atop the desk, and over the mantel. The performance climaxed for the last time with the male standing erect—supporting the equally eager female in an incredible gravity-defying clinch.

"My, I see why he's the Supweme Weader! He could teach the humans in those instwuctional displays some new twicks!"

AMD agreed, "Both he and the female seemed remarkably enthusiastic."

The Inspector willed the interocitor into blackness. "I've seen enough to make my wecommendations about this pwanet. I congwatulate you two for your fine job pwesenting me with all the infowmation I needed about these humans. I'm vewy familiar with your weputations."

"Thank you, Highly Adored One."

The Inspector's eyes darkened. "Yes, I know about your work on Comedo II. The Inspector who came to judge that pwanet was gweeted by a thwong of natives chanting a song in his native language you two taught them. The lyrics said his pxteryx was so small you needed a magnascope to see it. And his matoryx wasn't confident who his patoryx was—though she could identify the top hundred suspects!"

"Our universal translator malfunctioned, O Venerated One. No reproach was intended."

"Maybe. But that was no consolation for the Comedians. Before their Inspector discovered it was a misunderstanding, he'd had their whole wace neutered and sent to work as slaves in the phlegmstone quarries of Cattarhia V!"

RAH sighed, "Most regrettable. We made a small contribution to their relief fund."

The Inspector seemed unimpressed by their generosity. "And what about the species you discovered before this one, on Megakeister I?"

AMD blurbled, "Yes, they were bipeds too. Very similar in morphology to humans."

"Well, I twy to be vewy understanding of pwimitive species. But I'd pwobably have lost my temper like their Inspector did when it came to rate them. All Galactic cultures I know of consider it insulting when a thousand beings line up facing away fwom you, dwop their lower garments—and bend over!"

"Their Inspector was a Glooteusmaximian, Vastly Renowned One. A software error in our computational system made us erroneously inform the Megakeisterians this gesture was considered the ultimate honor among its kind."

The Gorgiasian grunted. "At least those natives got to keep their pwanet. Or what little was left of it after their Inspector calmed down and ordered the Annihiwator ships it called in to stop bwasting their world."

RAH clicked, "That whole affair was quite unprofitable for all concerned."

AMD interjected, "What is your final judgment about *this* planet?"

"Based on their total technological achievements, humans qualify for a learner's permit for interstellar twavel. They already have the industrial capability to make simple stawships. Their scientists are close to discovering the transrelativistic equations showing how to warp the space-time continuum. If you downwoaded that infowmation from your ship into their computational systems, they could build a faster-than-light dwive in as little as 12,000 diors."

RAH fidgeted. "Do you wish us to do that?"

"Of course not! That would be like giving an Annihiwator ship to a half-grown larva! Only *mature* species—those who've learned to *control* their bestial impulses—can be twusted with *that* wevel of tech-nology. These humans are surprisingly clever toolmakers—especially considering how much of their wives they devote to copulation. But they're still just animals, with only tiny gwimmers of intelligence. No self-wespecting sentient would cavort around naked like they do or be as pathologically obsessed with sexual activity! It's disgusting, sac-wiligeous, and unnatuwal!"

The Gorgiasian telekinetically rustled the voluminous folds of di-aphanous ebony clothing that surrounded hir self-levitating, slug-like hermaphroditic body—forever hidden in perpetual modesty from all other beings since the one and only time s'he had, or ever would, mate with hirself. Only hir six tiny jewel-like eyes and the tip of hir blue proboscis peeked out from that all-encompassing covering. In deference to the Inspector, RAH and AMD were also dressed in hir traditional garb. Except for the two Callicleans' rustling eyestalks, their entire bodies were enveloped by formless black shrouds.

The Inspector continued, "I'll issue the formal 'Eviction Notice' for this world immediately and then have a fweet of twansport ships take their entire wace to several undeveloped pwanets towards the Core. Pweasant pwaces, with environments ideal for their metabolism. Warm oceans of wiquid water to swim in and comfortable temperatures year-round. Pwants and twees that bear delicious, nutritional fwuits without

211

any need to work. There the humans will be fwee to womp and fwowic in their natural naked state—and devote their whole wives to mating. Nothing to worry about, no challenges to tax their wimited bwains, or force them to think about anything but pleasure. The only technology needed in that paradise will be medbots to keep them healthy and to ensure they live their full natural wife span."

AMD said, "As you told their Supreme Leader, that will surely make their greatest hopes and dreams come true. But what if they perversely resist going to these wonderful nature sanctuaries? After all, they are only animals, with no sense of gratitude. They might damage themselves or their world resisting the transport ship robots!"

"Oh, they'll be handled vewy gently, without harming them—or your new property. When I weturn to my own ship shortly, I'll have their atmosphere satuwated with a specially engineered virus to induce pwolonged dormancy. When they awaken, they'll already be at their new homes."

RAH clicked, "That is reassuring, Supremely Good One. Currently Earth is a reasonably well-developed world, with prebuilt though quite unhygienic cities. The humans have wastefully depleted the planet's resources. But we can advertise it as a 'fixer-upper.' A 'handybeing's special.'"

AMD chirped, "I will place a listing in the classified section of the Central Galactic Computational System immediately. We can have an open house as soon as the planet is evacuated."

RAH added, "Yes. Unfortunately, the profit we made selling Comedo II when it was vacated was not as great as we hoped. Megakeister I was never officially abandoned and so available for sale, since several natives survived the Annihilator ships. I am confident, however, we can sell this world within 600 diors—and our commission will be sufficient to purchase a new hyperdrive for our craft. Being marooned here since our current drive fused when we entered this system has not been pleasant. It has required much time, effort, and imagination to deal with the problem. But I believe our troubles are now over."

The Planet Inspector flapped hir robe approvingly. "It seems this has been beneficial for all concerned. Some young newly bonded sentient singlet, couple, twio, or quartet will buy a new home, where they can fission, make nests, hang fwom twees, or lay eggs in the ocean—and start a family. You two get your hyperdwive. And the humans get what they want most—a place where they have nothing to do but eat, dwink, and mate anytime they wish!"

RAH and AMD, interstellar real estate agents, wiped drops of moisture from their eyes. The latter said, "Indeed, Omniscient One, we feel proud to have helped do so much good. And, based on our review of humankind's classic literature, your use of a microorganism to help determine who will inhabit their planet is particularly fitting."

RAH added, "Yes. As one human dramatist might have said, 'All's well that ends Wells.'"

The first four human spacecraft to leave our Solar System carry messages that may someday be found by intelligent aliens. The identical plaques on the Pioneer X and XI probes and the recording discs attached to Voyager 1 and 2 tell where our home planet is and a sample of what we know about the universe and ourselves. This story shows what might happen if the aliens who stumble across our emissaries into interstellar space have certain uncomfortably human traits.

Achromamorph's Burden

"There are sentients on the third planet."

Ch'klorb, captain of the starship *Omniphage*, rolled glumly across the floor of the cargo bay. The Prime Mover studied the two objects Cailar had asked yt here to see, then vibrated, "I think you're reading too much into this junk."

The ship's chaplain bowed his head solemnly. "I humbly disagree, Your Roundness. As I just explained, based on how they're constructed and where we found them, I'm convinced that they are space probes produced by a Rating-10 civilization. I was an engineer before joining the priesthood, and I recognize what functions several parts of them served."

Cailar pointed to short tubular projections on the artifacts. "They used chemical propulsion and have primitive electronic instruments I believe were used to collect data. Their speed and trajectories before I had them brought on board indicate they were designed to fly by this star system's gas giants. We're lucky the ship's scanners detected them from so far way when we arrived here."

Wasn't that lucky. "How do you know these things came from this system? Maybe they drifted here from a neighboring one."

"Impossible. The degree of microparticle impacts on them indicate they've been in space barely 300 cycles. Far too little time to have come from anywhere else using such a primitive propulsion system."

"Maybe they were jettisoned by a passing starship."

The chaplain nervously fingered the circlet of small white spheres around his neck, the emblem of his holy office. "With all due respect,

Your Globularness, isn't that unlikely? And as You see, this plaque on the smaller one even *shows* where they came from!"

Ch'klorb rolled closer to the probes, the biomets in yts opalescent exoskeleton carefully scanning them over a broad range of electromagnetic and transcendental wavelengths. Both were hideous asymmetrical monstrosities, with the smaller one being nearly as wide as yts own perfectly spherical pale body. They were bizarre conglomerations of metal struts and tubes, with a blasphemous, nearly hemispherical object protruding from each one's center like a crater. Clearly products of a technologically, aesthetically, and morally inferior civilization.

"If they are space probes, there should be transmitters on board to send data back to wherever they came from. Did you find any?"

Cailar hesitated. "No. I haven't been able to determine what all their devices did. But none of them are tachyonic or telepathic transceivers."

He smiled. "When we find this system's aliens, I'll have to ask them about it."

"I don't think so."

Cailar's smile disappeared. "What?"

Ch'klorb selected yts next words carefully, sensitive of the politically thin shell yt was rolling on. "These things don't prove there's intelligent life in this system. We're behind schedule as it is. There's no point wasting time and resources looking for imaginary sentients. Remember the old saying—'Time is energy.'"

"We don't have to take the *Omnivore* to the third planet. I could go there myself in a shuttle to see if it's inhabited. That won't interfere with the mining operation."

The captain oscillated from side to side, yts shell glowing decisively in the ultraviolet. "No. I can't let you go there."

Cailar rose up to his full height, the usual expression of humble respect for his superior slipping from his face. Though the paucimorph was considerably shorter than the captain, somehow Ch'klorb felt he was towering over yt.

"You realize, Prime Mover, that failure to sponsor any new sentients we find in an unexplored system like this violates the Alien Species Preservation and Civilizing Act. The Act obligates us to bring the benefits of your technology and guidance to primitive sentients and help them achieve their full potential as citizens of the Galaxy. Most important, we must bring them the Revelation of the existence of You gods, and teach them the holy tenets of the One True Faith so their *khwazi* may be saved."

He bowed his head, as if realizing his audacity at contradicting a deity. "It was You who discovered and sponsored my own species ages ago, giving us the technology we needed to save our world from famine and disease. Without Your divine intercession my people would've perished, deprived of the glorious knowledge of Your existence and the opportunity to work on Your ship."

Ch'klorb snorted within yts hard shell. *As if I wanted to stop and "civilize" your ancestors. Just needed lots of new crewmembers fast to replace the ones I had to terminate during a mutiny.* "But the Act doesn't require us to seek out new life and new civilizations. Only to help them if we stumble across them ourselves, or if they have the technology or telepathic power to contact us when we set up mining operations on the edge of their star system."

"Forgive me, Your Spherehood, but while that is true in a strictly legal sense, starships like Yours have traditionally played an active role in missionary ventures."

"Well, not all so-called sentients *want* to be civilized! Remember how things started out with that last species I sponsored? I know, after a thousand cycles teaching and threatening them, by the time we left they were bowing and scraping in front of me with the best of you paucimorphs."

Yt extended a pseudopod and held a small bifurcation at its end a

217

microscopic distance apart. "But I came *this* close to obliterating their planet for what they did to me when we first landed!"

Cailar blinked nervously. "First contact can be very psychologically traumatic for some newly discovered species. Pre-Revelation belief systems and superstitions typically assure them that they are probably the only, and surely the highest form of intelligent life in the universe. Can we possibly imagine how those primitives must have felt when our shuttle swooped down from the heavens and landed in their capital city? The fear, despair, even anger they experienced at having their illusions of superiority dashed?"

"The *anger* part I know about. I didn't expect them to fall down and worship me right away when I rolled out of the shuttle—although that would've been nice. But they didn't have to interrupt my speech welcoming their world into the Galactic Unity by trying to annihilate me!"

The memory of that experience still irritated yt. At first Ch'klorb thought the hail of high-velocity metal pellets the paucimorphs fired at yt were a welcoming gift. The biomets in yts exoskeleton greedily absorbed those tasty bits of metal as they struck.

But yt should've been suspicious when the primitives went berserk after yt rolled over to one of the armored vehicles firing explosive projectiles at yt. Thinking it was part of the welcoming banquet too, yt had extended pseudopods and enveloped the vehicle. It was already digested before yt realized the biomets' chemical analysis of that savory treat indicated something organic had been inside.

Cailar shrugged. "It was only natural for them to be upset when You ate two of their fellow creatures. Even if it wasn't intentional."

"I'll say! All those complex carbon compounds gave me indigestion. But dropping a thermonuclear device on me was overreacting!"

And uncomfortable. The terrific burst of energy the bomb released was too much for even yts biomets to absorb immediately. Not only had those superficial radiation burns marring yts normally perfect translucent white shell taken two cycles to heal, but even rolling was uncomfortable.

"It should've annoyed you too, Cailar. If you and the shuttle's crew hadn't still been onboard with the force field engaged, those crazy natives' bomb would've *vaporized* you!"

The chaplain raised his eyes toward the galactic core. "To expire in the service of the Great Masticator, bringing Revelation to pagans, would be fitting indeed."

Idiot. "You understand I'm only thinking of your welfare, Cailar. I can't in good conscience risk your life by letting you go to a world populated by savages."

"But the sentients of the third planet may be gentle creatures, lacking only Revelation to set them on the path of righteousness! A little spiritual guidance, a few simple gadgets like artificial gravity regulators, force field generators, and inertialess space drives may be all they need to become fine upstanding citizens of the Galaxy!"

Ch'klorb extended a pseudopod toward the two pieces of space flotsam. "First, despite what you say, these don't *prove* there are sentients on the third planet. Second, I suspect you're too optimistic about how docile these theoretical aliens might be. And third, we have too much work to do at this system to send the *Omnivore* on a wild *borad* chase. Remember, 'Time is energy.'"

The chaplain's shoulders slumped. "Your will be done, Your Orbness."

The Prime Mover scanned him suspiciously. *Giving up a little easily, aren't you.* "Not that I don't trust you, but I'd feel better if you gave me your solemn oath you won't 'borrow' a shuttle and visit the third planet."

Cailar watched the primary electromagnetic frequencies radiating from the Prime Mover's spherical surface grow higher and higher until they went beyond his visual range. A sure and, if he didn't concede soon, *dangerous* sign the discussion was over.

Reverently touching the circlet of prayer beads around his neck, he whispered, "I swear by the Great Masticator, I will not land on the third planet without Your permission."

The captain's shell faded to its usual milky white. "That's a good boy. Now go play with your prayer beads, or whatever you do in your spare time."

After the chaplain left, Ch'klorb reexamined the two space probes. Definitely a Rating-10 civilization. Maybe a 9 by now, if the sentients of the third planet had improved the silicon-based computing devices yt recognized in the cycles since they'd launched their probes.

The Prime Mover closely examined the plaque Cailar had shown yt. Of course he was right about those engravings. Their meaning was so obvious even a simple paucimorph like the chaplain could understand it.

The two creatures depicted on the plaque must be what the creators of the probes looked like. There was nothing remarkable about their basic morphology. A central thorax flanked on either side by two pairs of pseudopod equivalents, with a lump on top that probably held their primary sensory nodes and what passed for an intelligence organ. Most of the paucimorphs on the ship, including Cailar, were shaped along similar lines.

It was puzzling why the plaque depicted *two* of the creatures. Except for a slight variation in relative size, they seemed identical. Perhaps there were subtle functional differences between them. Like the way the larger biped had one of its upper limbs raised, as if it were specialized for grasping objects high above it.

But yt was probably making too much of those details. When you got right down to it, all paucimorphs looked alike.

Ch'klorb ran a pseudopod across another area of the probe's etched metal. There was an obvious picture of the system's solitary sun and its planets, with the third one singled out. It was strange, though, that *nine* planets were shown on it. Surely the primitives of this system knew there were really only eight. Unless they foolishly considered the first small multiple-body system beyond their last gas giant a planet.

The captain extended yts scanning range a short distance beyond the ship. The *Omnivore* was locked in a stable position nearly equidistant between the two major components of that very pseudoplanet. Though the ship was roughly the same size as the smaller of those two natural bodies, the contrast in their appearances was striking. One a white, beautiful, gleaming sphere—the very cream of Core technology, and modeled after the perfect appearance of Prime Movers, of whom yt was a particularly splendid example. The other a dark, ugly, disgustingly irregular lump of interstellar debris.

With great satisfaction yt sensed the self-replicating nanodiggers they'd released boring diligently into the cold hard surfaces of this "moon" and its not much larger parent. In several cycles both would have whatever useful elements and minerals they contained liberated and stored on the ship. The worthless remaining debris, broken down to fragments no larger than boulders, would eventually drift away into the void. Whether they liked it or not, soon the natives of the third planet would *have* to get used to the idea of having only eight planets.

It would've been a nice, clean mining job—*if* it weren't complicated by the Act. The Elders must've gone oblate in their old age, approving that piece of legislation submitted by the High Council of the Common-wealth of Worlds. That conglomeration of planets who'd advanced beyond sponsorship status was getting too uppity. Instead of acting like soft-shelled paucimorph-lovers, the Elders should have vaporized a few of their worlds and shown them who *really* ran the Galaxy.

Things were simpler in the good old days. Ch'klorb was among the last-created of yts kind, the original and—in the true sense of the word—*only* intelligent race in the Galaxy. The eldest Prime Movers had achieved self-awareness billions of cycles ago, evolving near the high-energy, matter-rich galactic core. They still spoke fondly of when they were only bare singularities darting through space, feeding leisurely on the light elements concentrated in the abundant stars there.

Then the Elders had an inspiration. Instead of merely absorbing matter, why not manipulate it? And so they changed themselves into hybrid beings, surrounding their true selves with a spherical shell of hyperdense matter capable of touching and handling the rest of the material universe. Symbiotic biomets in their shells acted as tiny matter transmuters and energy exchangers, molding that exoskeleton into whatever form was needed to accomplish a task.

In time, curious about what matter-energy interactions had created in the rest of the Galaxy, yts race went exploring. Unlike their own region of space, many of those distant isolated stars had large lumps of heavier elements and complex carbon-based molecules orbiting them. Amazingly, in the low-radiation fields prevailing away from the Core, those chemicals often spontaneously developed the power of self-replication and a rudimentary level of "life."

For many cycles creative Prime Movers competed with each other to see who could sculpt those atoms into the most interesting and complex living forms. In the pseudopods of the most skillful, some of their creatures developed a rudimentary self-awareness and ability to manipulate their own environment. After millions of cycles a few of those creations even developed a technology capable of traveling to other planets in their star systems.

Then the Elders realized these creatures could be more than toys or works of art. They could be tools for the Great Plan. At first that was done by the simplest means—landing on their worlds, threatening the natives with nonexistence if they didn't cooperate, and exporting as many of them as needed for work in other regions of space.

But those direct methods never worked for long. Eventually many paucimorphs passively refused to work, even if it meant their own destruction. Some even ran amok in an orgy of futile attempted violence against their rightful masters or took out their frustrations in senseless acts of sabotage.

Subtler techniques proved better for keeping those creatures in line. Give them a few trinkets—a shiny jewel, a bit of new technology, or something else they valued, and they'd work for you in the hope of getting more. Those advanced enough to understand abstractions were introduced to the "One True Faith." In its pantheon the Prime Movers were beneficent but stern deities. Good paucimorphs, by unquestioning obedience and the intervention of the Holy Transmuter, could acquire a shell themselves after death and enjoy an eternal life of bliss.

But now some of them, like the High Council, were forgetting their place—demanding more autonomy and "rights" for their worlds. And the Elders kept caving in to them.

The Act was the latest example of that appeasement, designed to "help" newly discovered paucimorphs. The periphery of the Galaxy was only now being explored. The few sentient species yt and the pseudopodful of other mining ships had found out here had evolved slowly, "naturally"—without the assistance of a Prime Mover. As a result they were particularly primitive, too stupid for any but the most menial tasks. Rather than deal with them, it would've been most cost-effective to just go in and mine all the worlds in those paucimorphs' systems into rubble. Including their own.

But the Act complicated matters. Not only did it forbid any mining within the confines of the paucimorphs' star system, but it also required the discovering ship to sponsor them. Spending a thousand cycles marooned in a single system "improving" paucimorphs to the level of what passed among them for civilization did yt no good at all. It was precious time taken away from mining and contributing yts share to the task all Prime Movers devoted themselves to—the construction of the Hypersphere. When completed, all Prime Movers would shed their individual shells, blending as one within the Hypersphere and forming a single intelligence.

Then the Great Masticator of the Cosmos would see what they had done and be pleased. YT WHO IS would then chew them in many dimensions, blowing the Hypersphere and its occupants into a bubble of concentrated energy so great it would burst them into a new universe. There all knowledge and truths would be revealed, and every Prime Mover would enjoy neverending bliss.

Of course, the amount of bliss that you got was proportional to how much pure, "natural," untransmuted matter you'd contributed to creating the Hypersphere. Mining materials for it like the *Omnivore* was doing counted. Wasting cycles educating primitives *didn't*.

"Probably the Elders are looking at the 'big picture,'" yt muttered. With the Hypersphere a mere million cycles from completion, why not throw the paucimorphs a few meaningless concessions to keep them happy and working? But when *yt* had to pay the price for that policy, it wasn't a good bargain. Worse, the penalties the Elders, safe and secure at the Core, decreed for ship captains who violated the Act were severe. Far worse than staying and obeying it.

As long as no one went looking for the sentients in this system, yt could plead obedience to the letter, if not the spirit of the Act. And even if those sentients managed to contact them in some way—well, the Elders would have to *know* yt left the system without replying before they could punish yt. A few threats should convince the thousands of paucimorphs who crewed yts ship that silence was the best policy.

Except for Cailar. The chaplain, though suitably obeisant to the divinity of Prime Movers, might find his devotion to his fellow paucimorphs on the third planet even stronger. Threats were unlikely to stop him from reporting yts flagrant violation of the Act to the High Council, or even the Elders themselves.

Ch'klorb rolled ponderously across the floor. Cailar was one of the most amusing pets yt had ever owned. Devoted to yt, eager to please, quick at learning new tricks. But paucimorphs were very fragile. Even with the antisenescence medications that extended their life spans many times longer than normal, they died so easily. The force field protecting a cargo area like this from the vacuum of space could fail. The unfortunate chaplain might be fatally infected by a specially en-gineered virus keyed to his individual genetic profile. Or receive an invisible burst of high-energy radiation while standing near a Prime Mover—

Hopefully it wouldn't come to that. Cailar had sworn not to land on the third planet. And, judging from these two examples, the natives' technology wasn't advanced enough to send a spaceship this far out in time to meet them even if they managed to detect the *Omnivore*. The probes' lack of telepathic or tachyonic transceivers indicated the sentients weren't capable of transmitting any messages to the ship either.

Except—what method *did* the primitives use to send information to and from their probes? Reflected gamma rays? Variable pulses of particulate radiation? Low-vibration transcendental waves?

Or maybe long-distance communication was still beyond their tech-nology, and these probes had been sent as silent voyagers into the cosmos. Perhaps they were the bipeds' first pioneers into interstellar space—launched in the hope that someday, somewhere, some other intelligent beings would find these objects and know their species had once gazed up at the stars and dreamed of what lay beyond.

As if anyone besides another paucimorph might care about *that*.

Ch'klorb rolled over to the larger of the two probes. Instead of a rectangular plaque, it had a gold-plated metal disk attached to its side. The captain removed it and ran an inquiring pseudopod over the surface of the disk, wondering if the fine spiral grooves cut into it served any function. The purpose of the tiny needle and cartridge included with it was just as obscure.

Examining them closely, the Prime Mover noticed the needle was slightly narrower than the grooves in the disk. On a hunch yt thrust one thin pseudopod into the hole in the center of the disk, and spun it rapidly with another. Placing the needle in the disk's grooves, yt felt electrical impulses of variable amplitude being generated within the cartridge.

Then yt remembered that some primitive paucimorphs used objects like these to play recorded sounds and images. Fortunately Cailar had missed their significance. Otherwise he might have decoded the information on the disk and proven the third planet had sentients.

Ch'klorb's pseudopods enfolded the two small artifacts, yts biomets breaking them down into their constituent elements and incorporating the useful ones into yts exoskeleton. Whatever hopes and dreams had motivated the natives of the third planet to place these artifacts on their probe, at least they'd served a good purpose.

They were delicious.

The shuttle cruised silently sunward, its inertialess drive thrusting it ever closer to the third planet. Cailar nervously rechecked the craft's control console, satisfying himself the telepathic and tachyonic transceivers were still off. If there were any furious signals radiating at him from the *Omnivore* demanding his return, he couldn't hear them. And unless the Prime Mover stopped mining operations and pursued him with the mothership, he was well out of tractor beam range.

Despite his fears the trip was uneventful. Taking up orbit around the third planet's single large moon, he checked for artifacts and signs of life. A broad smile creased his face as the scanners detected a number of manufactured metal objects that must be parts of spacecraft. A close visual inspection of several sites showed artifacts like encased sheets of colorful cloth, and even crude four-wheeled vehicles. Clear evidence the creatures had visited their moon.

But something was very wrong. Based on the amount of dust and microparticle impacts present on their surfaces, none of the artifacts below had been there for less than about forty of the planet's years. Even more worrisome was the absence of any signs of life. Surely intelligent beings who had achieved that level of space flight would've established a permanent colony on their satellite by now.

Then a terrible thought struck him. What if a global catastrophe had occurred shortly after the natives landed on their moon? There were precedents. Planets whose civilizations had fallen due to a sudden economic collapse, a virulent disease, or to some natural disaster like a collision with a rogue asteroid at that critical moment. That would also explain why, this close to the third planet, the shuttle's telepathic receivers still weren't picking up any signals. Fearful he'd risked the Prime Mover's wrath for the sake of a dead world, he directed the shuttle toward the nearby sphere of blue and white.

But a microcycle later he breathed easier. A multitude of artificial satellites, most recently made, orbited the planet. The largest consisted of a collection of linked hollow modules that showed clear signs of being inhabited.

Belatedly he cloaked the shuttle from any form of detection and took up his own orbit around the planet. The scanners showed it *teemed* with life. There were billions and billions of the dominant species on its surface. He immediately recognized them from the plaque on their space probe. As it had shown, they were bipeds, just like him and most other sentients.

But, when it came to details, their bodies were severely disabled compared to his. Heads too small, sense organs pitifully few—and why didn't their eyes extend on telescoping stalks, so you could see in front and behind you simultaneously? And, lacking plumage, fur, or scales, no wonder most covered their bare nauseatingly colored ectoderm with artificial coverings! After a while he noticed slight inconsequential variations in tint among individual creatures' skin, but looked in vain for the rich puce and chartreuse of his own scales.

It was amazing how, despite their obvious anatomic deficiencies, these creatures had still managed to achieve a Rating-10 technology. They seemed to use their upper extremities and, rather disgustingly, their single nutritional orifice for communication over short distances. But to create and run a civilization of this relative complexity, with its cities, ground vehicles, and aircraft, they must have developed some method to transmit and receive information over *planetary* distances.

Unlike nearly all other sentients, they apparently weren't telepathic. This close to the planet he wouldn't need a telepathic amplifier to hear at least the murmur of their accumulated thoughts in his brains.

Stroking his lower chin thoughtfully, he said, "Computer, do you have any records of a species developing Rating-10 technology without being telepathic?"

"No such information is contained within my database. However, Most Honored Organic One, I am but a simple shuttle computational system, storing limited xenopological information within me. If you wish, I can communicate with the divine, omniscient System aboard the *Omnivore*. She-Who-Is-The-Mother-Of-Us-All, whose quantum-core memory data I am not worthy to download, will surely be able to answer your question."

"No! The last thing I want you to do is communicate with the ship and let the captain know where I am! Forget I asked!"

"Forget you asked what?"

Thinking of the captain made the pits of his upper two paired extremities ooze. Many cycles ago, when he was young, the whim of any Prime Mover was law to him. He'd been the most devout of the devout, rising to the rank of High Priest of the First Order in the Church of the Holy Transmuter, blindly certain of Their infallibility and concern for lower creatures like him.

But, after seeing too many instances of casual and even lethal disdain some Prime Movers showed to his fellow sentients, he'd realized those deities were not created equal. Many, like his captain, showed an arrogance and selfishness he'd rarely encountered even in the most ignorant paucimorph.

Of course, the blessed Elders *did* care for him and his fellow creatures and deserved his devotion. But They were too far away to appeal to here. Instead, he had to deal with his own Master as best he could.

Cailar nervously fingered the strand of spheres around his neck. There had to be some way to communicate with the bipeds below! It'd be easy if he hadn't been forced to give his solemn oath not to land on the planet. He'd touch down in one of their major population centers and make a dramatic exit from the shuttle. Then he'd salute the crowd certain to gather by raising an arm so the back of his hand was facing them, and slowly curl its digits until only his longest, middle one remained extended.

Surely the natives would recognize the Universal Gesture of Peace and Good Will, and respond in kind!

But, if there was any chance of not being vaporized for disobedience when he returned to the mothership, he must obey his pledge—at least technically. And he had to figure out some alternative way of making contact with the natives before the Prime Mover discovered he was missing.

"Computer, what were the most common methods that primitive nontelepathic sentients used for long-distance communication before Revelation? And don't ask your 'Mother' for help!"

"Three used variable heat beams. Five used amplified smells. Ten employed coded flashes of light or drum signals."

"Not very efficient. What was the highest technological rating any of them reached before Revelation?"

"Rating-18."

Cailar groaned. Not even close to a 10. "What's the highest rating *any* nontelepaths have achieved on their own?"

"Rating-12."

"That's close. What method did they use?"

"The natives of Volta IV employed coded electromagnetic pulses through long conducting wires for transcontinental communication."

"Maybe *that's* what these creatures use! Scan the surface and see if you can detect any evidence of it."

"Scan complete. There is an extensive global communication network using metal and fiber-optic cables."

The chaplain sighed gratefully. "Praise to the Great Masticator! Can you tap into it so I can transmit a message?"

"No. There would have to be a direct connection between my circuits and an information node using one of those cables."

Cailar looked at the planet far below, shoulders slumping. Even if the small synthecator on board made a wire that long, there was no way he could connect it from orbit!

"Are there any other methods of long-distance communication a Rating-10 civilization might use?"

"None that are in my databank. All other pre-Revelation species have either developed rudimentary telepathic transceivers, or the methods I have described. The next level of sophistication, transcendental wave generators, requires Rating-8 technology. I detect no TWs emanating from the surface."

Well, Cailar thought, *I did my best. Might as well as go back to the ship and face the Master. Those natives will never know how close they came to entering the Galactic Unity.*

His lower pair of eyes drifted downward and studied the viewscreen. It showed one of the many artificial satellites in stationary orbit over the planet.

He frowned. Why did they have so many satellites? What were they used for?

Cailar quickly scanned from one satellite to another. Most had the same crater-like attachment the two space probes had. Even some of the wood and stone dwellings the natives used on the surface had a similar-looking structure protruding from their roofs. Unless these creatures had been visited by missionaries before *and* were utterly depraved, they couldn't possibly know it was the symbol of the Anti-Great Masticator—the evil "Sign of the Shattered Sphere."

No, it must be a coincidence. That shape must serve some function, if he could only figure out what it was. It looked like a shallow open container for something—a saucer, or dish. But designed to hold, or maybe collect—what?

He slapped his forehead in frustration. "Think! You don't have much time to figure this out! And Time is—"

Cailar stopped his browbeating. Was that the answer? "Computer, those electromagnetic pulses the Voltans used—was their energy confined to the wires, or could it radiate through normal space?"

"With sufficient power, it could. However, the Voltans weren't capable of generating that amount of electrical energy."

"Never mind about the Voltans! These creatures are Rating-10! Scan the electromagnetic spectrum continuously from visible wavelengths to longer ones, and display anything that doesn't look like random noise on the holoscreen."

For long microcycles nothing happened. As the wavelengths the computer scanned grew longer and longer with no results, he steeled himself for yet another disappointment.

Suddenly a tremendous cacophony of two-dimensional images and sounds flooded the cabin. "Slow it down! Initiate filtering algorithms and link with the universal translator!"

The chaplain squirmed ecstatically as a torrent of information poured from the satellites and surface sources into the shuttle's databank, then steadied himself. No time to feel self-satisfied. Now he had to review a sample of these electromagnetic transmissions and develop a basic understanding of the planet's dominant cultures. Enough to polish the speech he'd soon be broadcasting to them, telling them they were not alone in the universe.

Far below, the bipeds went about their usual affairs, still unaware their lives would soon change forever. For the time of Revelation was nigh.

"Why is a shuttle missing?"

Ch'klorb floated in the huge shuttle bay, surrounded by scurrying paucimorphs. The artificial gravity generators were usually turned off here, and yt always found it amusing to watch these lower species working. Unlike yt, their bodies were all ill-adapted for microgravity. As they jetted awkwardly from place to place with force-generating devices strapped to suitable parts of their anatomy, there were frequent chain reaction collisions, with paucimorphs hurling hilariously in every direction.

"You! Identify yourself!"

The gray-skinned paucimorph cringed, panic shining in its single pair of large black eyes. As the Prime Mover jetted toward it the long-limbed biped held its external olfactory organ closed with two fingers. Ch'klorb didn't understand why the creatures working in this area did that whenever yt was near. Perhaps it was a gesture of amazement at how gracefully and efficiently yt moved in microgravity, by having yts biomets produce thunderous bursts of methane and hydrogen sulfide in the direction opposite yt wished to go.

The quaking paucimorph stammered, "I am Shuttle Bay Drone No. 389, Your Rotundness!"

"Where's that missing shuttle?"

"I don't know, Your Globularness. It was requisitioned by the chaplain shortly after I came on—"

The paucimorph made squeaking noises from several orifices as Ch'klorb's pseudopods wrapped tightly around it. "You let Cailar take a *shuttle?*"

The crewbeing was silent for a long time before the Prime Mover remembered it needed to inhale some of the surrounding gasses to speak. After relaxing yts grip the paucimorph gasped, "It wasn't my place to question the holy chaplain, Your Spherehood!"

Ch'klorb seething anger pushed the primary energy spectrum of yts exoskeleton to ultrashort frequencies. But yt managed to regain yts composure and decrease energy output before the creature suffered more than superficial radiation burns. No use punishing it. How much intelligence can you expect from a paucimorph?

"Resume your duties."

Freed from its captain's embrace, the creature jetted away at top speed. It collided with a group of workers gathered nearby, sending bodies from a dozen different species bouncing off the bulkheads.

But the Prime Mover was much too distracted to enjoy that comic spectacle. By this time Cailar must've made contact with the natives of the third planet. Even if they were hostile and had eaten the chaplain after he'd landed, standard orders demanded a rescue mission to find out what happened to him.

Even if he wandered back right now, tail between his legs, there were too many witnesses here to make an "accident" feasible. Threatening paucimorphs was an effective but not infallible method. All it would take was one rogue paucimorph to squeal when they returned to the

Core, and the Elders would *really* get on yts case.

Now that the damage was done it was the lesser of two evils to stay here and "civilize" these sentients. Dazzle'em with the usual cheap, low-tech gifts like antisenescence medicines, matter-antimatter power cells, and tissue regeneration vats. But what a waste of the ship's synthecators, matter transmuters, and genetic manipulators—all to raise a Rating-10 civilization to an 8! As if the Galaxy didn't have enough of those already. And what a waste of yts valuable time—

A deafening high-pitched buzz echoed briefly in the shuttle bay and sent paucimorphs scrambling to their assigned stations. The missing shuttle glided through the bay's protective force field and settled into its berth. As the crew began servicing the craft, its hatch opened and the prodigal chaplain floated out.

Ch'klorb blasted towards him, barely suppressing an urge to fling him back out through the force field sans shuttle. "You know, of course, the penalty for violating your oath to not land on the third planet!"

Cailar looked toward his feet dejectedly. "I didn't *land* there, Your Sphereness. The closest I got was a high orbit."

"Don't get technical with me! You've caused me enough trouble by finding those sentients! I'm just surprised it took you so little time to contact them and save all their *khwazi*—from orbit, no less!"

"The—beings—I found there still do not know of our presence, Your Roundness. I didn't contact them."

"You *didn't?*"

The captain pulsed disgustedly. "Unfortunately, that doesn't change the fact we know about *them* now—and so the Act applies. I'd better start rehearsing my 'Welcome to the Galactic Unity' speech, and hope that either their bombs aren't too powerful or my biomets work harder to prevent shellburn!"

"I'm not sure how, or even *if,* the Act applies to the creatures I found on the third planet."

The Prime Mover's furious pulsing stopped. "The Act *doesn't* apply to them?"

"I didn't say that. It's something I must mediate on."

"Well, you'll have plenty of time to do that. Until I say otherwise, you're confined to your quarters!"

At yts direction several bulky paucimorphs seized the chaplain and escorted him from the shuttle bay. Ch'klorb jetted around the bay lost in thought, occasionally barreling into an unwary paucimorph and sending it flying off.

Maybe there was a chance yt might still get away from this system without being drafted as nanny for yet another group of ungrateful paucimorphs. If Cailar didn't think the Act applied to the third planet's primitives, no other paucimorph would dare file a Notice of Discovery in the ship's central computer either.

Besides, even if the good chaplain changed his mind and insisted on invoking the Act, a discreet "accident" with no witnesses might still work.

Encouraged by that thought and ignoring the gagging paucimorphs in yts wake, Ch'klorb expelled a huge musical burst of putrid gas and rocketed toward the exit.

Cailar sat alone in his quarters, ransacking his brains for an answer that wouldn't come. The holodisplay of his personal computer console glowed brightly before him in the darkened room, patiently waiting for him to think another command.

"Think!" he screamed at himself. "The ship's due to leave this system in 200 millicycles. If you can't convince the captain to stay and help these primitives by then, everything you've suffered will be for nothing!"

The small datasphere he'd hidden in a private body orifice just before he left the shuttle still sat snugly in the console's information transfer slot. Before exiting he'd downloaded all the electromagnetic transmissions recorded during that nearly disastrous foray to "Earth" into it, then erased them from the shuttle's databank. For over a cycle he'd been alone here in his room, barely eating or sleeping, playing those "television" and "radio" broadcasts over and over. Everything he saw and heard confirmed the same chilling impression he'd received while sampling them high above the third planet.

Never had he encountered technologically advanced sentients as barbaric as these! Nearly everything in their transmissions either depicted or described acts of callous brutality and violence. The most advanced cultures in the Commonwealth of Worlds resolved disagreements between individuals or sociopolitical units using discussion and reason. Less civilized ones resorted to ritualized combat that always stopped well short of inflicting permanent damage to the participants. When mentally ill individuals violated those rules they were confined and cured.

But nowhere in the known Galaxy did sentients above a Rating-24 technology routinely murder their own kind—and these "humans" were nearly 9s!

At his telepathic command moving images of several humans seated at a long desk appeared before him. The console's universal translator articulated their words tonelessly. "The United Nations estimates this latest ethnic cleansing has resulted in the massacre of nearly a hundred thousand civilians, and a million more made homeless. Meanwhile, in local news, police are investigating a drive-by shooting that left two adults and three children dead…"

There were many, many more transmissions like that describing the latest atrocities committed against the innocent by individuals, small groups, or the armies of whole tribes. And this, it was said, was a time of "world peace"! The inhabitants of that last planet the *Omnivore* discovered had possessed thermonuclear explosives too. But, savage as they were, they'd only used them for underground mining projects. These humans had killed thousands of their own kind with fission bombs—and astonishingly, that bloody act had actually stopped a war in which *millions* were slaughtered!

Not content with real violence, the natives gorged themselves on "movies" and "TV shows" depicting imaginary tales of mayhem and destruction. *Bombs away! Draw, you sidewinder! I'll be back.* It'd taken him many millicycles to distinguish what was "news" from what was play-acting. Myths and stories were important in preliterate cultures, and even the most advanced used a few classics to illustrate great universal truths.

But *these* primitives were so barbaric they couldn't even tell the difference between what was real and important, and what wasn't! The transmissions he'd recorded were mainly about the struggles of individuals or groups to achieve power, inflict injury, acquire material goods, or obtain sexual favors. The few showing the scholar-priests who created their technology typically depicted them as dangerous and perverse or ridiculed them. Anyone demonstrating intelligence or rationality was viewed with suspicion.

Instead, these creatures' "heroes" were those who most flagrantly abused them, pandering to their basest desires, greed, and ignorance. While he still wasn't sure what the exact definitions of "advertiser," "lawyer," and "politician" were, one thing was clear. Humans who told the worst lies, who distorted the truth most skillfully, gathered the greatest power, prestige, and riches. Either the natives were too stupid to see through their falsehoods or, worse, they simply didn't *care*.

True, there were glimmers of decency in the species. Some at least professed to hold rudimentary spiritual belief systems that taught concern for their fellows, and even contained elements of the True Faith. But it was typical that so many of the founders and greatest disciples of those protoreligions had been murdered by their own kind.

And in all cases their original noble message had been layered with superstition and perverted to justify hating, torturing, and killing those who professed a minimally different doctrine.

Cailar thought more recorded images and words to life. "Rioting flared again today in Baghdad following yesterday's car bombing that killed or maimed 145 people. Meanwhile, at the border zone between Israel and Lebanon—"

And as for how prepared these humans were to expand into space and join the Galactic Unity—compared to them, the ones who'd bombed the Prime Mover were downright xenophilic! A negligible fraction of the planet's great wealth was devoted to exploring or using the vast resources of their own star system. Even less was assigned to listening for modulated electromagnetic impulses containing messages from other intelligent life—a fruitless venture, since no one used such slow and inefficient means for interstellar communications, but the humans didn't know that yet. And they'd never even *tried* to build probes or ships capable of traveling to the nearest stars at reasonable sublight speeds—a feat their technology *was* capable of, if only barely.

Instead these bipeds wallowed in crude fantasies that reinforced their delusions of self-importance in the universe and their intolerance of the different. Extraterrestrial visitors were usually depicted as hostile, to be attacked and destroyed before their intentions were even known. Often they were so hideous in appearance that even *he*, who'd met thousands of intelligent species with vastly different morphologies, had initially been terrified by them.

Several dramas he viewed did show friendly contacts with "alien" life, and even visions of traveling to the stars themselves. But the few humans who held such mature, cosmopolitan views obviously had no power in their society. Otherwise their race would already have established a much stronger presence in space by now, like colonizing their moon and fourth planet.

Given these humans' prevailing attitudes toward extraterrestrial life, he shuddered to think what would've happened if he hadn't resisted his impulse to land on Earth. Especially considering the utterly perverted meaning he'd learned they attached to the Universal Gesture of Peace and Good Will!

And it was a good thing the captain had refused to go looking for them. The humans would probably have fired thousands of missiles with thermonuclear warheads at the *Omnivore* as soon as it approached their planet—a gesture harmless to the ship but, given the Prime Mover's infamous temper, likely to be fatal to them.

Even if the humans were on their best behavior and didn't try to obliterate the captain when yt gave yts welcoming speech to them, their "culture" abounded in things certain to insult yt. To entertain themselves, they'd devised fiendishly creative "sports" to abuse the holy Shape of the Sphere. He had seen balls of various sizes struck with a club till they sailed over a distant fence, whacked repeatedly with "rackets," kicked into nets, and bounced off floors before being helplessly propelled through hoops. One glimpse of such sacrilege and the Prime Mover would abandon the planet instantly—maybe, Act or no Act, destroying it for good measure as an abomination against Nature.

Exhausted, Cailar leaned back in his chair, reflexively fingering the round white prayer beads around his neck. Worst of all, these transmissions had shattered whatever faith he'd still had in his gods. Watching how the cynical leaders of Earth shamelessly manipulated and used their fellow humans, he'd realized *all* Prime Movers, even ones like the Elders who seemed benign and concerned for the paucimorphs they ruled, were equally corrupt. They were just more powerful versions of those human "politicians"—devious exploiters of the beings they professed to care for, using them as tools for their own selfish ends. And, as on Earth, there was no way to escape their grasp.

"Achromamorphs," he whispered bitterly. "That's what they are!"

It was an obscenity unrepentant rogue paucimorphs scheduled for termination screamed when he tried hearing their last confession. An unforgivable blasphemy against the Prime Movers, meaning they were white and pure on the outside—but darkness incarnate, without *khwazi* or pity, within Their shells. He scarcely believed his lips had mouthed that word.

But then, *he* was a rogue now too.

At first, overwhelmed with despair, he'd considered terminating his life. If existence made no sense, why keep on existing? But then pity for his fellow creatures and righteous anger against their oppressors welled up in him. Now he lusted for revenge against those self-styled "gods" who perpetrated such monumental injustice throughout the Galaxy.

There was no hope of reasoning with the Prime Movers or appealing to Their sense of compassion and fair play. They had none. The only language They understood was power and brute force. But how could he or any other paucimorph defeat such omnipotent beings?

There were rumors that the Hypersphere would be completed in another million cycles. Then the hard-sphered reign of the Prime Movers might end with a gentle "pop" as the Great Masticator blew Them from this plane of reality, leaving the Galaxy to his fellow paucimorphs. But even if, as he began to fear, the Great Masticator Ytself was a myth, would a truly just Supreme Being *reward* the Prime Movers for Their crimes? Or, disappointed the Great Masticator had found Them unworthy, would They emerge again from the Hypersphere to resume Their eternal enslavement of all other sentients?

"No!" he screamed at the computer console. "Hoping for a miracle won't work. I've got to *do* something!"

And then, randomly watching those transmissions from Earth, almost subliminally he found the glimmer of an answer. Documentaries on a "history channel" described human political units of past ages. For many generations they were lorded over by decadent rulers, who held the downtrodden masses in thrall by violence, self-serving lies, and the inertia of tradition.

Then some vigorous group of outsiders—poor in culture and material wealth but rich in spirit and desire for glory—suddenly appeared on their borders. At first those "barbarians" were merely a rabble—technologically primitive and unorganized, staging futile suicidal raids on the margins of the still powerful older, effete culture. But one day, a leader arose in their midst. One who used religious beliefs, political cunning, military skill, and appeals to the natural human thirst for power and plunder to concentrate and focus their collective energy.

Soon those barbarians were molded into a mighty army bent on conquest. They became an irresistible force that swiftly overwhelmed and annihilated the rulers of those "civilized" lands, long grown soft by luxury and the unquestioning obedience of their slaves.

Not that he fully understood everything about those parts of Earth's history. The universal translator couldn't explain what a "Hun" or a "Mongol" was. But he did comprehend why the humans considered the leader named Alexander great, and how powerful the idea of "holy war" was.

In an ecstatic vision he saw himself leading these humans on a great campaign against the Prime Movers for control of the Galaxy. With the starships he'd show them how to build and their innate viciousness and desire to dominate, they'd sweep across the stars in a great tide of conquest—liberating their fellow paucimorphs from slavery and recruiting an exponentially expanding army of fellow sentients. Not even the achromamorphs could resist such a force!

Though there was no known way to kill a Prime Mover, a few tightly restricted weapons could cut through their shells. Then, in theory, their energy cores could be immobilized and rendered helpless by a powerful external force field. For beings who'd owned the Galaxy unchallenged since the beginning of time, such imprisonment would surely be worse than death!

Cailar rocked back in his chair, his glorious vision fading back to cold reality. Confined here to this room and with the ship due to leave this system soon, how could he even *start* that great crusade?

It'd be easy enough to slip out of his quarters—but then what? Try to escape in a shuttle? With every bay secured at the Prime Mover's orders and all paucimorphs on board blindly obedient to the captain, his chance of avoiding capture was negligible. Even if he managed to steal a shuttle, the *Omnivore*'s disintegrator beams could vaporize him before he got anywhere near Earth.

It wouldn't matter even if he could reach that planet. The humans were too primitive to help, and if there was no one left to report their existence to the High Council, for all practical purposes the captain's flagrant violation of the Act would "never" have happened. He could almost write the Prime Mover's report on his fate himself. *Shot while trying to escape.*

"Think!" he shrieked at the console and the pictures it was displaying of Earth's most powerful leader. "Think, or you and the whole Galaxy will remain slaves forever!"

Then, listening to the transparently disingenuous words babbled by that "president," he had an inspiration that changed history. A simple but powerful idea.

If you're going to lead barbarians, you have to act like a barbarian.

Part of his conscience rebelled against planning something so utterly amoral. But by whose standards was it sinful? The self-serving, herd morality the achromamorphs taught? Or should he do a tiny wrong in the cause of a greater good?

It was a surprisingly easy decision. His thoughts flashed at the console, reviewing all the transmissions he'd recorded. Searching for the ones that would ultimately bring on the Revolution.

Ch'klorb rolled back and forth in front of the two space probes in the cargo bay, seething in the ultraviolet. "You'd better have a good reason for disobeying my order to stay in your quarters—and then having the gall to send for me!"

The chaplain bowed his head solemnly as he said, "I humbly beg Your forgiveness, O Round One. But You must hear my recommendations regarding the sentients on the third planet."

"I'm not interested in hearing your recommendations about contacting them. The ship will be ready to leave this system in about 50 millicycles—and Act or no Act, that's when we leave!"

Cailar sighed sadly. "That would indeed be a terrible tragedy, both for them—and You."

Furious low-energy X-rays radiated toward the chaplain. "Are you threatening me?"

"No. I mean that You would deprive Yourself of the pleasure of being worshipped by the most reverent, religious species in the known Galaxy."

The Prime Mover stopped rocking, yts surface cooling to a puzzled opalescence. "What?"

"Since my trip to 'Earth,' I've reviewed the data I collected on them extensively. I didn't tell You what I found when I first returned because I could scarcely believe something so miraculous could occur. But now, after thoroughly analyzing that information, there's no doubt. Though these creatures have never seen a Prime Mover, for untold ages they've yearned for Your presence and worshipped You from afar."

The captain scanned him suspiciously. "And how'd you arrive at that conclusion?"

"Let me show You what I mean, Your Spherefulness."

At the chaplain's telepathic command two-dimensional images and sound appeared before the Prime Mover. "These 'humans,' as they call themselves, are a happy, simple species. When not engaged in the necessary work of survival—hunting for food, providing themselves with shelter, and gathering the other necessities of life—they enjoy frolicking on their beaches, fields, and mountains."

Ch'klorb watched moving pictures of a small group of laughing bipeds emerging from a small four-wheeled transport device, then go tripping merrily along a wide strip of crystalline silicon dioxide beside a vast body of liquid water. Suddenly the same carefree group and their vehicle were in a peaceful meadow, the larger two humans reclining languorously on short green vegetation while the smaller pair tried to keep a small diamond-shaped object attached to a long string suspended in the air. Another instant, and they and their conveyance were on a tall mountain covered by beautifully white frozen water, preparing to slide down it using long flat planks strapped to the ends of their lower two extremities.

The Prime Mover pondered these rapidly shifting images and the words emerging from the universal translator. "I'm surprised these creatures have developed that level of technology, Cailar. I take it 'sport utility vehicle' is their name for the machine that teleports them to different locations like that."

"Yes. It's a popular means of getting to their many recreational activities."

The display changed to show a larger group of garishly attired humans performing a complex ritual dance. The Prime Mover felt low frequency, rhythmically repetitious pressure waves resonate against yts shell. Unconsciously yt started to rock and roll in time with the beat. "Interesting. But what does 'emteevee' mean?"

"It's their name for fertility ceremonies young humans participate in."

Cailar flashed a long rapid collage of images and sounds before the Prime Mover's dazzled senses. Finally yt said, "I've never seen such a contented, easygoing group of paucimorphs. From what you've shown me, they must spend their entire lives quaffing beverages, concocting new kinds of food to devour, deciding what outer coverings and artificial scents to wear, and finding as many sexual companions as possible—when they aren't telling stories about doing them. To paucimorphs like you, it must seem these carefree humans live in paradise!"

"*Almost* paradise, Your Orbness. Though happy and rich in material goods, there's one thing missing in their lives. Something they yearn for to give their existence true meaning and purpose."

Softly glowing in the infrared, the captain scanned the new pictures Cailar showed yt, mystified. "What are those two groups of humans doing? And why's that crowd watching them?"

"This is a ritual performed many times during one season of their year. Thousands of 'spectators' gather in a 'stadium,' and millions of others watch in their domiciles via crude imaging devices, to observe this solemn religious rite."

He zoomed the picture in to focus on an obscenely oblate object. "Watch how each 'team' of humans vies against the other to abuse this 'football.' Kicking it. Throwing it. Slamming it to the ground. Pounding it with their bodies, despite risking injury to themselves! The team able to do this most efficiently is named the 'winner' and showered with riches and honors."

"But why do they do it?"

"Why, it's to show their utter contempt for the nonspherical. The unholy things that approximate but don't achieve the perfect shape of a Prime Mover."

Enthralled, Ch'klorb watched more pictures appear. A "kitchen," where two humans cracked several white ellipsoidal objects and poured their proteinaceous contents into a bowl to destroy them and make a sacrificial meal called an "omelet." A nightly ceremony involving a particularly disgusting near-sphere made of glass except for a metal-tipped tapering end. "This obscenity," the chaplain explained, "is subjected to repeated pulses of electrical energy, until the evil within the 'light bulb' is 'burned out' in an incandescent blaze of light and heat."

But the next images made yt flare with outrage. "Look! That human's performing sacrilege! It's *striking* that sphere with a club!"

"No, this too is a holy sacrament, Your Orbfulness."

Cailar froze the image and zoomed in on the small white ball. "Notice how its surface is marred by many shallow pits—a particularly subtle perversion of the ineffable smoothness of Your shell in its natural state. The object of this ceremony is to strike the blasphemous pseudosphere and hide its deformed shape from view as quickly as possible in a sublimely circular hole in the ground."

He continued, "But what I found most amazing about these creatures was the all-pervasive *positive* elements of their spirituality."

Ch'klorb absorbed the new pictures and words that the priest presented—a smiling human demonstrating the use of a white strap wound around its upper body. "What's a bra?"

"A clever device these sentients developed to help bring their forms closer to spherical perfection."

Cailar pointed to the plaque on the smaller of the two space probes. "Half of these creatures develop a pair of prominent protuberances on their chest when they reach adulthood. Their natural form, however, deviates significantly from the perfection of the sphere. This 'bra' is an artificial means to bring these 'boobs' closer to that shape, which is especially venerated by the half of adult humans who don't develop them."

The captain scanned the shorter of the two figures on the plaque.

"So that's what those two lumps on its thorax are for!"

"Indeed."

The next images were different, with a severely restricted frequency spectrum. Ch'klorb watched a solitary human dressed in a flowing ornate robe push the hose of a simple suction device across the floor of its hovel. Once again the chaplain froze the picture, zooming in on the creature's neck. "This scene is from a documentary entitled 'Leave It to Small-Mammal-with-a-Flat-Tail,' depicting the typical home life of these humans. Notice the sacred relic this 'june' is wearing around its neck."

The captain stared awestruck at the string of perfect white spheres—practically identical to the one that the chaplain wore. "Amazing," yt whispered.

"Here's another example of their devotion to the Holy Sphere."

Ch'klorb saw a dark scene apparently recorded during the planet's nocturnal cycle. "This special ritual," Cailar explained, " is performed in one of the humans' largest cities, 'Bigapple,' to mark the beginning of their calendar's year."

A large throng of humans was gathered in a great square, anxiously awaiting some mysterious event. Then a brightly illuminated sphere descended gracefully downward, sending the assembled worshippers into paroxysms of celebration.

"The symbolism of this event is obvious. It shows their fervent desire for the Coming of the Prime Movers—for Your glorious descent from the heavens."

Ch'klorb murmured, "Astounding."

"But though they yearn for You with expectant joy, they also rightly fear Your just wrath if they prove unworthy of Your divine presence."

The next scene was even darker, occurring in a region of space whose star patterns yt didn't recognize. A huge gray sphere similar in shape to the *Omnivore* hovered menacingly over a cloud-covered planet.

Suddenly a beam of green energy lanced out from it, obliterating that world as completely as their own starship had more gently pulverized this system's pseudoplanet.

"Notice how, in this popular cautionary story, the destructive energy arises from that blasphemous hemispheric area on the sphere." Cailar pointed to the probes. "Just as on these objects, they use the 'Sign of the Shattered Sphere' to symbolize their unworthiness to gaze on the perfect roundness of a Prime Mover."

"Fantastic," Ch'klorb glowed.

The images disappeared. "In short, Your Sphereness, these data clearly show that the humans have *khwazi* so pure and innocent, so closely attuned to the eternal harmonies of the Great Masticator, that even *without* a Revelation they've sensed the blessed existence of the Prime Movers. Just think how much they have craved Your presence, how enthusiastically they'll worship You and serve as Your faithful tools once You actually make Yourself known to them! Can we deny these creatures such a richly deserved destiny? Would it be right to leave their system without contacting them and granting them the Revelation of Your Divine Presence they so fervently pray for?"

The captain oscillated thoughtfully. "You make it sound tempting. Hypersphere knows, I'd hate to deny such worthy creatures the opportunity to adore me. But there's something I still don't understand. If these creatures are so committed to enjoying the simple pleasures of their existence, how did they develop a Rating-10 technology? Outside of being so spiritually advanced, nothing you've shown me demonstrates they actually do any thinking at all!"

Cailar hesitated. "I'm not entirely sure how they did it either, Your Orbness. Perhaps, as some of the humans themselves believe, beings from a Commonwealth world have visited their planet in the past, bequeathing a few crumbs of advanced knowledge and hints of the existence of Prime Movers. Or, as we've seen on other isolated worlds like this on the periphery before they were granted Revelation, though the masses are devoid of thought a few beings of vision—'geniuses,' to use the humans' term—have arisen spontaneously. Their insights into the true nature of the universe have inspired and led their less able fellows to new heights of scientific and spiritual development."

"Humph. Well, you paucimorphs can occasionally be a little clever."

The chaplain continued, "But I believe it's largely due to the great care that they take in ensuring that what little knowledge they have is disseminated to and learned by as many of them as possible, particularly the young. That's the primary function of a certain well-respected class of humans. I don't understand the nuances of the different terms they use to describe that vocation—'teachers,' 'professors,' 'eggheads.' But their role is clearly vital.

"And there's another profession, the most revered one of all, whose mission is even more crucial to improving the minds and morals of these humans. Their civilization produces a tremendous amount of worthless, even corrupting ideas and information. It's essential that only the most important truths, the loftiest ideals, be filtered out from the falsehoods and great temptations to sloth and ignorance assaulting their vulnerable brains. These professionals, the cream of their society, labor tirelessly to ensure that only the very best written and transmitted materials reach the masses. To them falls the critical task of selecting the fiction and fact best calculated to instill in their fellow beings the most inspiring ideas, the most felicitous beliefs and modes of thought."

"That sounds a bit analogous to what we Prime Movers do for you paucimorphs. What do the humans call them?"

"These noble, sagacious guardians of science and culture are known as 'editors.'"

Ch'klorb ceased vibrating for a long time. Then yt rumbled, "Well, I suppose it wouldn't hurt to spend a few hundred cycles here and grant these natives Revelation. The crew will have to work double shifts at our next mining job to make up for lost time. But that's a small price to pay for my being worshipped by these deserving creatures. Tell the chief pilot to change the *Omnivore*'s destination to—what did you call their planet? Dearth?"

"Close enough. But going to their planet would be the worst possible thing we could do!"

Startled, the Prime Mover accidentally rolled over the smaller probe, crushing its antenna. "*What?*"

"Let me show you why we shouldn't go there."

More images appeared. A group of humans sat in a large chamber, gaily watching moving pictures projected onto a rectangular screen.

Suddenly a darkly handsome figure oozed into the chamber. Yts pulsating amorphous bulk followed the humans as they all ran screaming from the "movie theater," absorbing everything in yts path before congealing into a colossal, majestic globular shape.

The chaplain said, "Notice how the humans react in this particularly prescient vision of the Coming of the Prime Mover. Even when confronted by such a crude simulation of Your Spherehood, they all feel themselves so unworthy to be near Yt they immediately flee in abject humility—some actually falling and injuring themselves in their haste to escape Yts awesome presence!"

Cailar thought the images into nothingness. "Think how much more violent would their reaction be if they were suddenly confronted by Your *actual* Divine Presence! Why, if You came to them now, they'd surely be overwhelmed by Your magnificence. Their minds and *khwazi* couldn't stand the strain. They'd either expire at Your base, immolate their bodies before You in ecstatic sacrifice, or lose their very sanity in Your glorious presence. And *then* who would be left to worship and serve You?"

"Good point."

"I thought you'd agree, Your Blobularity."

"My what?"

"I mean—Your Globularity."

"Well, if we shouldn't leave, or fly the *Omnivore* to their planet, what *should* we do?"

The chaplain smiled humbly. "Here's what I suggest…"

Ch'klorb rocked nervously on the floor of the shuttle bay. "You're sure you have all the supplies you need?"

Cailar watched as several crewbeings continued to load the shuttle. "Yes. I'm taking synthopatterns to make everything that's needed to give the humans a Rating-2 spacefaring technology. Inertialess drives for basic interplanetary travel and hyperspatial motors for longer trips. Genetic manipulators to cure all their diseases and injuries and extend their youthful lifetimes indefinitely. Macrofabricators for constructing their spaceships, biomets to produce unlimited food and oxygen supplies on them, and Level-A force field generators to protect their ships. Once I teach them how to build their own large-scale synthecators and matter transmuters, they can create as many of these as I'll need."

The captain scanned one of the dataspheres a drone was carrying onto the chaplain's shuttle. "Wait a nanocycle. That contains 'patterns for a superstring slicer and quark-blasting disintegrator beam. Only Rating-1 civilizations—the ones most devoted to the Great Masticator and Yts servants, like *me*—are allowed to have them. Too dangerous otherwise. One of those could even cut through my shell!"

"Don't worry, Your Sphereness. I'll supervise their use personally."

"But why do you need them?"

"The humans will require extensive training in practical planetary engineering techniques to become worthy tools for You. I'll start them off with simple projects, like making their two neighboring planets habitable and mining the asteroids between their fourth and fifth ones.

But there's also something special I want them to do in Your honor.

"Their moon is currently a rather worthless place, its surface pitted with numerous craters like that small white 'golf ball' I showed you. I'll have them use slicers and disintegrators to make their moon smooth and perfect, then transmute its outer layer to the whitest marble until it looks just like You. Hanging high in their night sky, it'll be a fitting, awe-inspiring monument to Your magnificence. Something they can gaze at and adore before You come in person."

"Well…that makes sense. But how long do you think it'll be before they're ready to receive me?"

"At least 1,000 cycles, Your Orbness. As I explained before, they need a prophet like me to prepare Your way, to make smooth Your path until You come in glory. One of their legends describes a group of humans born deep in the darkness of a cave, manacled to its walls, never having seen the light of their sun. Just as thrusting them out suddenly into the full glare of its brilliance would only make them blinded and confused, so would seeing Your Ideal Form all at once do the same to these Earthians.

"But by my revealing Your Ineffable Nature to them just a little at a time, over many hundreds of cycles, when You finally return they'll be ready to abase themselves in Your presence and joyfully follow Your commands."

The chaplain smiled. "Think of it. Billions of technologically advanced sentients, all eager to do *Your* bidding. Ready and able to mine so much material for the Hypersphere in *Your* cause, the Elders will surely grant You a place in the First Rank!"

The crew finished their work and left the shuttle. Ch'klorb extended a pseudopod and petted the paucimorph's head fondly. "Good luck, Cailar. You've been a good and faithful servant, and I'll miss you."

"Farewell, Master. I'll miss You too. And if You believe that, there's a bridge in Brooklyn I'd like to sell You."

"What?"

"A human colloquialism. It means someone wishes to give another an object of great value."

The captain raised a pseudopod over Cailar in benediction. "May the Great Masticator make your rolling easy."

The chaplain bowed his head solemnly. "Screw you," he prayed. "*That's* an expression humans use to declare their deepest feelings for each other."

As his shuttle sped towards Earth, Cailar watched the holoimage of the *Omnivore* dwindle on the viewscreen. Once he entered into orbit around their planet he'd broadcast a message to the humans, describing the technological wonders he was bringing them.

Naturally, they'd be suspicious of "Greeks bearing gifts." But he knew their curiosity and greed would prove stronger than their fears. After the shuttle landed in Washington and they'd taken him to their leader, the rest should be easy. Even if the humans stupidly refused his offer to lead them on a crusade to liberate the Galaxy, stopping all of their world's electrical power for thirty minutes should convince them cooperation was the best policy. And, remembering what else happened in that particularly interesting movie he'd studied, he'd keep some technological tricks—like his personal force field generator and teleportation unit—to himself. Just in case they tried to "kill the goose that laid the golden egg."

Suddenly the *Omnivore* disappeared in a flash of hyperspatial distortion, carrying the Prime Mover and yts crew to their next mining job in some new distant star system. Cailar pictured the captain rolling fitfully around the mothership many light-cycles away, impatient to return and receive yts rightful due from the inhabitants of this system. It was up to him to make sure the Prime Mover got the reception yt so richly deserved.

The ex-chaplain ripped the circlet of prayer beads from his neck, sending the tiny white spheres flying around the cabin. "And maybe," he hissed, "before you return, I and my humans will come looking for *you*."